PRAISE FOR NURY VITTACHI AND THE FENG SHUI DETECTIVE BOOKS

'Wacky, original and fun' *The Independent*

'Extremely funny' *The Daily Telegraph*

'Highly entertaining' *Time Out*

'Hong Kong's funniest commentator' BBC

'In common with the best satirists, his fantastical take on the world is only a heartbeat away from the real one' *Scottish Review of Books*

'Delicious stuff' *The List*

'Makes you laugh out loud and often' *The Age*

'Does for the flow of *ch'i* what Sherlock Holmes did for cocaine' *South China Morning Post*

'The man who made Lee Kuan Yew laugh' *The New Paper*, Singapore

'Clever and comic' *Sydney Morning Herald*

'The story is populated by a stream of eccentric characters and amusing examples of polyglot, multiethnic culture . . . a tasty smorgasbord of modern Asian life' *Japan Times*

'Unsurpassable mixture of humour, wisdom and whodunnit' *The Crime Forum*

'Should bear a large red label warning against its being read while consuming beverages, lest unwary readers wind up spitting tea through their nose as I did' *That's Beijing*

'To many, he is Asia's funniest, most pungent columnist and author. To others, he is a subversive threat who must be watched like a hawk' *Herald Sun*

'A wacky and hilarious whodunnit – you just have to dig in and hold on for the wild ride . . . Beyond the characters and zany plotting, one of the pleasures . . . is Vittachi's use of language' *Asian Review of Books*

'Comedy, pace and at the same time a certain philosophical calm' *Der Tagesspiegel*

NURY VITTACHI

Nury Vittachi is one of Asia's most widely published humour columnists – hailed by CNN as 'the beat reporter of the offbeat' and described by the BBC as 'Hong Kong's funniest commentator'. Born in Sri Lanka, Vittachi escaped the civil war and emigrated to Britain. He later returned to Asia and began his career with the *South China Morning Post* in the late 1980s. Well known for not pulling any punches in his journalism, his gossip column was deemed too dangerous to publish in the 1990s after Hong Kong was handed over to China.

Vittachi now lives with his English wife and three adopted Chinese children in Hong Kong. His whole life has been dedicated to breaking down cultural barriers and promoting freedom of expression, and he has written many fiction and non-fiction books for adults and children.

Nury Vittachi

THE FENG SHUI DETECTIVE'S CASEBOOK

Polygon

First published in 2006 by Allen & Unwin, Australia

This edition published in Great Britain in 2009 by Polygon,
an imprint of Birlinn Ltd

West Newington House
10 Newington Road
Edinburgh
EH9 1QS

www.birlinn.co.uk
9 8 7 6 5 4 3 2 1

ISBN 978 1 84697 109 9

British Library Cataloguing-in-Publication Data
A catalogue record for this book is available
on request from the British Library.

Typeset at Birlinn
Printed and bound by Clays Ltd, St Ives plc

Author's note

The feng shui techniques in this book are mostly from the flying star school and the form school of East Asia. The vaastu principles are from the northern Indian school. The ancient Chinese philosophy, stories and quotes from Confucius and other sages are largely genuine and come from texts up to 2,500 years old. The extracts from *Some Gleanings of Oriental Wisdom* are by CF Wong, with spelling and grammar corrections by Joyce McQuinnie.

Prologue: A quick bite

The tiger loping through the supermarket had blue eyes. It blinked them slowly as it languidly scanned the goods on the shelves.

Huge, muscular, and almost twice the length of a man, the 240-kilogram *tigris panthera sumatrae* paused. It appeared to be trying to choose between the Betty Crocker Super Moist Lemon Cake Mix and the Pillsbury Creamy Supreme Chocolate Fudge Frosting. It swung its massive head to the other side of the aisle to examine the First Choice Thai Fragrant Rice and the Golden Noodle Mee Goreng. Then it moved on again, heading inadvisably towards the Kraft Macaroni Cheese Dinner.

Spying an opening to the left, the beast impulsively powered its heavy body through the gap and found itself trotting down an aisle marked BREAKFAST CEREALS AND MILK PRODUCTS.

The tiger, an adult male with the white skin and dark stripes of a zebra, came to a halt. Slowly it surveyed the scene, its haughty, down-turned lips giving it the look of a jaded royal wine taster. Apparently bored, it hung its head slightly, making the bones of its shoulders stick up through its shiny white silk pelt.

In the corner of its vision there was movement.

A glow came from a glass cabinet containing fresh-chilled cold cuts, twenty metres away at the end of the aisle. A mother with a pushchair approached the fridge. The baby stirred in its sleep.

Smelling fresh meat, the tiger stared from a distance. Its tail, almost a metre long, twitched. It lowered its haunches to the ground. Its belly muscles tightened and its spine arched. Then it started to move, its powerful muscles shifting under its skin like zephyrs through a cornfield as it raced forwards, preparing to pounce.

'Wong-*saang!* Wong-*saang!*'

Madam Lin's cracked, piercing voice sang out over the noise of trucks reversing into a rubbish depot nearby.

'Wong-*saang*. Here!'

It was likely that there were several people called Wong within earshot of her penetrating yell, so a thin man of fifty-six hunched his head into his shoulders and tried to scurry away, praying that she was aiming her comments at one of the others. He recognised the voice as belonging to an irritating local landlady he had once encountered when he had done a feng shui reading for a community hall. On that occasion, he had been aghast to find she had placed a figurine of a plastic phoenix in a place where a *newborn* would have known that the only suitable animal was a rosewood turtle.

'Wong-*saang! Feng shui lo,*' she shrieked.

Aiyeeah! There was no avoiding it. CF Wong turned his head and feigned surprise. He pointed to himself, his index finger aimed quizzically at his nose. The expression on his face said: Me? You want me?

'Come. *Faidee-la!*' She beckoned him Chinese-style, with her palm down.

Pausing to let a taxi rumble past, the stick-thin feng shui master stepped into the road and reluctantly approached the opposite pavement, where Madam Lin Pui-yen, a woman of fifty in a black pyjama suit which stopped twenty centimetres above her ankles, was hopping with excitement.

'Come. Need you,' she barked.

'Hello, Lin-*taai*. Ver' nice to see you. Eat rice yet?'

'No time for chit-chat. Come. They have a white tiger in Sing Woo. Can you believe?'

'White tiger?'

'Yes. In Sing Woo supermarket.'

Wong rolled his eyes upwards. 'Must never put white tiger inside building. Wrong-wrong-wrong. Only outside, small statue only, on west only.' He shook his head in despair. Truly, the depth of ignorance displayed by the masses was bottomless.

The two of them walked towards a ragged store bearing the name Sing Woo Western and Oriental Supermarket and Property Agent. The front window was almost totally obscured by peeling hand-written posters in English and Chinese offering discounts on *bak-choi* and other grocery items.

'Tang should know,' Wong continued, a tone of severest disapproval in his voice. '*Never* put white tiger statue inside. Will bring bad fortune only. You tell Tang: I can change for horse statuette, very nice, very clean. Only ninety-eight dollar for big one, running horse pair in rosewood. Or have standing horse, imitation jade, twenty-five centimetre, only sixty-five dollar, special price.'

They reached the front of the store and Wong was surprised to see that it was deserted. Manager Wilfred Tang, who was normally found at the cash desk morning till night, was nowhere to be seen.

The geomancer stepped inside and peered curiously down the empty aisles.

'Tang is where? Lin-*taai*?' He was even more taken aback to notice that Madam Lin had not accompanied him into the shop, but was loitering nervously outside. He turned around and called out a question. 'Tang is where? And where is feng shui tiger?'

Madam Lin shook her head. Not feng shui tiger,' she called out. '*White* tiger. Can you get me some *gai-laan*? One catty.'

'Oh.' Wong was intrigued. Good white jade – if it was genuine – was expensive. Had Tang really invested in such a pricey ornamentation for this grubby, run-down store? Could he be persuaded to hand over a tiger of white jade for a cheap rosewood horse? Wong smelt profit.

His spirits lifted, the geomancer happily strolled along CANNED MEATS, looking for the supermarket manager. He turned left past FRESH FRUIT AND VEGETABLES, slipped along COFFEE AND TEA and then turned right into BABYCARE AND TISSUES. Baffled not to find a single living soul in the shop, he started to stride more quickly.

It was then that he recalled the look on Madam Lin's face as she stood shouting to him from outside the store. She had been biting her lower lip and there was a network of tension lines around her eyes. It was almost a look of fear.

But what was there to be scared of?

CF Wong turned a corner into BREAKFAST CEREALS AND MILK PRODUCTS, looked towards the COLD CUTS section, and found out.

Six minutes passed, during which he barely moved. Wong remained frozen to the spot, showing no more animation than the shoulder-high display of Buitoni Marinara Pasta Sauce to his right.

Standing next to him was a bespectacled woman, also as still as a statue. At their feet was a pushchair containing a sleeping baby.

In front of them, no more than three metres away, a large white tiger sat on its haunches. It weighed at least twice as much as all three of its human companions put together and was attempting to eat a packet of Spinelli's Spicy Chicken Poultry Sausage, tearing at the packaging and spitting out pieces of plastic.

The tiger was astonishingly beautiful. Its fur was short, creamy white, and had a reflective lustre that would have done a shampoo advertisement proud. The stripes running vertically along the length of its body were the deep, slightly purple black of East India Rosewood.

Yet it was not the lack of yellow fur that was startling about the beast, but the omission of the characteristic marmalade hue in its eyes. The orbs were unexpectedly large, and at the heart of the pupils were ovals the deep blue of summer skies.

The tiger glanced up and its audience tensed.

CF Wong was not an heroic man. Although motionless, he was having great difficulty in controlling outbreaks of shivers that kept starting at the top of his spine and running down his back and the length of both arms. His eyes remained so firmly locked on the head of the beast in front of him that his vision kept going in and out of focus.

The tiger looked down again at the difficult-to-open packet of chicken sausages.

The feng shui master's eyes darted around, looking for an escape. The only opening on this side of the building was a

5

doorless archway about four metres to the right of the tiger, apparently leading to a storage area.

The tiger, the doorway and the individuals trying not to be eaten formed an elegant triangle. The geomancer's brain worked at a feverish pace, fired by adrenaline. Can we reach the doorway? Which way will the tiger move? Or should we aim for the store entrance instead? Do we form an isosceles triangle or an equilateral triangle? Where is Tang? Has anyone called the police or the fire brigade or the zoo?

At that moment, he knew their only hope was to stay where they were. As long as they could keep absolutely still and silent, there was a chance that the tiger might leave them alone until help arrived.

At that moment, the baby woke up.

She stretched two tiny arms over her head and started to moan: '*Uhhhn.*'

'Shh!' the mother whispered.

'Mama!' shouted the child.

The tiger looked up and stared at the baby.

Wong knew that they needed to move immediately. 'I think we go that way,' he whispered to the woman, a *kebaya*-wearing *nonya* in her twenties. She had high heels and a row of bracelets, absurdly over-dressed for grocery shopping. Her hair was in a bun and her lower lip was trembling. His eyes pointed to the storage area.

'Cannot,' she replied, her voice trembling. Her eyes focused on a sign above the doorway. STAFF ONLY.

Aiyeeah! All Singaporeans were idiots! Rather be eaten by a tiger than break a rule!

6

Wong continued: 'I distract tiger. Maybe. You take baby, run to staff area.'

The woman shook her head. 'Too far. I think he will chase us. I think he can jump very far.'

The geomancer nodded. He too had noticed the tiger's long, muscular legs – if they tried to make a break for it, it would be on top of them in two, maybe three easy steps.

Wong strained his ears for the sound of arriving police cars, zookeepers, people with tranquilliser guns – but there was no sound from the front of the shop. Had that idiot woman Madam Lin even thought of calling the police? She was probably still standing outside the shop, angry with him for not returning with her catty of *gai-laan*.

It started to dawn on him that they had better assume they would have to solve this problem entirely by themselves. But how?

The tiger ripped another large piece of plastic from his package. Wong was unable to prevent his imagination visualising the creature stripping skin from a human victim. It tried to bury its snout in the pink meat of the torn sausages, but had difficulty: they were double-wrapped. Its eyes kept returning to the baby.

'Give me your phone,' Wong whispered, assuming that every Singaporean woman had one.

The woman, tears flowing freely down her face, slowly reached into her handbag and pulled out a tiny Nokia.

The geomancer tapped out the number for his friend Dilip Kenneth Sinha.

'Ye-es?' came a deep and elegant voice.

'Sinha!'

'Ah, hello, Wong. Are you already there? I'm just entering the compound and should be at our table in just a minute or –'

7

'Emergency! Please go to Sing Woo supermarket. Very urgent.'

'Sing Woo?'

'Near junction. Next to Long Kee's Pig Organ Soup. Don't come inside supermarket. Find Wilfred Tang, give him phone. Urgent.'

'I hear you.'

With a jerk of his head, the tiger abandoned the impenetrable packet of sausages and tossed it to one side. Then he started looking for an alternative meal.

'Ma-*ma!*' complained the baby, hands in the air, wanting to be picked up.

The woman, still crying, slowly bent down towards her child. She cringed as the safety buckle on the stroller opened with a loud *click*.

She lifted the child to her breast and began to breathe again.

The tiger gazed at parent and child. The baby went back to sleep, chin stretched over her mother's shoulder. Wong held his breath, looking at the tiger's blue eyes and trying to anticipate its movements.

For two long minutes, the beast merely examined the three humans in front it.

Then the phone came back to life. 'Wong-*saang*? Are you inside?' It was manager Tang. 'Where are you? Tiger with you, is it?'

The geomancer could hear several voices murmuring behind Tang. He assumed Madam Lin was bringing Sinha up to date with what was going on.

'We are in the back,' Wong whispered. 'Me and lady and one baby.'

'Can't hear you. Can you talk louder?'

'No.'

'Can you distract the tiger until police come?'

Wong gritted his teeth. 'Are there any other ways out back of shop?'

'Only through side storage area. I think.'

'You sure? Any door on other side? Tiger is in front of storage area.'

'Don't know-lah. I am not owner-one. Manager only.'

'Any windows or rear door?'

'No. Don't think so.'

Wong was silent for a moment, thinking. 'You see any feng shui item in this place? When you start work as manager, you ask this is what sort of dwelling?'

There was silence from the phone except for the sound of Tang's breath. 'Did not ask. Sorry-ah.'

'Did owner tell you it was Chi'en or Hum dwelling?'

'Aiyeeah, did not ask, if owner say anything, do not remember.'

Exasperation and amazement fought for control of Wong's face. How could anything but a stone take no interest in such an important piece of information?

He pressed on. 'See any feng shui item hanging up?'

'Er. Let me think.' A scraping noise suggested Tang was scratching his cropped head. 'Yes. There were some stuff. Turtle picture on outside front wall. Small dragon in warehouse next door, on dairy products side. More, don't remember.'

'Any red phoenix?'

'Felix is what?'

'*Bird.* Any red bird picture or statue?'

'Yah, is red bird picture hanging back shed where rubbish go.'

The feng shui master's eyes widened. 'Thank you.' He rang off.

Wong turned to the woman. 'Feng shui master who read this building decide shop frontage was really back wall of terrace.'

'So what?'

'It means there is opening towards red phoenix.' He pointed towards what was now the rear of the shop.

'Where?'

Wong pointed to a wall on their left hidden by tall shelves of canned meats. 'Maybe there.'

The tiger stood up and gave a short, sharp roar. The sound was lower and louder and more terrifying than Wong could ever have imagined.

Their hearts stopped.

The creature opened its mouth, revealing thirty off-white teeth, several of which were pitted and scratched. Most were canines and incisors. As its lips retracted, molars were revealed behind the carnassial complex in the upper jaw. The relatively short jaw, lined with thick, powerful muscles, was clearly designed to strip bones clean.

The tiger straightened itself, stretching its spine.

It shook its head once, and then took two steps directly towards the mother, its eyes still on the baby in her arms. As the tiger moved, its shoulder blades swung backwards and forwards in wide curves, enabling the beast to take huge strides. It trod elegantly, like a dancer: only the five soft pads of its toes touched the ground, with the rest of the foot raised slightly. Its claws were retracted, but their needle-sharp tips were visibly protruding through the white fur.

It took another step.

Wong reached one hand out to his left. His fingers snaked around the side of a cabinet, looking for the wall. Stretching

10

further, his fingertips touched cold, sticky, dirty, unwashed tiles. He moved his hand along the surface. He bent slightly and found what he was looking for: a power socket. A three-pin plug – furry and damp with a coating of oily dust – connected one or other of the freezer cabinets to the wall at this point.

The feng shui master strained his fingers and pulled at the plug. It obviously had not been extracted for a long time, and was stiff. Manipulating it from side to side, he eventually managed to work it loose. As he did so, he saw a yoghurt and cheese cabinet behind them start to flicker. There was a crackling, fizzing sound from the wall socket. The cabinet flashed again.

The tiger stared at the fridge. Discomfort registered in its eyes. Some deep instinct in its brain apparently associated bright, irregular light with fire.

Wong continued to manipulate the plug, and the neon tubes in the cabinet continued to flicker and buzz. Now there was a slight smell of burning. The tiger took four steps backwards, away from the three humans, its haunches moving into the STAFF ONLY doorway that Tang had said was their only escape route.

'Now,' whispered the feng shui master. 'Walk to *back*. Walk, don't run.'

The trio moved smartly to the shelf of canned meats at the back of the store.

Watched carefully by the unnerved beast, Wong put his fingers around the corner of the tinned meats shelving unit and pulled with all his might. It didn't budge. He tugged at it again. It shook slightly, but did not move forwards. The geomancer started to sweat. 'Stuck,' he groaned. *'Aiyeeah.'*

The mother put the baby down at her feet. 'Let me try-lah,' she said. 'Mothers carry twenty-kilo babies around all day.'

She pulled at one side of the shelving unit with two hands, while he yanked at the other.

11

She screwed her face up, let loose a long string of Chinese curse words and heaved with all her strength. It started to tip forward in slow motion. Cans of Libby's Corned Beef slid along the top shelf and tumbled into the air, followed by a shower of cans of Hormel Spam Lite from the shelf below.

They clattered and bounced and the air was filled with the angry sound of crashing tins bouncing and ricocheting off the tiled floor.

Behind them, they saw the white tiger raise its dark eyebrows, alarm in its blue eyes at the unexpected racket. It retreated further into the staff area.

The falling shelf wedged itself at an angle in the aisle, revealing an ancient, filthy door in the wall. Wong pushed at it and it opened – but only about thirty centimetres. There was something behind it, preventing it from opening further.

Still, the gap was big enough for two slim adults. The young mother slipped through first and then Wong handed her baby through the gap. The feng shui master then slipped into the semi-darkness, pushing the door shut behind him.

They found themselves behind a wall of cardboard boxes marked with the words: Che Foo. Next to it was a pile of boxes marked Great Wall. The original front door of the building evidently led into a temporary structure now used as the storeroom for a wine shop.

The woman put the baby down on a box of Dynasty Wine and started to move boxes aside. She noticed that one box to her left was already open and peered at the words on its side: YEO'S BRAND GRASS JELLY DRINK. 'Allah be praised. I need a drink. You want one?'

Wong took his usual stool at the nightmarket.

There was nothing obvious to differentiate this table from any of the others. It was a rickety round thing with metal legs and a topping of chipped fake wood. The table was covered by a stained plastic sheet bearing a pink and white gingham design – a cheap, disposable tablecloth that had been used repeatedly for months or years.

Nor was the table in a position that made it obviously attractive. While the front of the open-air seating area filled up first, Wong's table was almost the furthest back, and was angled off to one side. Only a feng shui master would immediately see that he had chosen the table in the command position. From his vantage point furthest from the dining area entry point, he could see all the other diners. But more importantly, he could see when Ah-Fat arrived to start cooking his legendary oyster pancakes.

The part he had just played in the White Tiger Incident (the creature had escaped from an over-authentic launch party for The Bak Fu Theatre Group) had left him drained of energy, and he was happy to just sit in a peaceful, familiar place and allow the world – spinning much too fast – to gradually settle back to its normal rhythm.

He and Dilip Kenneth Sinha, a tall Indian astrologer dressed in an immaculately-cut black Nehru-collared suit, had arrived at their table during the final minutes of dusk. As the feng shui master watched, night fell as suddenly as if a hand had turned a dimmer switch. The sky over the horizon of watching skyscrapers was navy blue. He looked over at Ah-Fat's stall – still empty. He glanced up at the sky again and it had turned black.

The absence of light from above seemed somehow to affect his other senses, too. Sounds became sharper, more vivid.

The murmur of conversation took a louder, more party-like tone, with a smattering of laughs and shrieks. Glasses clinked and plates clattered dramatically. A child being bathed could be heard laughing and splashing from a building nearby. A distant, constant hum rose from an overpass carrying lorries to the main road west out of town. And, incongruously in this humid, tropical scene, a music system was adding the melodious overlay of Bing Crosby singing 'Let It Snow'.

Desperately needing to excise the tiger from the front of his mind, the feng shui master concentrated on the array of comfort food that was about to arrive.

There were over thirty stalls in the marketplace, serving a variety of dishes from kapok kapok to fried kway teow. He knew them all. What other place in the world had such a fine array of cuisine? As well as Ah-Fat's Fried Oysters, there were other gems: Ah Lum's Hokkien Big Prawn Mee, Munch Munch Satay Hoon, Kang Kong Korner, Hong Kee Famous Chicken Rice and Tong Kee Fish Porridge. Tonight he would get a dish from each of them.

He took a deep sniff with his wide, flat nostrils. The smells also seemed to double in power as night fell. The night breeze carried with it the scents of candlenuts, turmeric, shrimp paste, daun salam, tamarind pulp and jaggery.

CF Wong was suddenly ravenous.

Hunger drove the original purpose of the meeting out of his mind. This evening's nightmarket dinner gathering of the investigative advisory committee of the Singapore Union of Industrial Mystics had been officially called by the feng shui master.

But if he had something urgent to relate to the other two members who had turned up, Sinha and Madam Xu Chongli, he wasn't immediately ready to share it.

Even before fortune-teller Madam Xu had arrived, Wong had already started to eat. This was certainly a faux pas in terms of etiquette, but it happened too often in Singaporean society to excite complaint. Eating was the holiest religious rite and diners were above having to follow the conventions of secular society.

Madam Xu, who was frequently late for appointments, was used to Wong's rudeness. But even she was taken aback by his cartoon-like blurring into a one-man eating machine, virtually inhaling the dishes before him. Expensively upholstered in silk and linen, she watched his technique with fascination. The geomancer barely chewed each mouthful of food before the pair of chopsticks hovering before his lips shovelled another pile into the breach.

'Goodness me,' said Madam Xu. 'Is he practising for one of those chilli-eating contests or something?'

'No,' said Sinha. 'He had a shock.'

'What? One of his clients paid a bill?'

The elderly astrologer smiled at the fortune-teller's witticism as he picked up a plate of assam pedas and spooned a generous portion of the tamarind brinjal fish onto her plate. 'A white tiger was being delivered to someone up the road and it decided to do a little shopping.'

Madam Xu, picking up a popiah pancake with her chopsticks, bit delicately into it, releasing the warm, pungent odours of fried lettuce, prawns, egg and turnip. 'A *real* tiger?'

Sinha nodded. 'Mee siam?' he offered, expertly lifting a small portion of vermicelli noodles in sour gravy with his chopsticks. 'Yes, a real tiger. And unfortunately, Wong decided to do some shopping at the same time and ended up stuck for some minutes discussing the price of rice with the beast.'

'Does sound rather distressing.'

The tall Indian astrologer stole a dish of chee cheong fun from Wong's side of the table and scraped the remains onto his companion's plate. 'Hungry tigers are not much fun,' he agreed.

Madam Xu shook her head. 'No, it's not the fact that it was a tiger that is distressing. It was the fact that it was a *white* tiger. You couldn't really complain if your friend is eaten by a white tiger. Such a rare beast. It's rather an honour if you see what I mean.'

'Ah.'

The astrologer looked to see if Wong would agree that it would be a privilege to be eaten by such a cat, but the feng shui master remained buried in carnal satisfaction, noisily slurping down the last drops from a bowl of black chicken herbal soup.

Wong placed the cracked bowl down with a thud and wiped his mouth with the back of his hand. 'Now is time,' he said.

'Time to tell us why you called this meeting?' Sinha asked.

The geomancer shook his head. 'No. Time for or luak. Ah-Fat is here.'

Sinha followed Wong's gaze and spotted the thin figure of Ah-Fat expertly whipping oyster pancakes out of his steaming wok.

Two minutes later, a large dish of or luak, giving off a powerful smell of singed, eggy seafood, arrived on their table, accompanied by a generous portion of extra-hot chilli dipping sauce.

Only after the serving platter was as clean as the day it came out of the furnace – which took these three diners less than six minutes – did Wong finally lower his chopsticks. He sat back, sated at last.

'Ahhhh,' he said, patting his extended belly and picking at his teeth with a bamboo toothpick. 'Better-better-better, yes.'

Sinha and Xu looked at the feng shui master expectantly. 'So?' said the astrologer.

Wong extracted the toothpick from his mouth and glared at the morsel of shredded chicken on it. He popped it back into his mouth.

'Have to go away,' he said. 'Mr Pun has plenty work for me outside. He call me today. I think I will go next week, maybe week after. Away I think for three-four week.'

'So long?' Sinha was surprised. 'Mr Pun must have bought a very big property somewhere.'

'No,' Wong said. 'Every year, Mr Pun gives Christmas gift to members of international board.'

'Oh?' Madam Xu inquired. 'He wants you to go round and deliver the gifts? You are the delivery boy now?'

'No. I am gift.'

Sinha chuckled. 'So he wraps you with a red ribbon and leaves you naked under a Christmas tree somewhere.'

'Unh?' Wong didn't get the joke. 'My service is gift. He offer free feng shui reading to each member of international board of director of East Trade Industries Company Limited. Five-six out of nine members accept the offer already. So Mr Pun paying me to visit their projects.'

Sinha lowered his chopsticks, scenting paying work for himself. 'You want us to cover for you?'

'No. Already I ask Mister Sum to cover for me. I want you to come with me for some of the jobs.'

'He'll cover our expenses too?'

Wong's brow wrinkled with irritation. His expression said: Would have I asked you otherwise? 'Of course. Three board members are in Singapore. I can do that no problem. One in

India. I told Mr Pun I need you to come help me with that, Sinha. Do some vaastu, you know?'

The Indian astrologer nodded. 'Of course. It would be my pleasure.'

'One in Australia, one in Philippines, one in Thailand, one in Hong Kong, so on – I hope you can help me with Philippines one, Madam Xu. Client there request fortune reading also.'

Madam Xu elegantly bowed her perfumed, coiffured head. 'I would be delighted, it goes without saying.'

Sinha chuckled. 'He's dipping deep into his pocket. If the next few weeks are going to be a no-expenses spared junket, I suppose that means Pun expects you to take Joyce with you?'

Wong plunged instantly into a deeply morose state.

He nodded gloomily. 'Aiyeeah,' he growled, under his breath. 'Yes. He want me to take Joyce also.'

Sinha laughed out loud and looked at Madam Xu. 'Ha. I think he'd prefer the company of the tiger,' he snorted.

The case of the fishy flat

A scholar sat on the Plain of Jars reading The Book of Changes.

He wanted to know where the Life Force came from. So he closed his book and made a vow. 'I will travel on and on and on, never stopping, until I find the primary source of ch'i.'

He walked across the city. He walked across the county. He walked across the kingdom. He could not find it.

So he decided to sail around the world.

He got into a ship and sailed far away. He saw many strange things. He saw in the ocean a great fish. The great fish was also travelling very far.

But he could not find the source of ch'i.

The scholar did not give up. He travelled very far, to the other side of the world. He went to the four points of the earth and the four corners of the lo pan.

Many times his path crossed with the path of the great fish, who also seemed to be seeking something.

But although he went to a thousand places, he could not find the source of ch'i.

One day he travelled to the land where people can talk to creatures and creatures can talk to people. He saw the great fish passing his boat.

He asked the fish: 'Are you looking for something?'

The fish said: 'Yes. Are you looking for something?'

The scholar said: 'Yes. I am looking for the source of ch'i.'

The fish said: 'What is ch'i?'

The scholar said: 'It is prana, it is the life force, it is Tao, it is the way, it is Heaven, it is God. You have travelled far. You have seen it?'

The fish said: 'No. I have been everywhere in the whole world. I have not seen the source of ch'i.*'*

The scholar was very, very sad. He cried very much.

After his tears dried, he asked the fish: 'What are you looking for?'

The fish said: 'I am looking for the sea.'

The scholar said: 'But you are in *the sea.'*

The fish looked around. He said: 'How can that be? I cannot see it.'

The scholar said: 'You cannot see it because it is every thing you can see.'

At that moment the scholar found enlightenment.

Blade of Grass, never forget the words of Confucius:

'Fish forget they live in water and people forget that they live in the eye of heaven.

'The world is heaven and heaven is the world. This is the beginning of understanding.'

From *Some Gleanings of Oriental Wisdom*
by CF Wong, part 21

He lowered his pen, blew on the page to dry it, and carefully shut the book.

Then, slowly as a golden rain-tree falls over in a paper-mulberry forest, he leaned way back in his creaking red leather- ette chair, cupped his hands behind his head and grinned.

CF Wong was a happy man. He felt like physically express-ing it some way. But how? Singing was something he hadn't done for years. Dancing was something he hadn't done for even longer – since his previous life or perhaps one or two

20

before that, he reckoned. Maybe he should celebrate by having a lion's head for lunch. But those devils at Tong Kee Fish Porridge were now charging $4.95 a dish: evil robbers from the fifth layer of hell!

Yet even as the feng shui master pondered the best way to celebrate, he was aware of a growing realisation that he probably wouldn't do anything at all. He had never been a demonstrative man. He had seen people expressing their feelings by jumping around and yelling, but had no idea how to do the same.

No matter. He was happy enough to just sink into his chair and let a smile play on his lips.

He would take it easy today. Perhaps do a little extra writing in his book of educational Chinese classics. And he might make a token celebratory action. He would order a portion of pan-fried wor tip from the Shanghainese coffee shop around the corner. Yes, that would be perfect.

The sudden burst of joy could be credited to a plan that had come to Wong as he had dragged his eternally suffering limbs into the office at 7.30 that morning.

Like all members of humanity, he had his crosses to bear. But this particular week, two particularly heavy weights were pressing down on him.

The first was a troublesome client. He had many of these, but this one was especially noxious. His assignment for the day was to examine the residential premises of Mr Tik Sincheung, the junior non-executive director on the board of East Trade Industries.

Mr Tik was a moderately successful broker with a medium-sized penthouse apartment in the Fort Canning area. Wong had been to the flat several times and each time almost nothing needed to be done. The businessman was highly conservative, and rarely altered anything. It was not impossible that he may have bought a new painting or a new bed. But even that was unlikely. The only changes between Wong's previous visits were alterations in the number of fish he kept and the precise spot in which he kept them. Mr Tik last time had had eight rare giant carp in a pond with a fountain on his terrace and twelve rare angelfish in a water feature in the south-west corner of his living room.

There was only one problem: the smell. The apartment stank of fish. Mr Tik stank of fish. Any unfortunate feng shui reader who had to spend more than an hour in the flat stank of fish. After Wong's previous visit, he had carried the odour around with him for three days. Even the local durian seller had complained, and had banned him from the store.

Wong, a life-long durian addict, had mentally sworn never to do Mr Tik's flat again.

The second cross was also supplied by the man who paid his retainer, property developer Mr Pun Chi-kin, chairman of East Trade Industries.

Pun had forcibly added Joyce McQuinnie, a student of British and Australian parentage, to the one-man-and-a- secretary feng shui agency operating on Telok Ayer Street, just off the business district in Singapore. The daughter of one of Mr Pun's property development associates, the young woman had initially been placed with CF Wong & Associates because she was writing a 10,000-word mini-thesis titled Feng shui: *Art or Science?* But she had found her first few weeks so enjoyable (to her temporary employer's amazement) that she had announced that she was going to spend her entire 'gap year' – whatever that was – in the feng shui master's office.

In theory, having a free assistant (a nominal salary payment for her had been added to Wong's monthly retainer) should have lightened his load. But she was too strange, too unpredictable, too *gwaai* to be of any use at all. Her thought processes worked in ways that baffled him, her manner was clumsy and insensitive, she knew nothing of the culture in which she worked, and to cap it all, she didn't speak English – at least, no form of English he had ever encountered.

The previous morning, she had burst into the office in a state of excitement at an article she had found in a glossy magazine. 'Cheese!' she had exclaimed.

She showed him a photograph, not of a stinky yellow Western foodstuff, but of a group of drunken young people. 'P Diddy's skanky ex is going full-on with Justin from The Dopes,' she explained. 'Unreal, totally.'

Wong nodded as if he had been about to say exactly the same thing. Yet there was not a single element of the sentence that had meant anything to him.

'What could a major slice see in such a pit?' the eighteen-year-old continued. 'I *mean*.'

Wong had no idea how to respond, but it didn't matter because she quickly supplied her own answer: 'Duckets, that's what, lucky bloody totty.'

The geomancer considered reaching for his *Dictionary of Contemporary English Idioms*, but decided against it. The book, although purchased only last year, had proved infuriatingly useless in analysing Joyce's speech. According to the text, she should be saying things like 'It is raining cats and dogs', 'Goodness, what a palaver', and 'The proof is in the pudding'.

When he was completely honest with himself (a rare event), he became dimly aware that there actually were some tiny-but-perceptible benefits of having her in the company. For a start, clients often reacted better to a gregarious young woman

23

than a taciturn old man. But he refused to let such dangerous thoughts take root. For on those rare occasions when she
appeared to be contributing something useful, she would inevitably say or do something that would irritate him to such a
degree that their relationship would go back to square one.

This week had been particularly hard work, and her impenetrable attempt at conversation the previous morning
summed up why. Communication was impossible. It was
undeniable: The gulf was too wide to be bridged. A feng shui
master's entire skill was creating zones of harmony – and until
he was rid of this noisy and pestilent *gwaimooi*, he would have
to endure the embarrassing fact that his own working life was
stuck in a permanently unsettled, inharmonious state.

So what had happened on that fateful sunny Tuesday to
bring such a heartfelt smile to his lips? He had suddenly remembered that Joyce McQuinnie hated fish. She loathed the
thought of them. At restaurants, she pushed away seafood
dishes with a look of horror. She steered a wide berth around
aquariums they encountered during assignments. She held her
nose when walking past a fish stall at the market.

Wong conceived a plan. He was going to make his two
crosses cancel each other out.

As soon as Joyce arrived at the office that morning, he
would assign the reading of Mr Tik's flat to her, to cover entirely by herself. If she had a miserable time of it and resigned,
he would be rid of her at last, and Mr Pun could not hold him
responsible. If she did all right – well, he might as well give
her all of his really difficult or unpleasant clients until she did
quit. Either way, he would win.

He bravely dared to imagine that this could be the beginning of a golden period. At best, he could be entirely free of
her within a day. At worst, he could eventually train her to do

24

ten, twenty, thirty per cent of his work for him. His workload would be significantly cut and, as a huge bonus, he would get her out of his office for most of each day. His two biggest problems would be solved at once.

And Mr Pun would be paying for it all. Now this was how capitalism should work!

A thud reverberated through the office as the door was kicked open. The insistent *shh-chka-shh-chka-shh* noise of personal stereo headphones became audible.

Joyce McQuinnie, a lanky teenager whose streaked hair varied between blonde and dark brown, ambled into the room, her face buried in a magazine. It was 10.10 a.m.: more than two-and-a-half hours after Wong had started work. She gave him a brief, nervous smile. 'Hey, CF!'

'Come. Job for you today.' He pointed to the paperwork in front of him.

The *shh-chka-shh-chka* sound grew in volume as she took off the headphones and stared at the plans and charts laid out on his table.

'You go see Mr Tik. Very nice man, quite old. Easy job. I give you records from last time. You check to see if any changes. Calendar changes I already calculate. I think no problem.'

She turned to him, her eyes widening. 'Cool. You mean I get to do this by myself?'

He bowed his head.

'Awesome, like totally!'

'Remember to count fish.'

'Fish? Yeeucch.' She wrinkled her nose.

'He has two fish pond. But no problem. Very easy.' He tried to recall a suitable phrase from his book of English idioms. 'This job is really bowl of roses.' Or was it cherries? Or apple pie?

She smiled and looked at the floor plan and pile of records from previous visits to the same premises. 'Neat,' she said. A cakewalk.'

'No cakewalk. Apartment. Two bedroom.'

'No, I meant it'll be a piece of cake.'

'You want a piece of cake?'

'I meant – never mind.'

Wong had the usual grim feeling that he was losing control of the conversation. 'Here is the address. From now on, I want you to do more job by yourself.'

'Cool.' Joyce wanted to set off straight away, but Wong was still a little anxious about letting her have full responsibility for handling a board member.

He sat her down and went through the actions that she would have to perform, making sure that she wrote it all down.

'Fish. You will check fish.'

'*Ewww*. Do I have to? I don't like fish. Except sometimes for ikura sushi with wasabi on the side if it's a *really* nice restaurant.'

Wong's face darkened. 'You must *not* eat Mr Tik's fish.'

'I was joking. *Geez.*'

He explained that the fish were not merely ornamental devices to attract good fortune. Fish of this sort cost hundreds or even thousands of American dollars each, and were regularly auctioned at high prices. Good breeding fish were sometimes fish-napped. Advising on fish security had become a distressingly common part of Wong's business in the past few months.

In the past year, thieves had regularly broken into homes and stolen fish while leaving money and jewellery behind.

'Fish very important. Importance of fish in feng shui of Mr Tik's apartment cannot be exaggerated.' Wong touched his fingertips together as he spoke. Ever since he had seen a picture of Confucius in such a pose, he had copied it whenever he had to deliver statements that needed gravitas.

She scribbled down his instructions in a notebook.

In a follow-up case such as this, a feng shui reader's task would be straightforward, he explained. First, ask if there had been any changes in the furniture, fittings, design or usage patterns for the various rooms. Second, check for changes in the number and type of fish. Third, check the birth dates of the home and the homeowner against the current feng shui calendar. Fourth, check the view for changes in external influences. Fifth, write lengthy comments on all the above.

'Most important is number six. But you don't have to do it.'

'What?'

'Write big invoice and wait for cheque. But this time, Mr Pun will pay direct. Special deal for members of his board.'

He made her get out her feng shui compass and tested her on *lo pan* readings.

The results, he admitted to himself reluctantly, were impressive. She had clearly learned a great deal over the first half of the year. Not that he had actively taught her anything. She had simply read through every feng shui book written in English she could find. And then she had watched him carefully on every assignment. By this time, he was satisfied that her technical know-how was not a problem, and she had the fundamentals down pat – the eight trigrams, the circles of destruction and creation, the yin-yang principles, and the interpretation of the flying star calendar.

But he had two further concerns. One was whether she had a feeling for the symbolism that was a key to Chinese mysticism. That sort of thing you couldn't get out of books. 'This shape bad, because looks like a Chinese grave,' he said, showing her a diagram which looked to Joyce like a ram's head. 'So anything this shape is bad.'

He pointed to the corner of the office where the kitchen items were. 'Knifes, waste bin, toilets, these things very negative. Things which look like those things, or which remind you of those things, also very bad. Understand? Never associate Mr Tik or his career or home with any of those things, understand or not?'

'Yeah-yeah. Peasy.'

There was one other thing he was nervous about: her use of English. 'Also, please try to talk so Mr Tik understand what you say.'

'He speaks English?'

'Yes, he speaks English.'

'So . . . ?'

The feng shui master took a moment to consider how to explain. He picked up his *Dictionary of Contemporary English Idioms* and tapped it. 'Mr Tik, he does not speak your English. He speak *this* English: It is raining cats and dogs. The proof is in the pudding. Goodness what a palaver.'

'Say *what?*'

'Speak in simple way to him, please.'

'No worries. I'm cool. This is so like groady to the max.'

He closed his eyes. A man could only pray.

Joyce gathered together all the papers, squashed them into her bag, and set off for the block on Fort Canning Road. The door slammed shut, the *shh-chka-shh-chka-shh-chka* noise vanished into the distance, and silence fell like a curtain.

Suddenly he was free of fishy Mr Tik, free of Joyce, and free of pressure. His secretary-administrator Winnie Lim had not turned up for work, so the stillness in the office was complete. It felt weird. It felt unfamiliar. It felt wonderful. He determined to attempt to arrange external assignments for Joyce on a daily basis, even if they were pro bono assignments.

Once more Wong started thinking of ways to celebrate. Singing and dancing were definitely out, he decided, but the second-breakfast idea was a winner. He picked up the phone and ordered a special delivery of dim sum.

Fu, the septuagenarian deliveryman, turned up twenty minutes later with three steaming bags. In traditional Shanghainese street-food style, the restaurant hadn't bothered with polystyrene boxes. Staff had simply thrown the dim sum into translucent plastic bags and sprinkled them with soy sauce and chilli oil.

While waiting, Wong had made a pot of green tea. The deliveryman let himself in and carelessly dropped the bags on the table. One tipped over. A yellow pork siu mai rolled across the table, leaving a trail of oil across the papers.

'Aiyeeah!' shouted the feng shui master. 'You nearly spoil cheque!' He grabbed an envelope containing payment from a customer, kissed the oil off it, and tucked it into his inside pocket.

Excitedly, he opened one of the bags and the cloying aroma of sweet glutinous sauces filled his wide nostrils. 'You have one,' he said generously, holding the bag out to the old man.

'Already got,' Fu replied, pointing to his stuffed left cheek.

Wong counted the dumplings in his bag and realised that the deliveryman had helped himself to a significant proportion of the meal as commission for bringing it. This was outrageous, but the geomancer couldn't bring himself to be in a bad mood today. He wiped up the oily residue from his desk with some tissues from a toilet roll in his bottom drawer and picked up a toothpick with which to stab the dumplings.

'Mmm, *ho mei*,' he mumbled to Fu's retreating back as he placed a whole har gow between his yellowing teeth and an explosion of grease filled his mouth. Life was improving and could conceivably get better.

Which was the moment Winnie Lim arrived.

She pushed the door open with such force that it bounced off the wall.

He was about to scold her for being late, but she was faster off the mark. 'Mean one you. Why you not share? Also I want,' she said, staring at his steaming collection of plastic bags.

The secretary scraped her chair over to his desk and started transferring the dumplings to her mouth at a steady, machine-like pace. Wong lifted his own game to match. For several minutes, the only sounds in the office were sloppy, competitive chompings from Wong and Lim.

Then the geomancer looked up at his secretary, putting on his sternest *I-am-big-boss* voice. 'Joyce this morning go to do Mr Tik. If no problem, then we give her plenty more assignment.' He spoke with his mouth full, oil dribbling down his chin. 'After a while, I do no work. Just count money. Ha ha.'

Winnie gave him a disapproving look and shook her head disdainfully.

He noticed her reaction with irritation and stopped chewing. 'So? What?'

'No good,' the secretary mumbled, also speaking with her mouth full. 'Joyce cannot do-ah. Bad idea.'

'Can.'

'Cannot. She mess up-lah. Joyce is foreigner. Everything also she do wrong.'

'Easy job I give her. Apartment of Mr Tik very easy.'

Winnie added a third dumpling to the two already in her mouth and spoke indistinctly, spraying grey goo over the desk. 'Not easy. She mess up. You see.'

He was angry. 'So many times already I do it, this apartment! Four-five over times. Only need to count fish. What can she do wrong?' He blinked crossly at her.

She shook her head and stabbed a toothpick violently into a chicken foot from another bag. 'Sometimes you are a bit stupid boss. Mr Tik move house already. Las' month. New house, very big. You don't know?'

CF Wong's mouth dropped open and a har gow dumpling rolled out, landing squarely in his bo'lei tea with a splash.

Joyce pressed the bell for a third time, and sighed. She told herself that she would patiently count to twenty and if there was still no reply, she would accept that no one was home. *One, two, three, four . . .* 'Bugger,' she said. Losing patience, she depressed the bell a fourth time, her fingertip turning white with angry pressure.

She was standing on the front step of an old, slightly crumbly block of pale green apartments on the southern side of a gently sloping road in Fort Canning. The address that Wong

31

had given her indicated that Mr Tik lived in the penthouse flat on the fifteenth floor. But there was no answer. Either he was out, he was deaf, or the buzzer didn't work.

As she stood in a state of confusion on the front step, one of the other residents arrived, keyed a four-digit code to unlock the door, and strolled in. In typical self-absorbed Singaporean fashion, the man who had arrived gave no indication that he had even seen Joyce. She grabbed the door before it swung back into locked position and followed him in.

The block was old, and there was no guard on the ground floor. Joyce summoned the lift and was carried slowly and creakily up to the top floor.

Arriving outside an apartment gated with a padlocked heavy steel shutter, she found herself stumped again. She rang the doorbell several times, but there was no response.

The bloody man must have dropped dead, she thought with sudden bitterness. How inconsiderate. This was a rare example of her having been given an entire solo assignment, and it seemed cruel of fate to conspire to make her fail. But what could she do? If he wasn't in, he wasn't in. She thought about wait- ing, but there was no air in the corridor, the space was humid, and she was sweating. Worst of all, there was a nasty odour of fish. She turned away and started to walk back to the lift.

Then she stopped. Hang on! This was the penthouse. She knew that whoever rented the top flat in this sort of apartment block nearly always got the roof as well. And space being at such a premium in the city-state, residents inevitably made use of the extra space, turning it into a picnic area or roof garden or something. There must be stairs from the apartment level to the roof – and possibly internal access, perhaps a spiral staircase or terrace or something.

'I'm gonna to do it,' she said out loud, her hands clenching into determined fists. 'I'm gonna bloody well get in and bloody well feng shui the place.'

Behind the stairwell door she found stained concrete steps leading upwards. She scampered up them into an ill-lit upper landing. Pushing open a metal door, she stepped onto the roof.

She shut her eyes against the glare – after the dark stairwell, the noonday sunshine was painfully bright. Squinting, she could immediately see that the roof space had been divided into three parts, each assigned to one of the three apartments on the top floor. The steps she had climbed opened into a small central area with a few structures that appeared to house electrical and mechanical installations for the whole building. But on each side were fenced-off roof gardens.

Although the tall gate of the roof garden on the north – Mr Tik's side – was locked, it only took a moment for the agile young woman to clamber over. She found herself on a pock-marked, clay-tiled surface irregularly covered with plant pots and plastic garden furniture. Most of the pots were empty and the few that still contained vegetation featured dry, papery brown leaves. The plastic furniture was cracked and broken. The whole roof garden had an abandoned look about it, as if no one had been there for weeks. Well, this was something she could write about in her feng shui report, for a start. Pots full of dead flowers were a definite no-no, *that* was for sure.

Joyce strolled over to the edge of the roof and looked over. She quickly found what she was looking for. There was a wide terrace running around the east side of the flat. She would be able to jump down to it without any danger. And even better, there were three windows facing the balcony. One was a set of French windows, and two were normal windows – one which was slightly open. Bingo! Breaking in might be surprisingly easy. Now *this* was showing initiative.

The young woman carefully lowered herself off the edge of the roof and dropped lightly on to the terrace. She couldn't see inside; heavy curtains blocked the view through the windows. But the lack of light escaping from the edges of the drapes suggested no one was home.

The French windows were locked, so she used an empty plant pot on the balcony to climb up and get onto the sill of the open window.

This is so easy, she thought to herself. She pictured herself reporting back to Wong. 'Actually, Mr Tik was out and there was nobody there. But I managed to break in and feng shui-ed the house anyway.' He would be like *so* impressed.

Moments later, she was crouching with difficulty on the windowsill, trying to push the curtain obscuring her view to one side.

Just then, her mobile phone started to ring in her left pocket. She awkwardly tried to reach it with her right hand. But the sill was slippery with some sort of lichen, and her right foot, which was bearing her weight, started to slide backwards. She reached out to grab the curtain, but it swung away as she attempted to get a grip on it.

'Bugger,' said Joyce as she fell forwards into the darkness and felt herself descending into tepid water. Her head hit something hard and cold and she blacked out. The last thing she remembered was the stench of fish.

'Aiyeeah!' said Wong, lowering the handset. 'No answer.'

He picked up his *lo pan* and put it into his battered case.

He would have to go to the correct address and do Mr Tik's apartment himself.

At the door of his office, he turned back to face Winnie. 'Phone Mr Tik. Tell him I am on the way. Little bit late.'

'Later,' Winnie mumbled, her mouth full of char siu so from Wong's abandoned celebratory breakfast. 'Eating, blind one, you can't see?'

He was going to come up with a rude retort, but didn't have the energy. What to do? He slammed the door on the way out and raced down the stairs, shaking his head at his ruined morning. Why did the gods hate him so?

The feng shui master's mouth dropped open as the taxi pulled up outside Mr Tik's new residence. The businessman now lived in a duplex apartment on the top floors of a sub-divided colonial house in Chatsworth Road. Definitely a notch up from the middle-class flat in Fort Canning. Mr Tik's family business must be thriving. This was odd, because he was a commodity broker, and that industry had been in a nosedive for the past twelve months.

Wong decided that he could definitely take some of the credit for the man's rise. He would have to let people know that this particular client's insistence on using a top-ranked not-at-all-cheap feng shui master was a key factor in his accumulation of riches against the odds.

'Must take photo,' the geomancer said to himself. He pictured a newspaper article in the *Straits Times*, with two images: a 'before' picture showing a humble Tik outside the crumbly block in Fort Canning, and an 'after' shot showing a wealthier-looking Tik leaning on a sports car outside his new mansion. The headline could be: BRILLIANT FENG SHUI MASTER TRANSFORMS SMALL BUSINESSMAN INTO WEALTHY TYCOON.

The geomancer took a lift to the third floor. 'Ah, Wong-*saang*, how are you?' Tik Sin-cheung, a small man in his late fifties with a barrel-shaped body, stepped out of the oak-panelled front door and shook both Wong's hands. 'Glad you came. Like the new place?'

The feng shui master forgot all the apologies for lateness that he had been rehearsing in the taxi. 'New place very nice. Very big. Very expensive.'

'Business has been good,' gushed Tik. 'Come inside. There are lots of nice things to show you.'

Wong wandered dazed into the marble entrance hall. In his mind, he had begun rehearsing a speech in which he asked Mr Pun for a fat surcharge on his original quote for the assignment, since the new premises were considerably larger than the old one. And he was feeling positive for another reason – amazingly, he could not detect the slightest smell of fish.

The apartment had water features in many rooms – far too much water, he realised. But he knew it would not be smart to say anything negative just yet. 'Ver' nice. You did a good job with new home.'

'I chose the colours and stuff myself,' Tik said proudly, showing his visitor into a room in which pink furniture clashed dramatically with orange walls. The hues were all wrong. It was a southeast living room, and there was lively *ch'i* energy in it. The room needed pale purple or lilac to calm the energy down, matched with fittings in light green or pale blue. It was obvious that it needed vertical stripes of green to support the tree energy present. But Wong kept his mouth shut.

There were fish motifs everywhere, of course, and the geomancer counted three separate aquariums in the main living area alone. Thankfully, they were not particularly odorous, although Tik himself smelt rather high.

On the upper floor, the client's homegrown colour-matching skills were again much in evidence. The master bedroom featured particularly dramatic hues. 'I did it purple and red. The two colours go together very well, don't they?'

'Hmm,' Wong replied. 'Very, er, something.'

'Yes, quite something, aren't they?'

The bedroom was in the northwest, which was a good location for a master bedroom, with its mature and steady energy. However, the feng shui master knew that Tik was single and a bit of a playboy, so using a bedroom to the west would have been better for his love life. He would eventually get the householder to switch bedrooms and decorate them in more suitable ways: rounded patterns in bronze, grey or pink would maintain metal energy.

After a fifteen-minute tour, during which Tik pointed out a number of innovative features, such as a bathroom with hessian walls already starting to turn green-blue with fungus, they returned to the dining room (full of spiky plants – very negative), where the householder laid out copies of the floor plans he had obtained from his interior designer.

'There. Now you can do your stuff. The first thing I want you to do, of course, is to look at the fish. I have fabulous new fish. I want you to check the security, too – especially of the fish on the terrace. You know there have been so many fish thefts in Singapore in the past few months. Any tea?'

'Bo'lei, please,' said Wong. As the client left his room, the feng shui master allowed himself the pleasure of a little cackle, and rubbed his hands together. He had completely forgotten about his pestilent assistant.

Joyce woke up. She was cold. She was wet. Her head hurt. It was dark. It was smelly. She appeared to be in a bath of some sort. There was something soft and spongy beneath her. Then something slimy and alive moved against her foot and she screamed.

'Aaa!' She reached for the edge of the bath, or whatever it was, and yanked herself out. She jumped onto the floor and stood shivering, miserable and wet on a hard wooden surface, trying to get her bearings. Water poured off her. What on earth was she doing, fast asleep, in the dark, in a cold bath? And the place stank of fish.

In seconds, it all came back to her. She had climbed through a window into Tik's apartment and fallen into something cold and wet. She saw movement in the black water and a shiver of horror ran down her spine as she realised she may have landed on something alive and crushed it. What *was* that spongy thing she had been lying on?

As her eyes grew accustomed to the dim light, she noticed in the low glow from the edges of the curtains that she was in a large room, and there were many tubs across the floor. Splashing and slithering noises came from all directions. The room appeared to be filled with fish tanks of various sizes. It was like a nightmare.

She scanned the dark walls for a light switch, but then decided that it would be unsafe for her to touch anything electric, since she was soaked to the skin. Instead, she carefully walked between two tanks to the curtains, and drew them open.

She turned around and gasped. Wong had told her to expect a couple of fish tanks. But instead, there were at least a dozen, and each was filled with sea creatures – ranging from thrashing giant carp to shoals of brightly-coloured clown fish. There must have been hundreds of fish in the room. *Eeew!*

She looked with disgust at the tank she had fallen into and noticed that a large spotted fish half a metre long lay flat and lifeless on the bottom. She must have crushed it to death, she realised with a spasm of repulsion.

To distract herself from that unpleasant thought, she looked into the other tanks. Many contained beautiful creatures. On her right, she saw a group of luminous fish, glowing green as they darted between strands of seaweed. And to her left, she saw a tank of what looked like tiny sharks. In another tank, tiny orange-tinted turtles swam over glowing, waving blue anemones.

Something about the blue glow reminded her of the mobile phone in her pocket. She plucked it out and was dismayed to see that it was soaked and the screen was dark. Water dripped from inside the casing. Punching the buttons produced no effect.

'Shoot. Oh well, one problem at a time,' she said out loud. 'I've got a job to do.'

The room was smelly but it was not cold. The air-conditioning was off. She was shivering from shock, not chills, she realised.

She took the *lo pan* out of her wet bag and carefully picked her way towards a flat surface. Although there was no furniture in the house, the kitchen counter would serve as a desk. She spread out her things upon it, and was glad to find that most of the stuff inside her bag was dry. At the bottom of her satchel, she found a pen that worked and some sheets of paper that were wet only on the edges, and started to work.

By 3 p.m., Wong had done basic readings for most of the main rooms in Tik's new residence. The colour scheme was

39

disastrous and would have to be adjusted and most of the furniture would have to be changed too. It would take a great deal of work to get the house right, but the feng shui master was pleased at how things had turned out. He knew he would have to be subtle about persuading Tik to make the changes, and they would have to be stretched out over a long period. With a bit of luck, Wong would have repeat fees which would carry him along for weekly visits for three to four months, if not longer. And if the house did start to smell of fish, he could assign Joyce to do all the follow-up visits.

It was time to head back to the office to start filling slots into his work diary. He rubbed his hands together.

By late afternoon, Joyce McQuinnie had finished analysing the fish-filled apartment. It had taken her a long time, but she was generally satisfied with her work. There were neat pages of diagrams showing the orientation of each room and the main influences working on the various spaces.

The rather obvious over-supply of water influence in the rooms had caused her a major challenge, but one she felt she had coped with. She had a list of recommendations that introduced salt, metal, fire and other elements into significant spaces to balance the elements to some degree.

The apartment, her compass told her, was in the north of the building, and most of the large tanks were grouped in the north or northwest part of it. Her plan proposed that a large number of potted trees be brought into the apartment, to absorb some of the excess water *ch'i* energy. For the northwest room, she knew that metal *ch'i* energy would be the right solution. A display of silver objects in that corner would do it, she reckoned.

She had concluded that the overall influence of the rows of tanks could be made positive. After all, in feng shui terms water was related to money. Wong had taught her that money flowed through modern society in exactly the same way that in ancient times, streams flowed and water gourds were exchanged in well-laid out human settlements.

Standing water was yin, since it could so easily stagnate. But moving water was yang. Every one of these tanks was full of live creatures, and the water was clean and looked like it had been regularly changed, so that alleviated the negative yin effects to a great degree.

It was a pretty amazing way to use a flat, she decided. When Wong had told her that Tik was obsessed with fish, she had not realised how extreme a compulsion like that could get. For example, there was no bed in the bedroom, only large tanks with more fish. Did he sleep with them? Or had he given up his whole apartment for the fish and gone to camp in a hotel somewhere? Water features in a bedroom were a big no-no, but since none of the rooms actually featured a bed, she had to assume that there were no rooms used for that purpose.

To get dry, Joyce had removed most of her clothes, squeezed water out of them and then left them on the balcony. She had done most of the work in her underwear. In the intervening three hours, the Singapore heat had done its stuff, and she would soon have reasonably dry garments to put on. She decided she had done enough work here, over and above the call of duty, and it was time to head off back to Telok Ayer Street.

That's when she discovered that she was locked in. Neither the front nor back door would open. Each was triple-locked. She recalled the padlock and chain on the gate outside the front door.

She was trapped. Her mobile phone still wasn't working and there was no landline in the apartment. How was she going to get out? She went out onto the balcony and tried to climb back up onto the roof, to see if she could get out the way she had entered. But it was too high. There were no chairs or ladders in the apartment on which to stand. She tried clambering back onto the slippery windowsill, but there was an overhang above it that prevented her reaching up towards the edge of the roof.

Perhaps there was something else in the house which she could stand on? But no: there was nothing suitable – not one chair except the low stool on which she had sat to do her writing in the kitchen. She searched every inch of the house and peered out of every window but could find no way of escaping. She was well and truly stuck.

Joyce felt panic welling up inside her. But she took deep breaths and forced herself to remain rational. She was in no danger, she told herself. First, Wong and Winnie both knew where she was. They would come and get her. Second, Mr Tik would eventually have to turn up to feed his fish. Surely they had to be fed once a day or so? Besides, she wasn't going to come to any harm through lack of food or water. The taps and electricity were still working. If she found herself actually starving, she could always find a cooking pan and eat one of the fish – if she could bring herself to do such a thing. No, there was no real danger. All she needed to do was stay alive until help came along.

But waiting to be rescued was boring. Watching exotic sea creatures go around in their tanks quickly lost its allure. And the place was stinky. After four hours, she was feeling half-asphyxiated by the smell. She'd have to throw these clothes away.

Joyce decided she might as well try to make contact with people outside.

She went back out onto the balcony and called out to passers-by below.

'Helloooooo,' she yelled to people walking on the street below. 'Heeeeeyyyy.'

No one looked up. She was fifteen floors above them, and her voice was drowned out by traffic that roared from a major road to the southwest of the block.

She wondered whether she should write a help message and send it down to ground level. But who would find a piece of paper on the ground and read it? It would probably be kicked into the gutter or get run over by a vehicle. It might not be read for hours, or days, if ever.

No. She needed something more creative. Perhaps she could lower something distinctive that would make people look up? She thought for a moment about throwing rainbow fish down until someone looked up, but then remembered that Wong had said the fish were very valuable and expensive. He might take it out of her pay.

Joyce went back into the apartment and walked around again, looking for something long and thin that would stretch fifteen storeys to reach the ground. What she needed was a really long rope or something that she could use to lower a message to ground level. In the movies people knotted sheets together, but there were no beds. What could she find to use as a rope?

She opened a cabinet under the sink in the bathroom and found two old rolls of toilet tissue. 'Got it,' she exclaimed.

She wrote a message on the first few sheets of paper: *HELP, CALL FENG SHUI MASTER CF WONG. TELL HIM TO COME TO THIS ADDRESS. URGENT. OR POLICE.*

Then she added the office phone number, attached a pen to the sheet to give it weight and gently lowered the long line of toilet tissue out of the window. Fortunately, it was a still afternoon and there was little breeze. Although it made her dizzy to hang over the balcony and watch the paper descending, she was pleased to see that a single roll of toilet paper took her message about two-thirds of the way down the building. She carefully knotted the last few sheets to the first sheets of a second roll and continued to lower the message.

Two minutes later, the message touched the ground. It dangled near the front door of the building, swinging gently from side to side in the breeze.

The first resident to pass, an elderly man, glanced at the vertical line of toilet tissue paper, but did not stop to examine it.

'*Oi!*' Joyce screeched from fifteen storeys above him. 'Idiot,' she added, as he disappeared.

After a few minutes, a middle-aged woman carrying bags of shopping appeared and strolled towards the front door. She noticed the swinging line of tissue and paused.

Joyce watched excitedly as she shook her head disapprovingly. Then she looked up to see where it was coming from.

'Heeey! Look up here,' the young woman hollered. 'I'm stuck.'

The woman gave no signs of noticing her or hearing her cry. But to Joyce's delight, she lowered her shopping bags and picked up the tissue, noticing the writing spread across several sheets. She started to read.

The phone rang at Telok Ayer Street. Winnie had disappeared and Wong was alone in the office, carefully calculating just how much money he could make from monthly repeat visits to Mr Tik's rainbow apartment.

'Yes?' said Wong, snatching up the handset.

'Are you CF Wong?' asked a young male voice.

'Yes.'

'Are you a feng shui master?'

'Yes.'

'Ha! I would have thought that toilet paper would be bad feng shui,' said the voice with a laugh.

'What?'

'Toilet paper. Do you know your name is on a long piece of toilet paper hanging out of a building in Fort Canning?'

Wong was speechless.

'Are you still there, Mr Wong?'

'You are who?'

'I'm calling from the news desk of the *Straits Times*. We just got a call from a lady who says that someone has draped her building with toilet paper with your name on it.'

'What?'

'Someone has written your name on a roll of toilet paper and dropped it out of the top of a building. It's a message fifteen floors long. In Fort Canning. Do you know anything about this? We're sending a photographer. Do you have any comment? Mr Wong? Are you there, Mr Wong?'

But the feng shui master had dropped the phone and was racing down the stairs to get into a taxi.

Twenty minutes later, CF Wong and Tik Sin-cheung arrived at the apartment block in Fort Canning Road. Tik, who had been roughly manhandled into the taxi by the desperate feng shui master, was still asking questions as they spilled out onto the pavement.

'But I don't understand. Why do we need to visit my old flat? I store my personal effects there. No one is allowed inside. It's very personal to me.'

'Someone is inside. You must get her out.'

'What do you mean? Who is inside? And how did she get there? No one can get in. It's locked. It's locked with three locks, and there's a padlock and chain on the steel gate. I'm sure there's no one inside.'

'She got in, I think.'

'Who? A burglar? Was she trying to steal my fish? I have fish inside. Just a few. They're mine. Honestly.'

'No, she is not burglar. She is my assistant.'

'Why did you send your assistant to my old flat? I didn't ask you to do my old flat.'

'Special service for old customer. We do your new flat and we do your old flat too, free of charge.'

Tik went quiet. 'Are you sure she managed to get inside?'

'I think.'

The businessman spoke slowly, carefully. 'I have . . . private things in there. I don't want people to know what's inside. I have a few new fish. I mean, *a lot* of new fish.'

Wong turned to look at him. There was an unmistakable tone of guilt in his voice. Tik spoke again, his voice betraying deep concern. 'If your staff member has managed to get in, then I will get her out. But you do . . . you do promise full confidentiality, don't you? You don't need to tell anyone what's in there, do you?'

The feng shui master said nothing.

'I would be willing to pay an extra fee, do you know what I mean? A special confidentiality fee? One thousand bucks?

One thousand-over bucks?'

Wong's mind was racing. Now here was a dilemma – not an ethical one, but a financial one. Clearly Tik had something serious to hide. And the geomancer could hazard a guess as to exactly what it might be. And he, Wong, was now being offered a bribe to keep quiet about it. This was where the math came in. If Tik's opening offer was one thousand Sing dollars, what would his final offer be? Conversely, what would be the financial effect on his feng shui consultancies if the spate of fish-nappings that had swept Singapore continued? In the past month alone, two frustrated customers had cancelled long-term contracts after they had installed expensive fish that had promptly disappeared. He glanced at Tik's garish clothes and decided that the fish-collector did not have a bright future. Better to put his trust in taking action to ensure the return of stability to the Singapore aquatic scene.

The geomancer marched swiftly through the main gates of the apartment block and then froze. He saw a young man in a multi-pocketed vest snapping photographs of the long string of toilet paper, swinging in the late afternoon breeze.

Wong hurriedly backed away, having a deep-rooted fear of the media. He positioned himself on the other side of the main wall, where the press photographer couldn't see him. 'You go inside. Unlock door. Let my staff member come out. I wait here,' he told Tik.

The businessman, looking ever more anxious, jingled the keys in his pocket and set off into the apartment block.

Keeping out of sight of the snapper, the geomancer tried to gaze up at the fifteenth floor. There was nothing to see.

A police car pulled up outside the block and a small, rather ruffled police officer climbed out. He straightened himself with some difficulty and stared up at the unravelled toilet paper. He chewed a well-masticated pen thoughtfully.

Spotting Wong, Inspector Gilbert Tan vainly attempted to pull his trousers over his round stomach, and ambled over.

'Ah, Mr Wong,' he said. 'Your call sounded so urgent-lah. What can I do for you? You summon me to tell me someone is dropping toilet paper out of a window, is it? Dropping toilet paper in private estate is not a crime, yet, I think, unless we try to use litter ordinance.'

The feng shui master shook his head. 'Ah, Inspector Tan. Have good news and bad news.'

'Tell me bad news first.'

'Good news for you. Bad news for me.'

'Oh. In that case, tell me good news first.'

Wong nodded. 'I think maybe we found fish thief.'

'What fish thief?'

'The big money fish stolen from all over? Carp, angelfish, exotic fish, like that? Remember? Fish thieves over past few months? In the newspaper?'

'Ah,' said Inspector Tan. 'Fish thieves, yes. Not most high profile case-lah. But yes, I did read somewhere that there have been a lot of stolen fish over past few months. You've found the culprit, is it?'

Wong pointed upwards. 'Man in this flat has suddenly got large number of fish. Small broker. Big money fish. Suddenly he is rich. Very suspicious.'

The photographer went back to his car and, after dawdling for a few moments, revved it up and raced away, tyres squealing.

Wong, seeing his opportunity, took hold of the police officer's elbow and steered him to the building's front step. They pressed the buttons of the flats at random until someone buzzed the main door open. 'So easy to get into Singapore flats,' lamented Inspector Tan. 'Nobody interested in security.'

In the lift, the police officer turned to his friend. 'So that is good news? You think you found a fish thief? And what is bad news?'

Wong looked gloomy. 'Bad news is I think I very soon lose customer. Also maybe upset Mr Pun, my biggest customer.'

As the lift neared the top of the building, an unmistakable odour seeped into the space.

'Eee!' said Tan. 'Hate the smell of fish.'

'Joyce the same.'

'And you?'

'Make me hungry only.'

As they stepped out of the lift they heard shouts.

'Murderer!' a man's voice shrieked. 'You killed my spotted plectropomus!'

The door was unlocked. They entered the room to see Tik Sin-cheung swinging a large, dead leopard-spotted fish by its tail. He was brandishing it threateningly at Joyce McQuinnie, who for some reason had stripped to her undergarments and trainers. Wong found her freckled, almost colourless skin repulsive; it looked like raw chicken.

There was some sort of fight going on. The young woman was gamely holding her own. She held her fists in front of her. 'You touch me with that and I kick this bloody thing in RIGHT NOW.' She tapped her Adidas trainer threateningly against a glass tank of rare pineapple fish.

'You dare! You just dare!' roared Tik.

'Bloody *will*,' Joyce spat, kicking it again.

'Ahem.' Wong coughed to interrupt the argument.

The young woman turned and spotted her boss. 'This guy's gone mad, just because I fell onto one of his bloody fish.

I couldn't help it. He shouldn't lock his flat up when people are trying to get in, should he? Tell him.'

Tik Sin-cheung lowered his spotted plectropomus. He had suddenly noticed the police officer standing in the doorway. His face fell. He looked around at all the tanks of fish.

'They're all mine,' he said. 'They're my family. They come to me. They call my name. I get people to liberate them, you see.' He dropped to his knees and put his hand in a tank of brightly coloured creatures, which fluttered away from him. 'These fish are Bodianus peppermint wrasse. They weren't being well cared for. So I got my people to rescue them for me. And all the others. I don't keep them. I find better homes for them.'

Wong barked: 'Joyce. You better come with me.'

'And you'd better come with me,' said Inspector Tan.

Fit for life or death

In all aspects of life there are mysteries. The crafty will take advantage of them. Even Zen masters do this sometimes. A commentary on Zen teacher Wang Shou-jen (1472–1528) tells this story:

Once a scholar went as a guest to a Buddhist temple. The abbot let him come in. But he was given no special honour. He was given no particular respect.

Then a prominent official arrived.

The abbot gave the official great respect. He bowed low. He escorted him around the temple himself. He arranged for the best food and the best drink to be given to him.

Then the official left the temple.

Afterwards, the scholar went to see the abbot. The scholar said: 'Why did you give me no respect but you gave the official great respect?'

The abbot replied: 'To give no respect is to give respect. To give respect is to give no respect. That is way of Zen.'

The scholar used his fist to hit the monk hard in the face.

The abbot said: 'Ow! Why did you hit me?'

The scholar said: 'To beat you up is to not beat you up. To not beat you up would have been to beat you up. That is the way of Zen.'

Blade of Grass, some people use crooked arguments to fight you. When they do this they are giving you a weapon. They have stepped off the path so the advantage is with you.

In his book, The Great Learning, Confucius said:
'The way of truth is like a great road. It is not hard to
find. Trouble is only men will not look for it.'
From *Some Gleanings of Oriental Wisdom*
by CF Wong, part 32

The gymnasium was filled with contradictions. Scented and bright, it was a soft and luxurious haven with a deep carpet and fine wallpaper. But at the same time, there was a hardness about it: the carpet was grey and the equipment was mostly steel with a dark, matt coating. The fixtures oozed class, consisting largely of shiny, ornamented brass fittings set into expensive Andaman padauk wood. Yet on the polished pine table on one side was scattered an untidy heap of dog-eared magazines and used paper cups.

Heavy air-conditioning kept the room uncomfortably chilly, but the man running on the treadmill was bathed in sweat.

Club executive manager Kees Luis de Boer had been running for seventeen minutes at ten kilometres an hour and was well into his stride, although his jerky speech was starting to betray a certain breathlessness.

'He's . . . here? Tell him to . . . come in.'

'He's already in the gym, sir, right behind you.' The membership secretary discreetly made an open palm gesture towards the visitor.

De Boer swivelled his bouncing head as much as he could to the left, which wasn't much.

Wong, trying to be helpful, leaned forwards to catch the manager's eye. 'Good morning Mr de Boer,' he said, pronouncing it *Deebo*. 'I am Wong.'

'It's d'Bo-*er*. Thanks for . . . coming. I'll be with you in a . . . few minutes. Just got to get up . . . to twenty. I'm out of sorts all day if I . . . don't get my run in, you know how it is . . . with the old endorphins.' The rhythmic thudding of his feet gave his words a staccato feel.

'Oh,' said Wong. He turned a questioning gaze to the woman next to him as if to say: *I'm afraid I do not know the Old Endorphins. Is this a problem?*

The membership secretary, a small grey-suited woman named Maria Runick, had a more urgent matter on her mind. She also tried to lean into de Boer's line of sight. 'Mr de Boer? A couple of the members are here at reception and they want to know whether they can come in. There's a sign up saying that it's closed from ten for an hour, but they are very, you know, insistent. And I already asked Mr Wong, and he says that he doesn't mind them being here while he's working.'

De Boer said nothing. The thump of his feet hitting the floor was the only sound in the gym for half a minute. 'Are they angry? Who are they? Anyone . . . important?'

'Yes, they are a bit . . . difficult. They say they didn't get the email saying that the gym would be closed for two hours today. Their names are Anthony de Cunha and Roger Eliott. I think you know Mr de Cunha.'

'Yes, yes, the petroleum guy.' He lapsed into silence. 'Shit.'

She glanced at the window between the gym and the reception area, where two unsmiling men in dark suits were waiting. After a polite pause, Ms Runick tried to press her superior again for an answer. 'Shall I let them in?'

'I'm thinking, I'm thinking. My brain . . . works a little more slowly when I am . . . running. But the answers it . . . gives are usually the right ones. If the word gets out . . . that we are having the place . . . feng shui-ed, people are going to ask . . . why. So we had better keep . . . people out.'

Ms Runick slowly breathed out and then breathed in again. She appeared to be attempting to gather courage to disagree with her boss. 'Yes, sir. But the news is already out. About the, er, unfortunate incident of last week. It was being discussed in the restaurant yesterday, and there was talk in the members' bar at lunch. I think if we let them know that we are dealing with the problem, it will be better in the long run. They'll all find out eventually. Three of our members work for newspapers, remember? And we have an ABC guy.'

She leaned over to catch her boss's eye for an answer.

It was difficult to tell if Mr de Boer was nodding, or if the vertical movement of his head was due purely to the fact that he was a heavy man pounding thunderously on a conveyor belt.

'I said . . .' he began with some irritation but then paused abruptly. The counter in front of him ticked over to the figure 20:00. 'Ah,' he breathed, and raised his hand to the sweat-stained console in front of him. He pressed an image of an arrow pointing downwards. *Beep!* it went. He thumped it repeatedly with his finger. *Beep-beep-beep-beep-beep-beep-beep-beep*. The high-pitched whine of the treadmill changed to a lower tone as it gradually slowed down.

'Okay . . . let them in, you're probably . . . right. You usually are,' de Boer said, his mood abruptly changed by his having completed his morning exercise.

It took another thirty seconds for the machine gradually to wind down to a complete halt. After that, the silence seemed heavy and uncomfortable. Wong stood by quietly, while Ms Runick scurried back to the reception to tell the members that they were after all going to be allowed to do their workout sessions, although a feng shui master would be working in the room at the same time.

De Boer used an enormous, monogrammed fluffy white towel to wipe his neck, where most of the sweat appeared to have gathered. 'I won't shake your hand, Mr Wong. But thank you for coming.'

The feng shui master gave a short bow. 'My pleasure,' he said.

Kees Luis de Boer, general manager of The Players, a high-class restaurant and sports club in a modern office complex in Perth, lowered his voice as he turned his eye to the door of the gym.

'It's all very negative when someone dies in a gym. We try to keep quiet about it. But at the same time, we do the right things. We had the police here. We had the family in for a party-wake-sort-of-thing, on the house. And we've got you here to clean out the bad vibes, get some good ones in. I know you won't mind me saying this – I'm an honest man, that's my biggest advantage and also my biggest shortcoming – but I don't believe in any of this sort of thing. I'm only doing it for the members. These days they're all into this bloody New Age stuff, crystals and feng shui and stuff. Need to keep the campers happy.'

With a creak, the door started to swing open.

'And talk of the devils, here they come now.'

De Boer put on a corporate smile and raised his eyes to the inlaid double doors, but the new arrival turned out to be a gawky young woman of about eighteen with her shirt-tail hanging out from under a shapeless sweater.

'Who . . . ?'

'My assistant,' the geomancer explained.

'Hi guys! Sorry I'm late!' Joyce said cheerfully. 'I went

through into the gym office instead of the gym and got talking to this guy – Jimmy? He's one majorly cool dude.'

De Boer's face twitched at the sound of the name. The corners of his mouth perceptibly turned down.

Wong wondered how to react. Who was Jimmy? One needed the birth dates of the managers of any facility to do a full reading of prospects for the business. 'Mr Jimmy is who?'

De Boer snorted his breath out through his nostrils. 'Mr Jimmy is no one. Today is his last day. He *was* the gym master here, but we feel his part in last week's, er, incident, was not satisfactory. The reception staff will be running the gym for a while, and we'll get a new personal trainer/manager as soon as possible. An advertisement goes in the paper tomorrow for a replacement.'

Wong nodded, pleased. So he could probably manage without Mr Jimmy's birth date. One less thing to think about.

De Boer gave Wong and McQuinnie a short, Teutonic bow and marched off to the shower rooms.

'Pants,' whispered Joyce, stamping her right foot.

'What?'

'Oh, nothing. It's just – well, it's just a shame that that Jimmy guy isn't going to be sticking around. He's like really nice! He's got this dimple – never mind.'

'I'm sorry,' said the dimple-chinned young man, wringing his hands. 'I don't think I'm going to be a very good lunch companion. I'm too, like, shell-shocked.' Despite his exaggeratedly masculine body, Jimmy Wegner's voice was light and somewhere in the alto range.

'That's all right!' said Joyce, a little too cheerfully. *I don't mind if you don't say anything. I'll just sit here and gaze at you.*

She suddenly felt her face tingle and wondered whether she had spoken out loud.

Jimmy did not react, so apparently she hadn't. *Phew.* 'Er. No worries! We can just sort of relax, and get into a state of, you know, like, relaxation!' She seethed inwardly at her inability to utter a half-intelligent sentence in front of this young man.

'Life stinks,' Jimmy said.

She gazed at the full lips from which those words emerged, and her eyes lazily travelled down to his jutting chin. 'Yeah, it really does!' she breathed. Then she realised that the sunny smile firmly attached to the front of her face was entirely unsuited to the conversation. She abruptly wiped it from her face. 'It really, really stinks, like *totally!*' As soon as the words left her mouth, she cringed so deeply that her eyes momentarily closed. Where had her *brain* gone?

It had been an interesting morning. Immediately after she'd learned that Jimmy was no longer going to be working at The Players club, she had found an excuse to go back to the gym office, where he was packing a pitifully small number of possessions into a box.

Astonishing herself with her gall, she thanked him for showing her the way to the fitness room that morning, announced that she didn't know a soul in Perth, and theatrically shared her bafflement about where she should have lunch.

The personal trainer appeared to be in a daze, but had picked up the signal and quickly agreed to show her the local cafés. He arranged to meet her at the corner of the street at 12.30. Thus, two hours after first meeting, they found themselves in Bev's Snags & Sarnies sipping cappuccinos and dipping French fries into mayo and sweet chilli sauce.

Her eyes scanned the coffee shop, as she became increasingly desperate to make some sort of comment worthy of an intelligent young woman. 'These coffee shops are like, really totally amazing. I mean, a couple of years ago, there weren't any, and now they're all over the place.'

'Do you have them in China?'

'Singapore. I'm from Singapore.'

'Oh yeah, right. So do you speak Japanese?'

'No. In Singapore people speak English mostly. They don't speak Japanese there.'

'Really? Weird.'

'Yeah. Did you know it's shorter to go from Singapore to Perth than to go from Perth to Sydney?'

'Really?'

'Yeah.'

'Oh. I guess it's 'cause of the curvature of the earth.'

'I guess. Or daylight saving time.'

There was a lengthening moment of silence that grew and threatened to become awkward. The chatter of people having more successful conversations at tables neighbouring theirs became problematic. They needed to be drowned out.

Joyce and Jimmy tried to fill the space at the same time.

'D'you – '

'How'd – '

Both stopped. Then both spoke together again:

'You fir – '

'Go o – '

They both halted. This time they laughed.

'You first,' chuckled Joyce.

'Can't remember what I was gonna say,' grinned the personal

58

trainer. 'Oh yeah, I know. How do they learn English in Singapore? Is it through all the video games like Nintendo and Playstation and that?'

'I don't know. Probably. But I thought Nintendo and that stuff was Japanese?'

'Oh,' said Jimmy. 'Yeah, maybe. But I thought you said they didn't speak Japanese?'

'No. Well, I suppose some do. I don't speak Japanese. That's what I meant.'

'Me neither.'

'That's interesting.'

'Yeah. It means we got something in common. That's very important in a – .' He looked away, suddenly embarrassed to have almost said the word 'friendship'.

Joyce was equally alarmed by the near-use of the word 'friendship'. The word was closely associated with the word 'relationship'. An instant friendship and/or relationship was precisely what she wanted from Jimmy Wegner, age twenty-three, unemployed personal trainer, of Perth. Yet she knew that the cast-iron, number-one, golden rule of dating said that at no stage of a developing relationship should either party ever admit that a relationship was developing, or that either party was remotely hopeful that a relationship might develop. To do such a thing would be to immediately forfeit all chance of a relationship developing. She didn't know why this should be so, nor who wrote these rules. But she felt instinctively that all human beings acquired knowledge of these rules in their teens by osmosis. They were built into the genetic programming of adolescents, and would just appear, like armpit hair and spots. They must be taken seriously.

'Er, what movies do you like?' asked Joyce, wanting to move the discussion on to safer topics.

Jimmy smiled, grateful to her for rescuing the discussion. He wrinkled his stubbly Clark Kent jaw as he considered this. 'Tough one,' he said. 'All of them, I guess.'

'Yeah, me too,' Joyce said.

There was another pause in the conversation, but the young woman did not want this conversational gambit to fail – it was usually a fertile one, and could often keep small talk going for hours. So she reinforced it with a bit of detail.

'What I mean is, I like most movies, except for ones with Kevin Costner in them. And Tom Cruise. And I just hate Alicia Silverstone. And Jennifer Love Hewitt. I don't really like movies at all, really. I prefer books. Much more intelligent don't you think? I read all the time!'

'Yeah. I suppose so. Movies stink. I'll tell you what I like much better than movies.'

'What's that?'

'DVDs.'

'I so totally agree with you.'

'They're cool.'

'Like totally.'

'How you can change the language into some language you don't understand and watch the whole movie in that language? And how Tom Cruise is talking in a squeaky voice in like Polish or Irish or African or, or, or Singaporean?'

'You do that? I do that. Movies are *way* better that way.'

'Yeah. You can understand them better.'

'Totally.'

'Strange, isn't it?'

'Yeah.'

There was another gap and Joyce wondered whether the topic was threatening to run out of steam. She looked for another subject. 'So what music do you like?'

Jimmy turned to look her squarely in the eye. 'I *hate* music. Music reminds me of . . . death.'

Joyce nodded furiously, although she couldn't see the connection. 'Oh! Right. I suppose it does, if you look at it that way! I mean they have music at funer – '

'There was music playing when that guy died last week, you see.'

'Oh yeah? Anything good?'

'I thought it was good at the time. 'You Die 4 Me' by The Booger That Ate the World?'

'Cool.'

'But ever since the guy died, I haven't been able to listen to it. It reminds me of death. It's terrible.'

'Yeah, I can imagine, it would be.'

'I mean, I lost my job, I lost my career, *and* I lost my favourite music. I mean, what else is there? Geez.'

Joyce thought about this. The right answer would be: Your friends. But that would be skirting dangerously close back to the 'R' word, which was best avoided. So she decided to take a different tack.

'You may have lost your job, but you haven't lost your career. You can get another job, can't you? There's loadsa gyms in Sydney, isn't there?'

He shook his head morosely. 'Not for me. I'm unemployable. Totally.'

'Why? It wasn't your fault. I bet people have died in gyms before. Was the guy very old?'

'Fifty.'

'Well that proves it. He just died of old age! Practically everyone dies when they get that old. It's, it's, *biological.*'

'That's what I think. But they keep hinting that I, like, worked him too hard. They were making out that it was my

61

fault. Like I killed him. Old Boa Constrictor said that I was lucky I wasn't charged with like *murder* or something.'

'Who?'

'My boss. My former boss.'

'That is *so* mean! That's slander and libel. You could sue him.'

'Yeah. I should.'

'Yeah. You really should.'

Another pause.

'Can't you go and work at some other club or some hotel or something?'

'Naah,' Jimmy replied. 'You see, if one person dies during a training session at a gym, it looks pretty bad for the trainer. But if *two* people die . . . well, that's serious business. It makes people think it's the trainer's fault.'

'But only one person died.'

He shook his head and turned to face her. 'Naah. I worked before at the Millennium Centre Hotel. Some old woman popped it during a training session then, about six months ago. Old de Boer hired me for his club three months ago. And now one of *his* clients has popped it. It looks like the problem isn't the old codgers. It's me. I'm cursed. That's what it is.'

Joyce realised that these sombre memories were badly de-railing the happy, light tone that she desperately needed this first lunch date to have. She determined to steer the conversation back to more cheery waters.

'So what DVDs do you like?'

'Dunno. All of them. Tom Cruise.'

'Me too. I *love* Tom Cruise.'

Wong trotted up the stairs. Why no lift? When he arrived at the doorway to the Millennium Health Centre, he saw a set of lift doors to his right and realised that there was a lift, but it ran up the opposite side of the building. He made a mental note to enter through the east wing of the hotel on his next visit – if there was a next visit.

He was on a mission. On returning to The Players after lunch, Joyce had excitedly related bits of her lunch conversation.

Wong had spotted a business opportunity. The club was part-owned by one of Mr Pun's board members, so Wong would only get his standard retainer for the two days' work clearing away invisible repercussions of the man who had exercised himself to death. But if Wegner's previous workplace, the Millennium Health Centre, had also suffered a death recently, he could very easily do some perfunctory readings, re-edit and re-present the work he had already done, and double his money.

So he had raced to a telephone and quickly made an appointment to see the manager of the facility, a woman named Dominique Alegre. He agreed to meet her at four o'clock that afternoon. To sneak out during a period when he was being paid by one client to try to set up some work with another client – well, it had a feeling of financial improp- riety that thrilled Wong. Getting one client to cover billable hours during which he signed up other clients – *that* was the only way a self-respecting independent businessman should run an operation.

At the Millennium Health Centre, he found loud, echoing music coming from a frosted-glass-walled room and he could see colourful shapes moving inside. It sounded more like a nightclub than a health facility. He swung the glass door open, took a step inside and then froze.

'Sorry-sorry!' he said. The room, it seemed to him, was full of women in their undergarments. He abruptly started to back out.

'Come in, Monsieur Wong,' the jack-jumping woman at the front shouted over the top of the music. 'We'll be finished 'ere in exactly twelff minoots. Grab a seat. Or join in, if you feel lack.'

The feng shui master gingerly entered the shaking, noise-filled room, gluing his back to the wall. Eyes down, he shuffled as discreetly as he could along one side of the gym where he found a cluster of seats, a bowl of fruit and some magazines.

Instead of instruments and singing, the music consisted largely of room-shaking bass notes, stuttering drum beats and a shrieking asexual voice half-talking, half-singing:

Push it
Push it
Push it
Push it
Git the fever git the fever git the fever git the fever
Come on down ya
Come on down ya
Come on down ya

The woman leading the dance, or whatever it was, continued to shout over the top of the pounding, jarring music. 'Knee-raise treeples, one last time, to ze right and back and back and back, to ze left and back and back and back. And repeat. And again. And one . . . last . . . time . . . And now we are going to take ze temperature down a leetle.'

The leader, a tall brown-haired woman who was dressed in a purple skintight outfit with a black bikini over it, turned around and fiddled with the controls on a music system. The jarring music disappeared and something more contemplative started to play.

Over the sound of electric piano chords, another female voice began to whimper:

Oooh, oh whoa yeah
Ooooh, whoa-whoa
You are the angel of my dreams
I loved you sight unseen
But now you've gone away
I need you more each day
Oooh, I'm your stalker babe, you better know it
I'm your stalker babe, not scared to show it
I'm your stalker babe, I'm gonna grow it
I'm stalkin' you, to-niiiiiiiiiiight yeah yeah yeah
whoa-oooh

The twenty or so women in the room immediately trotted over to the opposite side of the hall where each of them grabbed a thin, plastic blue mattress. They each found a space on the floor and lay down, like three-year-old children ready for an after-milk nap.

Wong watched fascinated until the women started lifting each leg up in turn. Suddenly he was faced with a forest of lycra-clad thighs and buttocks. This was much too indecent a display for him to watch. He hurriedly turned his chair so his back was to the aerobics class. Then he opened a magazine at random and buried his face in it. Unfortunately, the magazine – something called *Shape* – was full of pictures of underdressed young ladies, so was almost equally embarrassing. He eventually found a page of photographs of protein milkshakes, and read the recipe over and over again until the session came to an end.

The feng shui master's meeting with Dominique Alegre was not a particular success. For a start, he found it difficult to concentrate sitting in a small office with a woman in a leotard.

There was a certain physicality about her, a thrusting animal vitality that made him uncomfortable. She was glistening with sweat, although she smelt only of some sort of flowery oil. He kept his eyes on his papers in front of him.

Wong explained that he heard there had been a death in the gym, and he wanted to offer to help. But as soon as she started speaking, a second problem emerged. Ms Alegre, thirty-four, explained that she did not take feng shui at all seriously. She said it 'wasn't for her' although her mother-in-law was crazy about it and would be thrilled to know there was a real Chinese feng shui expert visiting town. 'I will tell *ma belle-mère,* ze mother of my 'usband. If you don't mind, I will give your number to 'er.'

As for her members, she said that it was true that they had been upset by the death of a woman being trained earlier that year, but an initial drop-off of attendance had only been temporary, and had barely lasted two weeks.

'We got rid of ze personal trainer involved. After zat, everyone felt a beet more relaxed,' she said.

'Was it his fault?'

Ms Alegre considered the question very carefully before replying. She tilted her head to one side. 'Yes and *non*,' she said, slowly. 'We always make sure older clients get medical clearance for personal training sessions. We have a tie-up wiz a medical agency called EDOC – Executive Doctors on Call – so zey get a full check-up before we start. And zen a doctor and ze personal trainer work together to design a suitable exercise programme. It was set up by Dr Frankie Brackish, who's quite well known in Perth. Ees all kept on a database 'ere.' She tapped her computer monitor.

'So what went wrong?'

'For ze club, fortunately, nothing. All clients sign a disclaimer zat removes any liability we may 'ave.' She paused.

66

'Sorry, zat came out badly. What I meant was, things went wrong very badly for ze client, of course, although ze club, fortunately for us, was not considered liable.'

She stopped there and folded her arms.

Wong was intrigued. What exactly had gone wrong? He said nothing, knowing that he could use his strangeness to get away with disregarding the rules of conversation. He said nothing but merely looked blankly at her.

After a few seconds, Ms Alegre continued: 'Ze personal trainer just over-did it, basically. I don't know. Perhaps he read ze chart wrong, or perhaps he's hopeless with numbers. Whatever, ze result was a disaster. Ze client was a woman of sixty-six. Ze trainer put her on an amazingly 'eavy schedule of exercises – too 'eavy for a client so old. She did all right ze first couple of sessions, but complained a bit. Ze third session, she was twenty minoots through on ze treadmill and simply – how you say? – keeled over. Hit her 'ead on ze railing as she fell. Infarction, Doctor Brackish said.'

'Why the trainer did not follow the instructions on the computer?'

'Don't know. He was an idiot, I suppose. Zey seemed clear enough to me. It was a shame. He may have been a liability, but he was a sweet kid – and *très* good-looking. He had ze chin of Kirk Douglas.'

After spending a further twenty minutes talking to Kirk Douglas's chin (this time on the telephone during a tea break), Joyce McQuinnie was convinced that this was a key moment in her life. Jimmy Wegner was the guy she had always dreamed of meeting. Okay, so he might not have been absolutely the cleverest fella in the world, but he was a nice guy, which was what really counted.

And they both adored Tom Cruise movies, so they were practically twins! Or perhaps they both hated them – she couldn't remember. Anyway, it didn't matter. What was important was that she had now known him for ages – *hours* – and had this really *really* strong feeling that he liked her as much as she liked him.

The timing was perfect. Here she was, stuck in Perth for a few days with not much to do, and there was Jimmy, suddenly unemployed and needing someone sympathetic to talk to.

Joyce did the rest of her share of work at The Players that afternoon in a daze, looking at the clock every two minutes, since Jimmy had agreed to meet her after work. She spent most of the time doing a *lo shu* chart for the owner of the club and the general manager.

But she was bursting to talk about any aspect of Jimmy Wegner with anyone. She was intrigued to find that Wong had sneaked out for an hour during the mid-afternoon to visit the personal trainer's previous workplace.

'We both like DVDs. Isn't that amazing? By the way, do the people at that club want him back? He needs a job.'

'They don't want him back I think.'

Joyce was surprised when her boss explained that Wegner had apparently committed precisely the same mistake twice – misread a list of clear instructions from a medical database. The question that was implicit in Wong's view of events was clear: Was Jimmy Wegner incompetent or was he just pretending to be?

Joyce found neither view acceptable. 'Okay, so he's a bit stupid-*ish*, but he's not *that* stupid. I mean, if the doctor tells you to make a guy walk at three kilometres an hour for four minutes, you wouldn't make him sprint at fifteen kilometres an hour for twenty-five minutes, would you? I mean, he's a fitness guy. He knows all this stuff. We talked about this. He did exactly what it said on his instructions.'

Wong was sceptical. 'If he knows this, why he keep killing his client?'

Joyce had a straightforward answer to this: 'The doctors' database has a page for each old person, with a list of mild exercises. But there's also an individual bulletin that the doctor writes sometimes. Anyway, this bulletin told him that the person needed a circulation boost and a super-heavy workout and a high-speed run or something. Jimmy did as he was told. It turned out to be too much for the person. But when Jimmy looked back at the website, the bulletin had gone and just the usual exercises were left.'

The geomancer shook his head. 'Impossible. Numbers is in health club computer. How will doctor get in? Will he sneak into health club and change the computer?'

She slowly shook her head. 'You really don't understand the Internet, do you, CF?' She pulled her chair over to where he was sitting. She placed a white sheet of paper on his table and started drawing a diagram.

'This is the doctors' computer in the doctors' office.'

'In office of EDOC.'

'What?'

'Executive Doctors on Call.'

'Whatever. Yeah. In the doctors' office. It has all the medical results in it. It is called a database. That's because all the data – that means numbers and stuff – is in it. That's the *base* where the *data* is kept. Now over here' – she drew separate rectangles on the other end of the sheet of paper – 'are the health club's computers. When they switch their computers on, they read what's in the database at the doctors' place. If the doctors add a bulletin here in their database, it would be read on the computers at the health club. It would be really easy to get someone at the gym to do whatever you wanted him to do. Jimmy says they sent him the wrong instructions. They added a note to his client's section telling him to double the weights and increase the speeds and so on. And then, after the guy died, they deleted that bit completely.'

Wong was not interested.

Joyce knew she had failed to convince her boss that her new friend had been grievously wronged, and was left in a state of frustration. How could anyone believe that someone with a face like Jimmy's was capable of wrongdoing? Just look at him! That chin could never lie.

As the working day drew to a close, the geomancer received a call from Dominique Alegre's mother-in-law, the elderly feng shui fan, and soon found himself on his way to a paying assignment for the evening. His Perth trip could after all prove to be pleasantly profitable.

Joyce, delighted to be left on her own, met up with Jimmy who told her about a former fitness teacher called Stan Eknath, who apparently had a similar story to his. Now knowing that young male gym instructors were more interesting in the flesh than on telephones, she asked Jimmy to track Stan down.

An hour later, the three young people met at Stan's father's restaurant, The Perth Indian Balti House.

'Yeah,' said Stan, over a rogan josh. 'The instructions I got on that fateful bloody day clearly said that she needed a great deal of exercise and had to be walked at a six per cent gradient for at least ten minutes at eight kilometres an hour.'

'Yeah,' said Jimmy. 'That's like what the report I got said about my guy.'

'And she had to cycle for twelve minutes.'

'Mine had to cycle for fifteen.'

'And she had to get her heart rate up to ninety-two per cent of maximum. I thought that was *way* dangerous at the time, but that's what the report for the day said. I had to do what it said. I would get in trouble if I didn't. Once she'd keeled over and the ambulance had taken her away – well, I went back to the website a couple of hours later, and the special instructions had disappeared. Just the usual ones were left.'

Jimmy shook his head slowly in wonder. 'This is what happened to me. *Exactly* what happened to me.'

Joyce, recalling what she had learned from previous cases, turned to Jimmy with a question. 'Who benefits from this? Like, who did the old geezer who died leave his money to?'

'I don't know, but I think it was his doctor. That's what I heard. There was a lot of gossip about the whole thing among the staff at the club.'

She turned to the other trainer.

He said: 'I don't know who the dead old bird at my place left her money to, but I remember her saying that she joined the health programme because her doctor told her to.'

'Why did your guy join the club?' she asked Jimmy.

'I think he joined for medical reasons, too.'

Stan bit into a poppadum thoughtfully, crumbs exploding over his chin. 'Just supposing both were sent by their doctors – and both left their money to their doctors. That would mean – '

'A motive!' the young woman said.

Jimmy asked, 'What was the name of the doctor at your gym?'

Stan's brow wrinkled. 'I don't remember. I don't think we ever got individual names of doctors. The reports were on a website. The company paid some money and we got access to it. It was called Executive something.'

Joyce interrupted. 'Hang on a minute. Lemme think. Er – what was it? Was it – Executive Doctors on Call?'

Stan nodded. 'Yeah – I think – yeah, that was it. You got it.'

'I think maybe we really have got it,' she replied, her mind racing.

Dominique Alegre dropped Wong off at her mother-in-law's residence at precisely 6.30 p.m.

The seventy-two-year-old woman lived in an apartment block three storeys high on a steep slope on the outskirts of town. It was called The Regalia and had become a popular haunt for the elderly, since it was not far from a hospital specialising in outpatient services with a Senior Citizen Clinic.

'I don't sink *ma belle-mère* wants you to feng shui her place tonight,' Ms Alegre said as she punched a four-digit code into a panel at the main door.

'Just have a look-see,' Wong agreed.

'*Oui.* She wants you to meet a few friends, too. Zey're all interested in feng shui these days.'

'Ah.' Wong felt like rubbing his hands together. The stars were in his favour and his luck was in. He visualised two or three little old ladies, all of whom would hire him to poke around their apartments for a couple of hours each at his usual outrageous fee.

Arriving at flat 3B, Dominique Alegre introduced him to a tiny, wrinkled woman named Eleanor Mittel. She jabbed a quick kiss onto her mother-in-law's cheek and fled. '*Au revoir,*

Eleanor. Look after Monsieur Wong and make sure 'e gets back to his hotel safely, will you? See you Sunday.'

Old Mrs Mittel grabbed Wong's upper arm unnecessarily firmly and steered him along a neat little hallway containing two slim tables, each bearing a bouquet of flowers.

'The second door,' she muttered. 'They're in here.'

Keeping a tight grip on him, she kicked the door open and swung Wong into the room. 'I got 'im,' she crowed.

The feng shui master was aghast to see there were fifteen women in the room, aged from about forty-five to well over Mrs Mittel's age.

'Oh!' he said. 'You are having party. Very sorry. Maybe I come back tomorrow.'

'Oh no-no-no,' said his hostess. 'You don't escape that easily. I've invited the entire membership of the North Perth Handbag Society to meet you and we've got a forty per cent turnout, despite the fact that I only started making the calls mid-afternoon.'

'You're a very persuasive woman, El,' one of the women called out, and the others laughed.

'Harry would have said so,' said another, triggering a louder laugh.

'Behave yourselves girls,' said Mrs Mittel, tightening her grip on Wong's arm. 'We don't want to scare him off.'

The geomancer was forcibly placed in a dining chair in a position where all the women could see him. Sixteen pairs of eyes stared at him and gave instant feedback.

'He's kinda cute.'

'Skinny though.'

'Needs one of Bessie's two-ton Lamingtons.'

'Yeah, then I don't have to eat them.'

'Does he speak English?'

73

'Prob'ly better'n you, Milly.'

Mrs Mittel clapped her hands sharply together to get her audience's attention. 'Come now, ladies, we need a bit of quiet here. Mr Wong has kindly agreed to give the North Perth Handbag Society a talk on feng shooeee. As you know, from the talk that Mrs Nimmo gave us last year, this is the ancient Oriental art of placement. Mrs Nimmo, God bless her, was just reading out of a book, but this Mr Wong is your genuine article. A real feng shui master who just happens to be in town and is a friend of my daughter-in-law.'

'I don't think – ' said Wong, trying to rise to his feet.

Mrs Mittel put a hand on each shoulder and pressed him down. 'Come now, Mr Wong, no need to be shy. We don't bite.'

'Julia does,' said a cheerful woman with a red, blotchy face.

This inexplicable remark caused hoots of laughter from the other side of the room, and one elderly woman had a coughing fit and had to be helped out of the room to recover.

'Maybe she does, but we are not gonna let her bite you, don't you worry,' Eleanor Mittel told Wong. 'Now how about you give us a five or ten minute talk, and then we do Q and A and general discussion?'

So saying, she spun herself round and squeezed herself, with a wriggle of her bottom, into a tiny space left on one of the three sofas in the room. 'There. We're ready.'

The geomancer loathed speaking in public – and was generally mistrustful of *gwaipoh*, an aversion that his time spent with Joyce had only reinforced. So the idea of addressing a whole roomful of them – well, it was one of the most hideous ways he could imagine spending an evening. He tried to calm himself by imagining that it was possible that several of the women in this room would hire him at exorbitant rates over the next few days to look at their houses or apartments.

But in the meantime, what was he going to say? Maybe he could do a basic introduction to feng shui, as he did when he occasionally found himself with a client who knew nothing about it.

'Feng shui man use a compass first. This is to find out which direction.'

The blotchy-faced woman shouted out: 'Show us your tool.'

'Yeah, get yer tool out,' her neighbour added.

This caused a riot of laughter, and a stern admonition from Eleanor Mittel. 'Behave yourselves, girls.'

A woman of about eighty with white hair cackled. 'Hands off, girls. Eleanor wants him for herself.'

Wong's lack of experience in making speeches in English proved to be no disadvantage at all. Whatever he said sparked off spontaneous and quite unintelligible comments that baffled him but greatly entertained his audience.

After five painful stop-start minutes, in which he had explained almost nothing about his science, it occurred to him that some of the women in this group were roughly the age of the people who had died at the fitness clubs.

'In feng shui, health associated with yellow colour,' he said. 'Anybody here is healthy?'

The blotchy-faced woman, who was the quickest comedienne in the group, said: 'I have a healthy appetite, but that's all!'

Eleanor Mittel sniggered back: 'The healthier your appetite, the less healthy your fat gut.'

'Oooh,' murmured the other women at this personal attack.

Wong pressed on: 'Anybody here use health club?'

'I do,' said a woman of about seventy. 'Do I need to get them to paint my club yellow?'

'You never belong to a health club, Bee,' said a woman with grey hair.

'I do. I did three K on the cycle yesterday.'

A fifty-something woman in a long, green, earth-mother dress raised her hand. 'I'm doing a course with a personal trainer. I've only been once and it nearly killed me.'

There was general laughter at this, but Wong raised his eyebrows. 'He make you work hard?'

'It's a she. And hard is not the word for it. I think she's trying to polish me off.'

'The lamingtons will get you first,' said the blotchy-faced woman.

Two hours later, Mrs Eleanor Mittel placed CF Wong in a taxi.

'Thank you, Mr Wong. You were a star.'

'Ah. Okay. What time I do your flat tomorrow?'

'Early. Nine-ish would be good.'

The taxi pulled off into the road, leaving Wong with a welcome moment of peace.

It had been a stressful and strenuous evening, but it had worked out fine in the end. Four of the women had hired him to visit their apartments over the next two days.

During his talk and the general discussion over snacks later, he had learned that three of the women present were active members of a health club. One of them, an attractive woman in her mid-fifties introduced to him as Mrs Lavender, had recently embarked upon a course with a personal trainer that was proving to be extremely strenuous. 'Getting healthy is going to be the death of me,' she laughed.

Of course, it was possible that she was just out of shape, Wong realised. Perhaps there was no connection at all with the incidents at the Millennium Health Centre and The Players, but it would be intriguing to check it out.

'You have doctor?'

'Yeah – and he specialises in sports and fitness.'

'A good man?'

'Very good. He does a lot of work for kids' charities and stuff. If you haven't written your will yet, Mr Wong, you could do a lot worse than write a bequest for him, as I've done.'

At 11.45 a.m. the following morning, the juice bar of the Stretch Yoga Centre was occupied by six people – five of whom were women, the sixth being Wong. The feng shui master had long been proud of his traditional Asian misogyny and was irritated to find himself constantly in the company of females during this particular mission. Was it Perth that was at fault? Did Australian men all move to Sydney, leaving this side of the country over-supplied with the pestilent sex? Or was it something to do with health clubs? Maybe only women in Australia were healthy?

'Are you married, Mr Wong?'

Mrs Lavender's question brought him abruptly out of his reverie.

'I know you're not wearing a ring, but I didn't know whether people in your country had the tradition of wearing rings.'

The geomancer shook his head. 'Not married. No rings, no, no, don't like it, Mrs Lavender.'

'Call me Jackie.'

'Yes, Mrs Lavender Jackie.'

'Just Jackie.'

'Mrs Jess Jackie.'

She reached over the table and took hold of his hand. 'I can do a bit of palm reading, you know. I was taught by my aunt, who had a bit of Romany blood.'

She ran her fingertip over his palm, tickling him.

'There are seven different categories of hand, you know,' she said. 'You have what is called a philosophical hand, gnarled with pronounced knuckles. This type of palm indicates – '

The geomancer snatched his hand back. 'I think maybe we do this later.'

Jackie Lavender leaned back in her chair, still supremely calm and confident, despite his nervous, hostile manner. 'Okay, you tell me, what is it you're after? Why are you here? It obviously isn't my body.'

Wong wasn't sure what she was talking about. He thought for a moment before replying. 'I have a feeling about your training course. Sometimes people die from training too much. I am a bit worried, that's all.'

She looked at him. 'Did your compass tell you I was at risk? How did you work out that I was in danger?'

Again, he found himself baffled as to how to reply. He didn't want to go into detail about the deaths at the other health clubs. The chances were that this had no connection. He decided to take the simplest option. 'Yes, my compass needle point at you. It show me you have danger. Need to check your training program.'

She rose to her feet. 'Come. I'll show you.'

She led him down a white corridor to an office containing an untidy desk and two computers. 'Ashanti's not here, but I'm sure she won't mind. Ashanti's my personal trainer.'

'Is this computer link – '

78

He stopped as a small, wiry young woman with brown skin stepped into the room.

Jackie Lavender gave a small cry of pleasure and kissed her on both cheeks. 'Hello, dear,' she said. 'I want you to meet Mr Wong, a friend of mine. He's very interested in my training regime. Mr Wong, this is Ashanti Carle, my trainer, and managing partner of the Stretch Yoga Centre.'

Ashanti Carle gave Wong just enough of a smile to be minimally polite, but no more. 'Can I help you, Mr Wong? What is it exactly that you need to know?'

'Ah. Er,' Wong stammered. 'I, er, want to know what is the doctor connection for your health programme.'

'Are you a salesman from some sort of consultancy?'

'No, no, nothing like that. I am feng shui master. I am interested in health of Mrs Jackie Lavender.'

'Oh. Well, I am also interested in her health, and since I am paid a considerable sum of money to improve it, I hope you don't mind if I get on with that job.'

'Yes, yes, of course.'

'So, goodbye, nice to have met you.' Ashanti Carle spoke dismissively.

'Ah. Goodbye, yes, goodbye.' Wong did not move. 'Just one question. You use group called Executive Doctors on Call?'

'No, we don't,' said Ashanti. 'We have our own doctor, retained by our group. Goodbye.'

The personal trainer slipped her arm into Jackie Lavender's and whisked her to the aerobics room where something called Hi Lo & Sculpt was about to begin. He turned away but managed to catch Ashanti's comment to Mrs Lavender.

'He's either after your body, or Dr Brackish's consultancy contract. Either way, he gives me a bad feeling.'

'I think he's rather cute,' Jackie replied.

Wong froze. Where had he heard that name before? He recalled the name being spoken with a French accent. Dominique Alegre must have mentioned it. He was somehow connected with Executive Doctors on Call. That meant that all the same factors were in place: a young trainer, an aging client, an over-strenuous programme, a connection with Executive Doctors on Call – it might just be all coincidence. Or perhaps it wasn't – in which case, Mrs Lavender's life was in danger.

The feng shui master turned around and marched into the gymnasium. 'Ms Jackie Lavender,' he said. 'I think you should not to do this program. Maybe not safe.'

Ashanti Carle, tiny though she was, tensed her muscles and suddenly looked very dangerous indeed. She grabbed Wong, spun him round and picked him off the floor with pincer-like grips on his upper arms. She marched with him to the entrance of the room. 'I've had quite enough of you, Mr Wong. I know exactly what you're after. Kindly don't darken our doorstep again.'

She carried him protesting all the way to the front door of the Stretch Yoga Centre and unceremoniously heaved him outside. He landed heavily on the pavement.

She theatrically dusted her hands. 'Goodbye and good riddance.'

It was very bad feng shui to sit in the dust, so Wong quickly picked himself up and brushed himself down. His bony bottom hurt. Then he sneaked around to the front of the building and peered through the window.

He saw Jackie Lavender on a treadmill. She was running very fast, and her face was bright red. Even from this distance, he could see a throbbing vein standing out from her left temple.

Ashanti Carle was watching the woman run with her lips down-turned and a puzzled look on her face.

Wong wanted to march in and turn the machine off. But he was frankly terrified that if he as much as showed his face near the door again, the tiny woman would grab him and beat him to a pulp.

Jimmy and Joyce were back in Bev's Snags & Sarnies.

They were sipping milkshakes.

Joyce was just about to make an attempt at a joint period of silence. This was a relationship test she learned about from her greatly accomplished man-killing older sister, who said that a friendship only became a true friendship when the two people involved could be silent for 120 seconds together without feeling awkward.

She and Jimmy had now had several hours of small talk if you counted lunch yesterday, dinner last night, and now this mid-morning meeting. But she wasn't sure that they were ready to try out a two-minute silence yet.

And even if they were, her mouth wouldn't let them – it kept opening and filling up the slightest gaps in the conversation. And since Jimmy was not a great conversationalist, there were lots of pauses to fill.

They had both stopped talking to slurp from their striped straws, and it had become too quiet. Joyce said to herself, I should just let this silence remain, see what happens.

'So what's your favourite food?' asked Joyce's mouth, taking the decision into its own hands.

Jimmy thought about this. 'I don't know. I don't really like food. It's bad for you.'

'Yeah! You are so right! It has calories.'

'Yeah. Bad for your health.'

'Yeah. I hate food too! It's *so* like, calorific.'

Jimmy tried to nod his head and slurp at the same time, which resulted in the straw slipping from his mouth and a dribble of chocolate milkshake snaking down his chin. 'Oops. Ha ha.'

A similar fake laugh echoed out of Joyce's mouth, but she misjudged it, and ended up with some strawberry milk going down the wrong way. She had a coughing fit. It took a few seconds for them both to recover.

As another silence threatened to descend, Joyce's mouth again took the initiative, racing to plug the gap.

'What are you doing for lunch today?'

'I dunno. What are you doing for lunch?'

'I dunno! Fancy something to eat? Any good places round here?'

'Yeah, loads. There's a brilliant burger place and there's Hot Dawg which is a hot dog place, and there's a totally amazing kebab place which does these totally amazing turtle wraps or whatever it is.'

'Tortilla wraps.'

'Yeah, and them.'

'I love tortilla wraps!'

'Yeah, me too.'

Jimmy looked up and gazed into Joyce's eyes. 'You know something, Joyce?'

'Yes, Jimmy?' she said, her voice jumping an octave and turning breathy.

He gradually leaned towards her. 'I feel like I've known you all my life.'

'Yeah, me too! Like ages and ages!' She leaned towards him.

'Yet if you think about it, we only met yesterday.'

'Yeah, just a few hours ago!'

'It's just been like minutes only.'

'Yeah, and it's flown by!' said Joyce, moving her face closer to his. She didn't know whether to gaze at his eyes, his lips or that gorgeous chin, so she scanned them all in turn. 'It's all flown by in like a few seconds!'

'Yeah. Like ten seconds or something. Time flies when you're having fun.'

'Yeah.' She noticed that he was looking at her lips.

She focused on his lips.

They moved closer together.

That was when Wong interrupted them. 'Come! Quick-quick. Plenty urgent work.' The feng shui master, who had appeared from nowhere, painfully tapped her shoulder with his index finger. 'Quick. I think problem is happening again. Come, come!'

'It's Saturday,' complained Joyce, turning to glare at her boss. 'I'm having a day off. Tell me later.'

'No,' said Wong. 'Need help now.'

'Trust your boss to lob in just then.' Jimmy looked up at him. 'What's the sweat, guv?'

'Some trainer in Stretch Yoga. She is following instructions from Dr Brackish. Same doctor wrote your special bulletin. Same trick. Maybe even might kill Lavender, Jackie, I think. Trainer won't let me in. You must go stop her. Ms Carle will listen to you. You are also one of them.'

'What?' Jimmy said. 'What on earth is he going on about?'

'Dunno,' said Joyce. 'I'll ask him. What are you saying, CF?'

'*Come.*'

He beckoned them with his hands.

Joyce reluctantly started to move. She reached for her purse. 'I'll pay.'

'No, I'll pay,' said Jimmy.

'No, you're unemployed. I'll pay.'

Wong turned around and thumped a twenty-dollar note onto the table. 'Quick. Must go *now*.'

'Geez,' said Joyce, astonished. 'This must be really important.'

At two o'clock that afternoon, a thin man in an ostrich-leather coat hurried into the ground floor entrance of Stretch Yoga.

Although there was a CLOSED sign on the door, Ashanti Carle stood waiting in the reception to let him in.

'Thank you so much for coming, Doctor. It looks really bad.'

'Have you called an ambulance?' Doctor Frankie Brackish asked.

'I just did. They should be here in five minutes. But I think it's too late.'

'Where's the bod – the patient?'

'Still in the gym,' said Ashanti, wiping her eyes and sniffing. 'I followed the special bulletin for Mrs Lavender on your database really, really carefully. But it seemed to be too much for her – '

Doctor Brackish marched sternly down the corridor. 'I hope you haven't been foolish. Jackie Lavender is not a young woman. She has a heart condition. It would be madness to overdo the exercise.'

He opened the gym doors and stepped into the cool, sprung-floored room. The lights were off and the curtains were shut.

84

'Now,' said a voice he thought he knew.

Switches were flicked and the room was suddenly ablaze with light.

'Surprise,' said half a dozen voices.

Doctor Brackish, blinking, stared at the individuals who stepped out from their hiding places behind the gym equipment. There was Jimmy Wegner, whose voice he had just heard. And Dominique Alegre, a client from the Millennium Health Centre. And Kees Luis de Boer, general manager of The Players. And Stan Eknath, another fitness trainer whose career he had ruined. And his patient Jackie Lavender – not collapsed on a treadmill as alleged but looking perfectly fit and smiling. And two other people: a teenage girl and an old Chinese man.

Ashanti Carle came up behind him. 'Sorry, Doctor Brackish, but it's over. The game is up, as they say in the cop shows.'

'What – what – what are you talking about?' he stuttered. 'What's going on?'

'We compared notes, that's what. Stan and Jimmy and me. You added bulletins onto the instructions on your website, sent us heart patients and tried to make us work them to death. Mr Wong says he is going to ask the police to examine the wills of patients of yours who have died. I don't know exactly what you're up to, but I know you've been using us as saps.'

'I did no such thing. The notes on my database recommend very mild exercise. Check it and see.'

'I bet they do. I bet they do *now*,' said Jimmy. 'But you add special individual bulletins and delete them, don't you? You tried to make Ashanti kill Jackie – and as soon as you got the call from her that her client had collapsed, you deleted the individual bulletin in the database, didn't you? Removed the work-her-to-death stuff, so that all that was left was a mild list of exercises.'

'You can't prove any of this.'

Jimmy held up some sheets of paper. 'We printed the bulletin. And we have witnesses to everything.'

'You couldn't have. You're lying. My bulletins are in a graphic file format. You can't print them out. They would come out blank.'

Jimmy gestured at Joyce with his hand. 'We got some expert help.'

Joyce blushed. 'I wouldn't call myself an expert. But I can find and install shareware and I can reverse fonts and I can do screen dumps and all that sort of thing. It was really easy, anyone could do it.'

'Bugger,' said Doctor Brackish. He turned around and faced Jimmy Wegner. 'I'll fight you in court. You haven't a chance.'

Jimmy turned to Stan. 'Hear that? He wants a fight.'

Stan grinned. 'A fight? Bloody fantastic idea.'

The dark-skinned trainer peeled off his shirt in one easy movement, revealing a wiry torso with muscles rippling like a panther's.

'Let me help,' said Jimmy. He pulled his shirt over his head, to reveal his equally impressive bodybuilder's physique.

Joyce's eyes bulged, her jaw dropped open and her tongue slipped out. 'I think I'm going to faint!' she whimpered.

The cars that flew away

The King of Qi was having trouble governing, and needed some help.

So he called the Governor of Xue Di. The Governor of Xue Di was a tough man whose name was Meng Changjun.

The King of Qi said: 'I will give you a post in my government.'

So Governor Meng Changjun moved to the Kingdom of Qi.

The time came for tax to be collected in Xue Di. (Meng Changjun remained Governor of Xue Di.) He called his servant, Feng Yuan.

Governor Meng said: 'Go back to Xue Di. Collect the taxes for me.'

Feng Yuan said: 'Shall I bring the money back here?'

Meng Changjun said: 'No. Buy something with the money.'

Feng Yuan said: 'What shall I buy?'

Meng Changjun said: 'You know what I have. Buy something I do not have.'

So the servant looked all around Meng Changjun's house in the capital of Qi.

Then he travelled in a chariot to the district of Xue Di.

Later he came back to the Kingdom of Qi.

Meng Changjun said: 'What did you buy with the money?'

Feng Yuan said: 'I looked in your house. You have gold and silver. You have wine and food. You have women and heirs. I bought something you did not have.'

Meng Changjun said: 'What is it I do not have?'

Feng Yuan said: 'The love of your people.'

Meng Changjun said: 'How can you buy love?'

Feng Yuan said: 'I told the people of Xue Di that you were cancelling their debts. This will help them to have love for you.'

Meng Changjun was very angry. He said: 'You have done a bad thing. You have lost my money.'

But later the King of Qi said to Governor Meng Changjun: 'I do not need you any more. You can go home now.'

Meng Changjun went home. He was still angry with his servant. He reached Xue Di.

He found all the Xue Di people lined up on the street to greet him. They all loved him. They cheered. They sang his name.

He was happy. He turned to his servant. He said: 'The servant has taught the master.'

Blade of Grass, simple minds think earthly treasure only is valuable. Wise men know that treasure of the spirit is harder to find and far more valuable. The younger the age you realise this, the sooner you are born.

From *Some Gleanings of Oriental Wisdom*
by CF Wong, part 42

Wong read through the chapter he had just written and pondered. The story of the wise servant Feng Yuan reminded him of a related tale, and he was feeling creative. Perhaps he could write another chapter this morning – or even two? It was 10 a.m. and he didn't have any appointments until a reading of a new Szechuan restaurant at 1 p.m. It appeared that neither Mr Pun nor any of his board members was in need of his services today.

He flipped to a fresh page of his journal to begin writing again, but then noticed a movement from the corner of his eye. His secretary Winnie Lim had adopted a curious posture. She was sitting up straight behind her desk with her arms spread out in front of her. Her hands, palms down, were stretched out flat with the fingers splayed. She looked as if she were performing some sort of spell.

'What?' he inquired.

'Drying nails. Two colour holographic blend. Mus' keep fingers horizontal for ten minute.'

'Oh.'

'You answer phone.'

'Okay, okay.'

Joyce looked up from the magazine she was reading. 'No probs. *I'll* answer the phone. He's the big boss. He shouldn't have to answer his own phone. People'll diss him. I can do all that secretary stuff, easy.' The young woman beamed a 100-kilowatt smile at her boss and yanked the phone off his desk on to her own.

Wong did not return the smile. Instead, he gave her a malevolent glare.

Joyce was in disgrace and he wanted her to know it.

She had brought a group of friends into the office the previous night. They had apparently missed the 7.30 showing of a movie and she had decided to kill some time by giving them a tour of her workplace.

As a result, Wong arrived at the office at eight the next morning to find that it stank of stale beer and was littered with small polystyrene boxes from the hamburger store. But worst of all, there was writing on the wall – a Chinese character drawn badly *in blood* – a shocking sight, and extremely negative *feng shui*. After he had got over his fright, he had become puzzled.

89

His knowledge of Chinese characters was encyclopaedic, but he was unable to identify precisely the one on the wall, and had wasted half an hour going through his old stroke-order dictionaries to try to locate it.

When Joyce finally arrived at the office at 10.25, looking the worse for wear, she had apologetically explained that it wasn't a Chinese character at all, but an accidental splash of burgundy, a type of red wine from the land of the *gwailo*.

'But why is wine on *wall*?' Wong had asked.

Her eyebrows came together crossly, as if he had asked a totally unreasonable question. 'Well, you know, you open some wine, you have a bit of a party, the wine gets splashed all over the wall, you know how it is.'

Wong did not know how it was, as was evident from his irritated expression.

Joyce, clearly feeling guilty as well as hung over, wearily tried to make amends. She promised to get some super-strong stain remover. 'Mind you, the way I feel now, I wouldn't know whether to splash it on the wall or drink it,' she'd said.

An uneasy silence had descended.

So later that morning, when she offered to man the phone, the feng shui master assumed that she was attempting to make up for her sins, which remained startlingly obvious on the office wall. Then he remembered that Joyce's mobile phone was out of order – water had short-circuited the electronics. He realised that the real reason she wanted maximum access to the office's single phone line was to keep her social life going. Pestilent *mat salleh*.

After this, an uneasy peace was maintained for precisely seven-and-a-half minutes. And then the phone rang.

'Hello?' said Joyce. 'Yeah, this is CF Wong's office. Oh.

Well, I'm afraid he's in a meeting. Can I help you? I'm his personal assistant.'

Wong was surprised to hear this. What meeting was he in?

'A what? A garage? No, we don't do garages. Who is this? Sorry, but Mr Wong is a busy man. He has to do a lot of important offices and shops and homes. He doesn't have time for garages. Try one of the cheap ones. There are lots in the phone book, probably. Look under 'Feng Shui People' or 'Mystics' or something. Good luck. Bye-ee.'

She lowered the handset and gave her boss a self-satisfied smirk. 'There you go. Got rid of a time-waster for you. He wanted you to do his garage. I *mean.*'

Wong was confused. 'I am not in a meeting.'

'Yeah, yeah, but that's what secretaries say. Good ones anyway.' Joyce threw a dirty look at Winnie, but she didn't seem to be listening. 'You mustn't make it too easy for people to get hold of you.'

'But who was it?'

'Dunno. Some idiot. I told him you didn't do garages. You don't, do you?'

Wong thought about this. 'First you ask price. *Then* I decide if I do it. Better.'

Joyce lifted her feet on to her desk and picked up her magazine. 'Okay, but I bet you couldn't charge much for something like that,' she said, flicking through the pages.

'Depend on who belong to it.'

'It belonged to some bloke called Young. Nevis Young or something like that.'

Wong leapt out of his chair as if he had been scalded. 'Nevis Au Yeung?'

Joyce peered over the top of her magazine at him. Unnerved, she had difficulty keeping her voice steady. 'Yeah, that's it. D'you know him?' She quietly took her feet off her desk.

The feng shui man was instantly short of breath. His bony chest appeared to be constricted. He couldn't speak. He found himself stiff and swaying like a poorly-assembled scaffold, his mouth wide open. He began hyperventilating.

'Uh-oh,' said Joyce, dropping her magazine and sitting bolt upright. 'I guess I did something wrong.'

Wong clamped his mouth shut and took three deep breaths through his nose. He spoke quietly. 'You mean the secretary of Nevis Au Yeung called to me?'

'No.'

'Who was it?'

'It was the guy himself. Nevis wotsit.'

Wong's eyes bulged and he looked as if he was about to fall over. 'Aiyeeah! Aiyeeaaaaah!' The feng shui master's thin body started to tip backwards. He was about to faint.

Winnie, her fingers still spread in front of her, shrieked. 'Get him! I think maybe he will fall over and break his head.'

The geomancer again swayed steeply backwards.

Joyce shouted to Winnie: 'You get him – you're closer.'

'Cannot-ah! Nails not dry!'

But Wong didn't fall over. His knees buckled and he merely collapsed heavily into his seat, his eyes still glazed. Thirteen seconds passed.

Then he jerked himself to his feet again and spoke urgently: 'Call him back! Find the number in the book. Quick! He is the vice-chairman of East Trade Industries Company Limited. Also, he is the thirty-ninth richest man in Asia.' (Wong, like many of his friends, obsessively memorised the *Forbes* listing of the world's wealthiest people every year.)

'Yes, boss,' said Joyce, suddenly suffused with guilt.

'Phone book is there,' said Winnie.

'I'll see if I can do a last-call-received redial thing on this phone,' the young woman said, punching a few buttons. She bit her lower lip and crossed the fingers on her free hand. Success! 'There you go. It's ringing.'

All three held their breath.

'Hi. Is that Nevis? Yeah? My name's Joyce. I'm the assistant of CF Wong, the feng shui man? You called just now?'

'Give me the phone.' Wong, still emotional, spoke with difficulty, his voice husky.

'Well, I'm just calling to say that he's just come out of his meeting. He said he doesn't normally do garages but he might do yours, cause you are on Mr Pun's board and all that.'

'Give me the phone.'

'Is it an urgent job? You want him to come today? He probably can, but we'll have to charge a one hundred per cent surcharge for express service. As a board member, you are entitled to one free normal visit, but we have a surcharge for urgent assignments.'

'GIVE ME – '

'Yeah, one hundred per cent. And if you want Mr Wong himself to do it, instead of one of his staff, that will be a further one hundred per cent. That okay?'

Wong lowered the hand that was reaching out to the handset. Two hundred per cent surcharge? It sank in that Joyce seemed to be handling this rather well.

The young woman, starting to relax, leaned back in her plastic seat. 'If money is like not really a major problem, I would suggest you go for the annual package price. You get a monthly visit from Mr Wong himself. It's way cheaper than booking individual visits.'

Nevis Au Yeung's tinny voice could be heard coming out

of the handset, but not loud enough for Wong to hear what he was saying.

The frantic feng shui master knew that Au Yeung was one of the wealthiest members of Mr Pun's board of directors. But he had never shown any interest in feng shui. What had changed the tycoon's mind?

Wong tiptoed around to the side of Joyce's desk to eavesdrop. All he could hear was an unintelligible buzz from the handset.

'Yeah,' she replied. 'Sounds good. What's the address? Ridley Park? Yeah. What number? Got it. See you at eleven. Bye-ee.'

She put the phone down with a self-satisfied smirk.

Wong, McQuinnie and Lim stared at each other. The feng shui master spoke first. 'Well?'

'He's expecting us at his place in Ridley Park at eleven.'

'How much he is paying?'

'The first visit will be the free one he gets because he is one of Mr Pun's board members. But he'll pay the surcharge. As for the follow-up visits, well, he said he'd pay whatever we asked. Make up a number, CF.'

Wong tried not to smile too broadly, but it was difficult. He grinned and his hands turned to fists. His eyes were wide as rice-bowls. His cheeks lifted themselves so high that his wrinkled-nested eyes almost disappeared. The room seemed filled with heavenly light.

Nevis Au Yeung. He had to make up a number to put on an invoice for *Nevis Au Yeung.*

Oh, were there enough numbers in the universe?

For most people, a garage implies a small, single-storey construction for one or two cars. But Nevis Au Yeung had a seventeen-car classic collection, and then another ten cars that he actually used. The tycoon's cars were worth more than the average Singapore apartment complex. His family members had another three dozen vehicles between them, and then there were some forty or fifty spaces for staff cars. The garage Au Yeung had asked Wong to deal with was more like a three-storey municipal parking lot – but, of course, this being Ridley Park, the building was an elegant, architect-designed, steel-sided structure disguised behind a bank of trees.

'Oops, sorry,' said Joyce, peering upwards as they stepped out of the taxi. 'He said a garage. I didn't realise he meant a bloody great building.'

'No problem,' said Wong, his eyes shining with pure, unadulterated greed. 'We charge by square metre.' He was already making a mental estimate of the floor space of the parking lot – four or five thousand square metres – and huge numbers of dollars were running through his mind. This was going to be a nice, fat job that would cover his office expenses for months.

A loud, musical toot exploded clownishly behind them. They quickly stepped out of the drive as a vintage car rolled up and stopped three metres in front of their knees.

'Hello, chaps,' said the driver, a debonair man of about forty with thinning red hair and one arm dangling out of the car. A younger man, with pale brown hair and a freckled face, waved a greeting from the passenger seat. The car in which they sat appeared to have been driven straight from an Edwardian postcard.

'Waah. So old,' the feng shui master said.

95

'Chitty Chitty Bang Bang,' Joyce said.

'Hmm?' Wong asked, unsure what language she was speaking.

'Can we help you? Come to see the motors, have you?' The man spoke with a cinematic London accent, pronouncing 'motors' as if it was two words: Mo. Uz.

While Wong was searching for the right words, Joyce got ahead of him. 'Morning. Do you guys like work here? We want to get in. There's no bell. We're here to do some work for Mr Nevis Au Yeung. This is Mr – '

'No problem,' said the cheery motorist, whose accent and dark tortoiseshell glasses gave him the air of a cut-price Michael Caine. He held out his hand, thrusting a business card at Joyce. 'The name's Dick Curdy. This is my brother Petey. Say hi, Petey.'

'Hi, Petey,' said Petey.

'We look after the Chairman's little collection of motors for him. The ones he's got left, anyway. Hardy-har.'

Joyce showed the card to Wong. CURDY'S CLASSIC CARS, it said, next to a picture of a vintage car.

'That's one majorly cool car,' the young woman said. 'Is it one of his oldest?'

'What? This little number?' Curdy slapped the car door, which looked as if it were made from green enamel. 'Naah. This ain't his. This is ours. Replica. Made about thirteen years ago. It's younger than you are. It's younger than Petey's mental age. No, it's our clients who own the vintage cars, not poor us. Me and Petey have to schlep around in cheap copy cars, or use Shanks's pony. We're workers, the unwashed masses, the lumpenproletariat and all that.'

Petey man leaned out of the window. 'You a motorist your-self, miss?'

'No,' said Joyce. 'I can't drive! I use the MRT – and Shanks's pony, like you.'

Wong turned an amazed face at her. 'You use *horse* to come to work?'

The eyes of the men in the car changed focus slightly and the feng shui master realised there was someone behind them.

The two visitors turned to see a stocky, unsmiling man in a dark uniform approaching. He greeted the Curdy brothers with a courteous wave and opened the high security gates for them to drive through.

Then he introduced himself as Alyn Puk, day-shift security guard. 'You're the people he called? From the feng shui company, is it? Follow me.'

The Curdys waved a cheerful goodbye as their replica car roared past.

Puk, a tired-looking man who seemed too heavy to be in his present profession, led them to a small office set into the ground floor of the car park. While they were walking, he used his walkie-talkie to summon someone else. 'Harris Wu there, is it? This is Puk. Could you get him to come over to my office? Tell him the feng shui people are here. Yah. Now. Over.'

They heard a roar as Dick Curdy drove his elegant, low-slung replica vintage car into the garage block. It made a purring noise that kept changing in tone as it drove up a network of ramps to the third storey.

Wong had already noticed that people on the site, like the ancient Israelites, refused to utter the name of their leader. He was referred to simply by the reverential pronoun 'He' – clearly spoken with a capital initial.

The three of them sat down at a desk in a tiny office.

'The usual rules apply,' Puk said. 'You know already, is it?'

'No,' Joyce said.

'Yes,' Wong said. 'You mean stuff is confidential?'

'Yah, man. *Nutting* you say or hear while working on His premises can be pass' on to anyone else – media or newspaper man, broadcaster, like that – and no photography or recording of any kind is allowed and all that stuff, et cetera, et cetera, you know? Just sign here.'

Puk made them both sign a privacy contract that was far too long and boring to read. Then he threw it carelessly into a filing cabinet.

Another man arrived, a tall, thin, bow-tied man with Shanghainese features and an educated Singaporean accent. He was wheeling an office chair in front of him. He squeezed through the doorway and handed his name card to the two visitors. 'Harris Wu,' he announced. 'I'm the architect for all His Ridley Park buildings. You the feng shui consultants, is it?'

After they all shook hands, Wong aimed his attention back to the security officer. The sheer depth of the gloom emanating from the man drew his eyes like a magnet. The man was so filled with depression that he looked as if he might implode. 'Okay. What do you need from us?'

Wong leaned forwards. 'Is there specific problem? Or he just want general feng shui reading?'

For a few seconds, Puk did not answer. Then he tilted his head back and surveyed the ceiling. His expression changed slightly, from misery to irritation. 'You mean He didn't tell you?'

'Tell what?'

'There *is* something specific you have to handle.' Puk clasped his hands together, suddenly serious. 'I guess the Chairman want *me* to brief you only. Well, this may sound crazy, but

98

. . .' His voice trailed off and he turned to the window, as if the words he was seeking might be etched on the glass.

They waited.

He abruptly turned back. 'Three cars have been stolen. He doesn't like it when His cars are stolen. He doesn't want any more cars to disappear. If more cars are stolen, He will be very, very angry. We do not want to see Him very, very angry. That's the size of it, really.'

'Ah. Stolen. Bad. Mr Au Yeung call police?' Wong asked.

Puk nodded. 'Oh yes, we did all the obvious stuff. We call police. We call private detectives even. And that's after His own staff did a comprehensive check. The Chairman has His own police force, sort of thing, you know?'

'Find anything?'

Puk looked uncomfortable again. 'No. Couldn't work out how it was done. How they were taken. All three cars disappear – *poof* – in broad daylight. We have security cameras at the only one exit-entry station, and yet we have no video record of cars being driven out. Somehow they were taken out of the building, but not through driveway.'

'What cars was it?' the feng shui master asked.

'Jaguar XK160, 1930 Aston Martin and 132 Bugatti. All very rare one.'

'What other ways are there out of the building?' Joyce asked.

Architect Wu volunteered an answer: 'There aren't any. Well, there's the fire stairs.'

'But cars can't go down the stairs.'

'Correct.'

'So how did the thieves get them out?'

Wu shrugged his shoulders. 'We don't know.'

Puk clasped his hands together again and gave the frozen smile of a man forced to speak nonsense. 'They vanished into thin air.' He clicked his sweaty fingers. 'One moment they were there, the next moment they were gone. How did they do it? I don't know. Ask David Copperfield. Maybe Mr Copperfield took them. For me, that's the only sensible suggestion.'

'So you contact this Mr Copperfield?' Wong wanted to hear more about this suspect.

Joyce whispered much too loudly: 'He's joking. David Copperfield doesn't nick cars. He just makes like aircraft disappear.'

'He is aircraft thief? Corporate jet of Mr Au Yeung?'

Puk stepped in. 'I'm sorry. I shouldn't have confused the issue. The jets are fine. Just the cars are gone. Three of them, anyway.'

Wong pulled at the little hairs on his chin. 'Maybe some-one tamper with video cameras?'

'Naah,' said Puk. 'I thought of that. No one has tampered with those things. I check them myself every morning. Besides, there are human staff as well as cameras at the in-out ramp.'

Joyce excitedly turned to the architect and gestured with her hands as she spoke. 'Maybe there's a secret tunnel some-where, and they drove the cars away down them. Or maybe someone lifted them off the roof with a helicopter.'

Harris Wu just stared at her. He seemed to be wondering whether to dignify her ideas with a reply. 'I built this place,' he said at last, an icy edge to his voice. 'I think I would probably know if there were tunnels or helicopter landing pads.' He closed his eyes and his lips thinned. His expression said: God give me patience to deal with fools.

She bit her bottom lip and nodded apologetically. 'I guess so,' she whispered, feeling one centimetre high. 'Sorry.'

Wu opened his eyes and took a deep breath. He moved forwards and his office chair creaked. 'It's like this. We don't know how the cars were spirited out of the building. Puk and I, we checked and rechecked every single possibility. So then . . .' He looked to the security guard, unsure of how to continue.

'Tell them,' said Puk. It was not an instruction, but a challenge.

'Okay, I will. You see, the Chairman's, er, latest, er, wife, comes up with a new idea. She says they were stolen by mystical means. Black magic. Wacky stuff. Anyway, the amazing thing is that the Chairman takes it seriously. So He says He will sort it out by Himself. The next thing we know was half an hour ago, when the Chairman's secretary calls me to tell me that some feng shui masters are on their way. They're going to solve the problem for us. That's you guys. So go on then. You better get started.'

Wong was worried. He slowly shook his head. 'Finding stolen cars is job for police, not for us.' He was concerned that the outrageous fees he was planning to charge would become contingent on the cars being recovered – and finding stolen property was much harder than simply doing a reading of a car park.

Puk seemed to read his mind. He said: 'We're not expecting you to find the cars, I think. I think the Chairman is just covering His, er, just anxious to cover all possibilities. You just need to make sure that no more cars are stolen. If anyone tries to drive one out, I'll stop them. But if anyone tries to take one out through, er, mystical means, that's your job – to prevent it, I mean. To make sure that mystical means cannot be used to steal cars in the future? See what I mean?'

Wong felt reassured. His income, in that case, might be safe.

The heavy security guard rose awkwardly to his feet, signifying that their briefing was over. 'Come,' he said. 'We'll give you the tour.'

The four of them walked up the ramps that took the cars between the various levels. Puk explained that there was a staircase they could use, but they would get a better feel of the place by using the vehicle access routes.

It was immediately apparent that the garage was a hot and unpleasant place. There was no cooling system, although there were extractor vents that took some of the fumes out of the air. The place smelled of cars and gasoline, and you couldn't spend five minutes there without feeling damp and uncomfortable.

As they slogged their way up the slopes, Wu gave them a run-down of how the garage worked. The three levels had different functions. The ground floor was used for the cars Nevis Au Yeung used most often – four or five luxury sedans, a stretch limo, a couple of sports utility vehicles and a few two-seater sports cars. The middle floor and half the upper floor were used for cars belonging to other members of his family, plus the staff cars and minivans. The rear half of the upper floor housed the tycoon's collection of classic cars. On the east side of each floor, there was a cluster of rooms. The small ones on the ground floor were the car park management offices. The tiny, windowless ones on the middle floor were used for storage. And the large, sticking-out ones on the third floor were staff quarters for Allie Ng, the night guard, who was the only employee who lived on the site.

Wong wrote everything down in a notebook, and asked several questions about the flow of cars through the building.

Wu, surprised and thrilled to find someone interested in car park architecture, spoke at length about construction de-tails, boasting about how the building had been completed in a record fifteen weeks. 'When you build a car park, you start off with some basic questions. Do you want two-way flow or one-way flow?'

The feng shui man nodded. 'Same with *ch'i*. Flow very important.'

'People assume that straight lines, quick in and out, is the best. But in fact, that would result in the vehicles moving too fast. Quite dangerous. So we actually deliberately build in a few twists and turns to slow people down.'

'Movement of *ch'i* energy just the same. Must flow, but not too fast. Just the same.'

'How interesting. Another issue is the angle of the actual car park lots. There has been a big fashion for angled spaces, but as you can see, I've opted for ninety-degree spaces in this car park. I find that angled spaces confuse drivers, and if you go for a one-way flow, you can't risk that. Someone drives the wrong way around a one-way system and – crash!' He clapped his hands together for effect. The sound echoed in the hard-surfaced space.

Warming to his subject, Wu spoke in detail about the particular challenges of accommodating his employer's car collection. 'In the old days, car parks were for junior architects. Every slot was 2.4 metres by 4.8 metres. A monkey could do it. But these days . . .' He shook his head sadly. 'You wouldn't believe how complicated it can be. The traditional luxury car, like a 230 Mercedes-Benz, would just about fit into a standard slot. But now His children keep buying these fancy four-wheel drive cars – you know what I mean? – which are almost two metres wide. Stick two of them next to each other and neither can open their doors. And the Chairman bought a Jaguar XJ8 last year. It's even wider than an SUV and has a turning circle of 11.5 metres. That means a major change in the way we design the ramp entry points.'

'Flow at corners very important,' Wong agreed.

'Two-way flow systems achieve more turnover, but turnover was not my prime interest with this particular project. My dream was to achieve the most flexible car park possible within the limitations set.' Wu's eyes filled with passion as he spoke.

Joyce watched the two men with wide eyes. She found it astonishing that people could possibly become so enthusiastic about anything as boring as a car park.

Fortunately for her, an exhaustive tour didn't take long. On the ground floor and the middle one, there was not much to see – after all, a car park was a car park. But then they reached the top floor, and could feel both Puk and Wu start to become tense.

'And here we have His pride and joy,' said Puk. 'The classic collection and the vintage collection.'

Before them were more than a dozen cars which looked like they had come straight out of a museum. There were boxy vehicles on thin, spindly wheels from the early twentieth century. There were curved, gangsterish cars from the 1930s. And there were over-sized, angular sedans that evoked America in the 1950s.

'Phwooah! These are *sooo* cool,' the young woman said.

'Yeah. And wait till you see the last one,' said Harris Wu. 'It's fabulous. It was built before 1920. A royal blue Alfa Romeo 24. Gorgeous.' He pointed to an enclosed area with a heavy metal shutter lowered over the entrance – a garage within a garage. 'It's in there. I'm sure the Curdy boys won't mind. It's a dust-free climate-controlled area. Probably the most hi-tech garage in Singapore.'

Security guard Puk held up his hand. 'No. The Alfa 24 is a very valuable car. We keep a record of every time that door is open and closed. We can't just open and close it when we feel like, just to show visitors. I think – '

Wu threw up his fingers in surrender. 'Hey. I'm cool. You can see it another time. Perhaps when the Curdys are finished for the day.'

The dispute, although trivial, somehow raised the level of tension in the group. The thread of the conversation broken, the sound of the birds outside and the scraping of the cicadas suddenly seemed curiously loud.

Joyce decided to break the awkward silence. 'These ancient cars are like so amazing. I mean, do they like actually *work*? Does old Nevis, I mean, your chairman-geezer, drive around in them?'

Wu thought about this. 'Well . . . yes, they do work, but, no, He doesn't drive around in them. He used to. Usually what happens is that He gets one, and He's very excited, and drives around in it for a day or so, and then He puts it in here and more or less forgets about it. Then He goes off on his travels, and gets busy with other stuff.'

'What a waste.'

'Yeah. But when He's in town, or has guests, He likes to come up here and look at the cars. He strokes their hoods. He talks to them. They're nice to have. And they're an investment. They accumulate value. The cars in this building are worth almost as much as a decent-sized skyscraper.'

Wong was prowling around the floor. 'What are in those rooms?' He pointed to the doors on the east side of the building.

'Those doors lead to the stairs, and those lead to staff accommodation,' said Puk. 'On the second floor, we have some rooms – we keep junk in there. There's a laundry room with spare uniforms and stuff, and a storage area where we keep car parts and that sort of thing.'

'I need somewhere to work,' said Wong. The feng shui

105

master had subcontracted his afternoon appointment and those of the following days to a fellow practitioner named Sum, so that he could concentrate on Nevis Au Yeung's garage for as long as needed. 'I need a room to work from, small table, two chairs, good light.'

Puk looked dismayed. 'There are no rooms with decent light in this building. There are just the cubby holes we use for offices downstairs . . . I know – you can use the table in Allie's flat. We play mahjong on it sometimes.'

He led them over to a door that appeared to have been badly painted with leftover grey primer. Puk hammered on it. After two minutes, a thin, small man in striped pyjamas appeared. 'Morning, Puk,' Allie Ng said, his voice thick with sleep. 'Or afternoon, is it?'

'These are feng shui people,' Puk said. 'They're going to use your table for their work for a couple of days, can or not?'

'Yah, sure, no problem,' said Ng. His nostrils suddenly whitened, and it was clear that he was trying to suppress a yawn. ''Scuse me,' he said to the visitors, putting his hand to his mouth. 'I'm a shift worker.'

'Poor you,' said Joyce. 'What hours do you work?'

'I'm on from six in the night to six in the morning six days a week.'

'That's terrible,' she exclaimed. 'Is that allowed? That's – er – let me see – seventy-two hours a week. Don't you have unions and stuff?'

'I don't mind,' said Allie Ng, yawning again. 'Especially in a difficult situation like now, with the cars disappearing.' He put his arm on his colleague's shoulder. 'We are in this together. We are brothers.'

Puk turned to Wong. 'Allie and I *are* in this together. The

Chairman said that if one more car gets stolen, we're both going to lose our jobs.'

'Why don't we let the poor guy go to bed?' Joyce said.

The diminutive night guard ushered Wong and McQuinnie into the three-room flat. His wife Suma had gone out to the playgroup with their child, so the living room was empty. A small table was cleared of plates and toddler playthings for them to work on. Then he went back to his bed.

Wong began the long process of examining the floor plans and mapping the directions of the influences. He started by making notes on the structure with the help of Harris Wu. The garage was well designed, with a total floor area of 4,500 square metres on four floors, including the roof. It had two hundred and forty vehicle spaces, plus the large enclosed work-shop for the Alfa 24, staff accommodation and some small offices on the ground floor. It was steel framed with a façade of mesh panels, architectural bracing and insulated cladding. The floors were pre-cast concrete, covered with a watertight membrane. The roof deck was covered with mastic asphalt.

The geomancer thanked Wu for his help, and the architect bowed once and left the room.

Looking at the floor plan, Wong noted with approval that Wu had cleverly managed to minimise the use of columns – not only were these irritating to drivers, but they sometimes chopped up the flow of *ch'i* into awkwardly small tributaries.

The structure was basically very simple – each floor was a rectangle of just over 1,000 square metres, with parts of the east and north sides closed off for other purposes. There was a forty-square-metre set of rooms used for offices on the ground floor, twenty-five square metres of storage rooms on the second level, and forty-two square metres of space used for staff accommodation on the top floor. Wong calculated that the flat in which he was sitting was a thin rectangle, having a frontage of about 12.5 metres and a depth of about four metres. The living space in which he sat was four metres wide, and contained a kitchenette. The main bedroom next to it was also four metres wide, part of which had been hived off to form the unit's only bathroom. Then there was a small room about one-and-a-half metres wide, which housed the baby's cot.

Wong smiled as he noticed that Allie Ng's flat was facing due south. It wasn't an ideal location, but it was better than Nevis Au Yeung's accommodation, which faced northeast, precisely the wrong direction for a tycoon born in the year of the rat, 1940.

Joyce, quickly bored, made a token effort at helping her employer, and then went for a walk. Allie Ng's flat was airless and filled with the rank odour of sleep-breath and the sour milk smell of babies.

At first, she had no idea what to do. They were stuck in a car park for the entire day – perhaps for two days or more. There were no shops, no people, no coffee bars. Why on earth did no one have the idea of putting CD shops or boutiques into car parks? To her, that would be such an *obvious* thing to do, and what was really needed to brighten up the place. Perhaps she should suggest it to the tycoon? He might be really grateful to her for the idea.

She wandered around aimlessly for a while, not knowing what to do with herself. Then an idea came into her head. Suddenly she knew exactly what she was going to do – sneak a peek at that rare car that Harris had talked of.

She looked behind her guiltily as she turned a corner to-wards the back of the third floor – and walked straight into Harris Wu.

'Oh. Sorry.'

'No harm done,' said the architect. 'Where are you off to? Can I help you?'

'I was just – I was just wandering around a bit, you know, getting a feel for the place.' She gave an involuntary glance at the shuttered workshop.

He smiled at her, a grin that said he knew exactly what she was doing. 'You want to have a look at the Alfa 24? It's really quite something.'

'Can I? Will we get into trouble? Have you got the key?'

'Come.'

As they walked towards the enclosed area, he patted his pocket. 'There's no key. The only way you can open it from the outside is with a dedicated remote control device. The front door works like a shutter, but it's four times as thick – I designed and installed it myself. Impossible to break through.' He pulled a pair of small metal devices out of his jacket. They looked like miniaturised television remotes.

She expected them to go to the shuttered front, but when they reached the walled-in area, Wu beckoned to her to move past the door and round to one side. 'The Curdy boys are doing some work in there today. Replacing something on the dash. They're very temperamental about being disturbed. The air in that room is kept at a certain temperature and all that. Let's just have a look through the window.'

He led her around the side of the enclosed area where there was a window, about two metres long, set into the wall. Peer-ing in, she saw that everything was a bright orange-yellow colour, as if at the bottom of a sea of artificial fruit juice. She saw a slightly blurred image of Dick Curdy sitting in a car which looked as if it was a century old.

'Why is everything orange?'

Wu said, 'The Curdys installed a yellow filter to protect the paintwork against fading. The Chairman looks after this car better than He looks after His children or His staff, if you ask me. Don't tell anyone I said that. The inside of this particular garage has its own climate control station – cost more than fifteen thousand dollars.'

'Sing?'

'US.'

'Geez.'

She peered through the glass again. As her eyes got used to the scene inside the orange sea, she could locate both men. Dick Curdy was adjusting the left side headlamp, while younger brother Petey was in the passenger seat, with his arm half-buried in a hole in the dashboard. Petey turned and saw her looking at him. He gave her a smile and a wink.

Joyce was astonished. Cheeky! She decided not to respond. But somehow her face had its own ideas. Before she could stop herself, her mouth opened to reveal a bright, toothy smile, and her right eye winked back.

Petey lasciviously licked his lips with the tip of his tongue and then puckered them in her direction.

Joyce, shocked, again decided that she wouldn't react. But still her features appeared to be in a state of mutiny. She heard herself laugh, and her lips drew themselves together and blew him a kiss back.

Amazed at herself, she blushed painfully and raised her hand to cover her mouth. Her face was burning. She hoped that her red cheeks wouldn't show through the tinted window. Why on earth had she done that? And in front of a witness, too! She thanked Wu and fled to the safety of the room in which her boss was working.

The following day, Wong arrived at the car park early in the morning. It was a hot, glaring morning, and the building was baking when, a little after 9.45, he was handed a written message from Alyn Puk. It had been faxed to the security guard's office from Winnie Lim. 'Friend of Joyce came yesterday afternoon to try to fix stain on wall with stain remover,' it said. 'He made it worse. Now big red splodge on wall. Splodge is shape of cow.'

'Aiyeeah.' Things in his office were going from bad to worse.

Meanwhile, Joyce McQuinnie arrived at work at 10.30 a.m. in a state of acute embarrassment at her exchange the previous afternoon with Petey Curdy. She found it hard to even think of yesterday's encounter without blushing. Yet at the same time, she could think of nothing else. It was so strange. She had barely swapped two words with the guy in her whole life – and he had blown her a kiss. Was he saying that he had fallen madly in love with her? Or was he just teasing her? And what on earth had she been thinking of, blowing him a kiss back?

She spent the rest of the morning carefully avoiding the sealed workshop, walking long distances around it when she went out to take measurements, and using the stairs at the north end of the building when she needed to change floors.

But as noon approached, Joyce started to question whether she was taking the right approach. She tried to visualise what her older sister – a spectacularly successful tormentor of the male sex – would do in such a situation. Melanie certainly wouldn't skulk around in a state of abject embarrassment.

Joyce asked herself why she should feel cowed. She was a single adult, and so, presumably, was Petey. There was absolutely no reason at all to be ashamed about a mildly flirtatious exchange. The truth was, Petey might well be very attracted to her. She was an attractive young woman, after all. Her dad always called her 'Beauty' and 'Princess'. You couldn't blame men for fancying a young woman like her. It was biology.

But as for herself, she had no interest in him whatsoever. She and Petey could be friends or not friends. It made not the slightest bit of difference to her. She was far too busy to be distracted by stuff like that. She had a job to do. So for her, the best reaction would be to continue with her life exactly as normal. If they bumped into each other at any time in the next few hours, so be it.

But they didn't. By mid-afternoon, Joyce found her attitude had changed yet again. His face kept popping into her mind. In her mind, she replayed yesterday's scene continuously, zooming in on the way his lips slowly puckered themselves up and then – pop! – a little kiss shot out in her direction. She was soon longing to see Pete Curdy again – but only so she could show by her cool, detached expression that she had absolutely no need whatsoever to see him again.

By four o'clock, she found herself sitting outside Allie Ng's flat, on the hood of one of Nevis Au Yeung's spare BMWs, trying to think of an excuse to revisit the workshop. But even if she thought of something, what would she say when she got there? And anyway, how could you strike up a conversation with a gorgeous guy through a soundproof glass window?

No solution presented itself until Wong had nearly finished his work making feng shui charts for the building, its owner and the missing cars. She had an idea. She strode into Ng's living room, where the geomancer was sitting, poring over twenty pages of *lo shu* charts he had drawn.

'You know, I was thinking. If that Alfa thing is the most valuable car in the building, you better see how it fits into the calendar,' said Joyce. 'Remember how you told me that cars have birthdays and ages too?'

'Ah,' said Wong. 'Yes. How old is it? I think he say made in 1910.'

'We'd better make absolutely sure. I'll go and ask the Curdys for you. They'll know.' Before he could say no, she raced out of the door and headed for the sealed workshop.

She pressed the button at the garage's front door. A buzzer sounded, but time passed and there was no response. The shutter did not move. She tried to lift it, but it was firmly locked. So she walked around the side. She found the tinted window and raised herself on her toes to peek through.

'Huh?' This time she couldn't see anything at all in the room, except some tools hanging on the wall. The lights were off. Had they gone home already? Bother!

Perhaps she just needed to get a better angle. She gripped the edge of the sill and pulled herself up. It was hard to see, but there appeared to be nothing there – not even the car. 'Bugger,' she said. 'Missed 'em.'

'Can I help you?' said a voice.

She looked behind to see Alyn Puk standing next to her.

'Oh, er, yeah, hi!' Joyce stammered. 'I was just looking for the Curdys! Are they in today? Mr Wong needs to ask them something!' She flashed him a pleasant smile. 'I'm just taking a message!'

Joyce bit her lip. Why did she suddenly have to speak like a child doing an errand for a grown-up? Why did she feel she needed an excuse? She was an assistant feng shui consultant, and was fully entitled to walk around the premises.

Puk looked coldly at her. 'I suggest you stick to your job, which is wandering around with a compass, and keeping black magic out, isn't it?'

'Okay,' she said, suddenly meek. 'I didn't mean any harm. Just wanted some info from them about the age of the Alfa. I didn't know they'd taken it out.'

She had taken a few steps away when Puk spoke again. 'What did you say?'

'I didn't know the guys'd taken it out,' she repeated. 'It's not in there.'

'What do you mean *it's not in there*?' Puk suddenly looked alarmed.

Joyce, wondering why this was so difficult for him to understand, spoke slowly. 'There's nothing in that garage. It's empty.'

His eyes full of horror, Puk leapt to the workshop window and peered through.

'No,' he breathed. 'Dear God.'

He fumbled with a leather pouch hanging from his belt to get his communicator out. He was so nervous that he couldn't open it with his fat fingers.

'Want me to help?' Joyce offered.

'NO!' he shouted. Finally managing to open the latch, he snatched out the walkie-talkie and yelled into the microphone. 'Harris. Come up to level three, now, urgent, code red. Run, damn you. Bring the remote key for the workshop.'

They waited in silence until Wu arrived at a sprint, pointing the remote at the front shutter of the garage.

For twenty agonising seconds, the three of them waited until the metal garage doors swung upwards to reveal what they had all already realised. It was empty. The Alfa had gone.

Harris Wu was speechless. His jaw dropped open and he stopped breathing. Beads of sweat sprouted from his forehead. He wandered through the yellow-lit workshop and then wandered out again in a daze. 'Oh my God,' he whispered.

Joyce tried to comfort the two of them. 'I'm sure it's fine. Maybe Dick Curdy has taken it out for a test drive. To see if whatever he did to it was okay. Or maybe Nevis Thing's gone for a drive in it himself.'

But Puk was inconsolable. 'Dick and Peter both left early today. Dick went to collect a pre-war spark plug from a parts store and Pete's gone to their home workshop to reline the clutch friction plate.' He reached out with a fat arm to steady himself against the wall. 'The Alfa's gone. And so am I. I'm bloody history, man.'

He was right. The car had vanished. And Puk and Ng were given notice of termination immediately by Nevis Au Yeung himself, over a mobile phone, in the most colourful of language.

Dick and Petey Curdy, who had left the premises at one and three o'clock respectively, had been summoned back to the site immediately. Dick was close to tears as he wandered around the empty workshop. 'I've been working on that car, on and off, for ten years,' he said. 'It's like losing a family member. Bloody, *bloody* hell.' His younger brother, his face heavy, put an arm around his shoulder to comfort him. Any glimmer of flirtation between him and Joyce was forgotten. The missing car was the only object of adoration now.

Minutes later, Puk, Wong and Harris were summoned by telephone to a meeting with the chairman in conference room AY-1.

'Come,' sighed the distressed security guard, gesturing for Wong to follow. 'Let's go.'

The feng shui master was confused. Puk was moving away from the house.

'We should go to house for conference, yes?'

'No. The meeting is in conference room AY-1. That's Mr Au Yeung's car.'

'Oh.'

As they walked across a set of lush, carefully trimmed lawns to an open area containing a silver stretch limousine, Wong thought back over the past minutes of panic. The search for the car had been thorough and heartbreaking to watch. Allie Ng had once more been roused from his daytime slumber – clearly he was having a bad week, and it wasn't going to get any better.

Puk, Ng, several other staff and a group of police officers had crawled over the building, peering into every corner of the car park for clues. They had even stuck their heads into the small room where Wong had spent two days comparing measurements and drawing charts.

There was no sign of the vehicle. It wasn't to be found anywhere in the building. And yet both entry barrier guards – the 6 a.m. to 3 p.m. man and the 2 p.m. to 11 p.m. man – were adamant that it had not been driven out of the only exit. An initial examination of the tapes from the security cameras backed up their assertions.

As Wong, Puk and Harris reached the limousine – an eight-metre-long stretch Lincoln Towncar imported from Chicago – they could see that it contained Nevis Au Yeung in a state of apoplectic fury. He was a short, fat, volcanic mountain of anger.

Four large bodyguards surrounded the car.

There were two rows of three seats facing each other in the passenger cabin of the limousine. A small, walnut coffee table lay between them.

Puk, Harris and Wong climbed in and sat with their backs to the driver. Nevis and a silk-clad woman sat opposite them. Joyce waited politely outside the car not knowing what to do, until the woman, whose body was twenty-ish and parts of whose face were thirty-ish, reached out and grabbed her hand, dragging her in to sit next to her. 'I don't know who you are, dear, but you might as well sit next to me,' she said. 'I'm Foo-Foo.'

Joyce was stunned by the sheer opulence on display inside the car. The seats were cream leather and as soft as cushions. The inhabitants were sumptuously dressed. Nevis Au Yeung had a Jhane Barnes camel-cashmere blend one-button jacket over Polo Ralph Lauren double-pleated golf trousers and A. Testoni caramel tasselled loafers. The woman was wearing a Kay Unger light and dark pink paisley strapless crinkle dress with matching scarf, over Cesare Paciotti honey-suede bunched boots.

It was almost impossible to breathe. The air in the car had been entirely replaced by designer perfume, as Nevis's Bulgari BLV Pour Homme did battle with his girlfriend's Clandestine by Guy Laroche.

The four new arrivals sat in terrified silence as the tycoon growled a lengthy monologue. 'Idiots. You *idiots*. I am surrounded by incompetence. Do I have to do absolutely everything myself? Do I have to stay up *all* night guarding my own car *by myself*? Do I pay security staff a huge fortune to do ABSOLUTELY NOTHING?' He continued in this vein for ten minutes, his statements heavily decorated with bursts of Cantonese Joyce could not follow (curses by the sound of them and by the way Wong winced).

The only person who remained calm throughout the tirade

was the woman who was always referred to outside her presence as 'His latest – er – wife'. The implication, Joyce decided, was that she was the girlfriend of the moment.

Whatever her status, the woman – who went by the name Foo-Foo Au Yeung – was not only unperturbed by the tycoon's outbreak, but was positively beaming. She felt that the latest disappearance totally justified her theory. She was having an absolutely wonderful day.

'I told you,' she said, during a pause in her partner's thunderous ranting. 'Black magic. The only explanation. I said this all along. Now perhaps you'll all believe me.'

Everyone else remained frozen in their seats, except Wong who had started scribbling in a notebook.

Foo-Foo turned to look at him. 'Well? What about you feng shui people? Since we are dealing with black magic, only you can help us.'

Wong bowed his head deeply to indicate that he accepted this fact. 'Yes,' he said. 'We can help I think.'

Joyce blinked in surprise at his answer. What was he going to suggest? Should we hold a séance to get rid of some invisible wizard spiriting away cars?

Nevis went quiet, seemingly struggling to deal with his own beliefs. He leaned forwards and spread his thick, bejewelled fingers on the walnut platform. 'I am a businessman,' he growled. 'I deal with hard facts. Yet even I cannot imagine how this was done. I don't normally believe in black magic, but . . . well, I can't explain how this happened. And neither, it seems to me, can you,' glaring at Puk and Harris. Then he turned back to Wong. 'Maybe you are our last hope, Mr Wong. As Foo-Foo says.'

The feng shui master, in a state of sheer terror, nodded far too much, looking like an executive toy.

Nevis continued in a voice that was two degrees quieter than before, but somehow ten degrees more dangerous: 'But don't fail me. If you fail me, I won't forget it. Do you understand? And I won't pay you either. Not one cent. Is that understood?'

'Yes-yes-yes,' Wong stuttered. 'We can help. I think. But first have to do more work. More compass readings. More study. More charts. Very busy.'

So saying, he rose to his feet, bowed once, and crept out.

Joyce, terrified to be abandoned in the car awash with Au Yeung's anger, gave Foo-Foo an embarrassed smile and crept out behind him. 'Gotta go, gotta help,' she said in a tiny girlish voice that she recognised as her own, circa age nine.

'*Geez.* So how did the car vanish? Was it a helicopter, like I said? Harris and me, we checked all round here but didn't find any signs of anything.' She squinted in the bright sunshine as they stood on the roof deck of the car park.

Wong shook his head. 'Car has not vanished. Cars do not vanish.'

'Where is it, then?'

'Still here.'

Joyce looked irritated. 'But we looked *everywhere.* I mean, a car is a huge great thing. You can't just tuck it behind a dustbin or something.'

'Correct,' said Wong. 'Need a big space. So we need find space that we have not check yet.'

'Are there any?'

He bowed his head. 'There *are* spaces we not yet check. Not many.'

'Like what?'

'Like next to baby's bed.'

Joyce wondered if he were joking. 'Doesn't she sleep in a cot?'

'She has small room, about two metres wide. Dining room of flat a little bigger, about four metres wide, same size as mother-father room.'

'So I don't think you could hide a car in there. You're joking, right?'

'A car is not so wide as you think. I walk around. I measure cars. Average car is 1.6 or 1.7 metres wide. Not too big.'

'But come on, CF. Where could you hide a car in that tiny flat?'

'Look at map. Total width of inside rooms of apartment is eight-nine metres only. Four metre and four metre. Outside frontage is bigger. Total width is 12.5 metres. I think possible is secret room there.'

'A secret garage, where a car could be hidden, you mean?' He nodded.

Joyce said: 'But how could they get it into the apartment? The doors are so tiny.'

'Not through the doors. Did you notice this?' Wong pulled two small remote controls out of his pocket.

'Where did you get those?'

'Borrow from Mr Harris.'

'You stole those from him?'

'Just borrow them. Noticed something. Always he carry two remote controls. But why? Only one garage door that needs remote control. Officially.'

'So the other control opens something else . . . ?'

They walked briskly down the ramp from the roof level to the third floor. Joyce trotted quickly around to make sure there was absolutely no one around. Looking over the balcony, she noticed that the staff were having a meeting at ground level.

Wong placed himself at a distance of about six metres from Allie's apartment and pressed both the remote controls. Nothing happened. Then he turned to his left, jabbing the button and waiting to see whether there was any reaction. When he pointed one of the remote controls to the extreme right, there was an audible click coming from some distance away.

This was followed by a gentle whirring noise. Wong and Joyce watched amazed as an entire section of wall lifted itself up and tucked itself into the ceiling cavity. There, in a secret room built beside Allie Ng's apartment, was a vintage car.

'That's amazing,' said Joyce, rushing up to the vehicle. 'You've found it!'

She touched it to make sure it was real. Then she happily surveyed her reflection, which appeared upside down in the gleaming chromework. 'CF, this is wonderful! Old Ben Nevis will be like *sooo* pleased. *And* we'll get paid. Phew!'

Wong looked smugly happy with himself and strolled over to join her at a leisurely pace.

But then Joyce turned to him and her face fell. 'Hang on a minute. Maybe we won't. There's a problem. This isn't the 1910 Alfa Romeo 24.'

They raced down the stairs to look for Alyn Puk. Joyce was told by the entrance guard that the security chief had gone to the Ridley Park main security chamber. This was a small outhouse tucked behind a glade of dawn redwood trees in Nevis Au Yeung's front garden, occupied by two uniformed guards and a bank of twenty-three video screens, two of which were focused on the car park entry-exit point.

The fat, unhappy guard was standing with Nevis and Foo-Foo, running through the security videotapes of the past three or four days. Although the room was air-conditioned, Puk had sweat stains running from his armpits to his waist.

Foo-Foo used her elegantly manicured index finger (with a purple-painted, jewel-encrusted false fingernail) to press the fast forward and rewind buttons, Puk scribbled down a record of the cars coming and going, and Nevis slumped in a corner, a mumbled trickle of Chinese curses flowing from his lips.

On the largest screen, a string of cars could be seen being driven in and out of the car park at fast-forward rates, but none of them was a royal blue Alfa Romeo.

Wong and McQuinnie joined the watchers as the stultifyingly boring video ran on and on. A grey car passed out of the building. A black car passed out. A white minivan drove in. Peter Curdy's green replica car passed out. A brown van passed in. Suma Ng's yellow hatchback passed in. Nevis Au Yeung's sister's dark purple Lexus passed in.

'Try another tape,' hollered Nevis.

The guard slammed another videotape into the machine and the same scenes began repeating themselves, but in a different order. A white car. A grey car. A burgundy car.

Joyce had never seen anything so boring in her life, but so conditioned was she to giving her attention to any active television screen that she found herself focusing on it. Three minutes later she was rewarded by a glimpse of Petey Curdy driving across the screen. She started singing: 'Chitty Bang Bang, Chitty- Chitty Bang. Chitty Bang Bang, Chitty-Chitty Bang Bang . . .'

Foo-Foo looked at her. 'I remember that movie! Dick Van Dyke.'

'Yeah,' said Joyce. 'Brilliant movie. My dad gave me the video when I was six.'

'I saw it at the cinema. Of course, I was *very* young at the time.'

The two women sang together: 'Oh, you, pretty Chitty Bang-Bang, Chitty-Chitty Bang Bang, we love you . . .'

Nevis Au Yeung looked at Wong. 'They are saying what?'

Wong looked blankly back at him, screwing up his lips and shaking his head as if to say: I know nothing.

'Hey!' Joyce suddenly stopped singing, screwed up her face and moved closer to the screen. 'That's not Chitty Chitty Bang Bang.'

Wong, as usual, had no idea what his assistant was talking about, or whether she was merely uttering nonsensical noises. But it seemed she had observed something.

'What?'

She pointed to the screen. 'Curdy's changed his car. Look.'

'Stop TV please,' the feng shui master said to Foo-Foo.

She pressed the pause button and the picture froze, shivering slightly, and missing a section along the bottom.

Wong barked at his assistant. 'What do you say, Joyce?'

The young woman pointed to the green car. 'That's not the car that the Curdys have been arriving in. That one had running boards.'

'Running boards?'

Joyce pointed to the car on the screen video, to the space beneath the doors. 'See here? There below the doors? He had a car with running boards under the doors before. That's very important. That's where the wings are hidden, you see.'

Nevis Au Yeung rose heavily to his feet and joined the small group clustered around the television. 'What wings?' he asked in a curiously high voice, forgetting to be angry.

'The wings that make the car fly,' Joyce explained, as if she was talking to an idiot.

The chairman's wife nodded enthusiastically. 'Right,' said Foo-Foo. 'I remember. Wings come out of the running boards when you go off a cliff and you can fly.'

'This car can *fly*?' Au Yeung asked, incredulously.

'Of course,' said Joyce. 'How else could they escape from the pirates?'

Nevis straightened up and looked even more aggrieved. 'How come no one told me this car could fly?'

'This car looks similar, and it's the same colour, but it's different. A bit, anyway.' Joyce stabbed the play button and the car on the screen disappeared off screen.

'Cute,' she whispered to herself, as Petey's face whisked past.

'The car or the driver?' said Foo-Foo with a laugh.

Joyce bit her lip, not realising she had spoken out loud.

'Mr Au Yeung. You think you have one big problem in your garage: disappearing cars,' Wong began. 'But this is not true. Really you have two big problem in your garage.'

They were standing on the third floor of the car park. The evening sun was shining low in the sky at an angle where it slanted into the building. Everyone was squinting.

The feng shui master waved his hand at the diminished row of collectable cars and the empty climate-controlled workshop, its shutter open like a shocked mouth. 'You think thief using black magic was disappearing your cars. Between nine o'clock morning and eleven o'clock morning, the cars vanish. But no cars leave the building at that time. So where do they go?'

Wong picked up the remote control. 'Answer is nowhere. They do not leave the building.'

He pointed the remote control at the wall of Allie Ng's flat and put his thumb on the button that triggered the infra-red beam. 'Allie Ng is cousin-brother of Harris Wu, the architect who built this building. Ng and Wu is the same word in Chinese. Different dialect. Same character. Same name. Harris Wu built two automatic doors, not one. First is for workshop. Second is secret door built on side of Allie's apartment.'

The wall began to rise, tucking itself in to the ceiling revealing the 132 Bugatti secreted there.

There was a gasp from the assembled watchers.

'First, your Jaguar XK160 disappears. But was not taken out of garage. Just stored here. Everybody looks for clues at exit doors, can find none. Because car has not gone out of exit.'

He turned to stare at the suddenly terrified Allie Ng, who looked wide-awake for the first time. Harris Wu tugged uncomfortably at his shirt collar, his eyes turning to stare at Wong.

'Car stays in secret compartment for a while. Maybe one day, maybe few days, I don't know. But when Ng is on night shift and no one else is here, in the middle of the night, video is switched off and car is quietly driven away.'

Allie Ng started to walk backwards but Puk, who had already hung up his uniform, grabbed him firmly by the arm.

Nevis Au Yeung spoke in his deep, rumbly voice: 'I don't understand. Where did that secret wall come from?'

Wong said: 'Architect who built building built it. Who else? Few days after, 1930 Aston Martin taken, same system. Stored for few days, then taken away when everything quiet. A week ago, 132 Bugatti taken. But still here. Not taken out yet. Hidden in apartment space.'

Harris Wu fell in a slump to the grimy floor and put his hands over his face, a picture of misery.

'That's amazing,' said Au Yeung. 'And my Alfa? Is that hidden here somewhere else?' The short, fat tycoon snatched the remote control out of Wong's hand and clicked it at all the walls he could find. 'Here maybe? Or here? Or here? Give me a clue, Wong, where is it?'

The feng shui man said nothing, and the businessman's attempts to use the device to make other walls tilt upwards produced no movement.

'Alfa is different problem,' said Wong. 'Not hidden behind walls.'

Joyce piped up, grinning. 'We didn't solve that one through feng shui methods,' she said. 'Actually it was something I noticed that helped us find out what happened to that.'

The feng shui master continued: 'Alfa was not stolen today. It was stolen two days before.'

Nevis and Foo-Foo gasped.

'But how?' Puk asked. 'It was here this morning. I saw it myself. We checked on it every morning and every night, me and – '

'Will explain,' said Wong. 'The two Mr Curdys came every day for past two weeks. They arrive in their own replica classic car. Spend all day working in sealed garage on Mr Nevis Au Yeung's Alfa. But they are not really servicing it. They are removing pieces. They take out engine cover from Alfa, put it on their car. Next day they take out mudguards, swap with

126

their car. They do it very carefully, so no one notice. In small-small steps, they swap most dis- dis- dis . . .'

'Distinctive?' suggested Joyce.

'Thank you. Distinctive bits of Alfa. They put distinctive bits of Alfa on to their car. Two days ago, they leave their car here and drive off in Alfa. Car in workshop still looks a bit like Alfa.'

Dick Curdy spluttered, in a faux upper-crust British accent: 'I say, steady on.'

Puk was baffled. 'But how? I don't get it.'

Wong turned to the security guard. 'When you look through yellow-tint security window every morning, you see old car. You think is Alfa. But really is their car with a few Alfa pieces on it. They gamble that you don't notice any difference between one old car, another old car. Looks almost the same. They think you and Mr Au Yeung too stupid to notice difference.'

The tycoon growled: 'So they've taken my car away and left me with theirs?'

'No. This afternoon, they drove off in their car. So there is nothing left in the workshop – nothing at all.'

The tycoon nodded, the truth slowly dawning on him. 'They drove off with my car and their car, the car your girl refers to as a Chitty. The flying car.'

'Yeah,' said Joyce. 'That's just my nickname for it. 'Cause it looks like the car in the video? Caractacus Potts'?'

Dick and Petey started to walk away.

'Stop them,' Nevis Au Yeung said.

Curdy turned to Wong. 'You can't prove any of this in court.'

'I don't need to prove anything in court. I am my own court of law,' said Nevis.

The four large men who always hovered near the tycoon moved swiftly to grab hold of the Curdy brothers.

Security guard Alyn Puk was a changed man. He sucked his stomach in and somehow managed to suspend it at chest level. He strutted around, hands behind his back, chin high, pigeon-chested and proud.

'The barskets,' he kept repeating under his breath as he watched Harris Wu, Allie Ng and the Curdy brothers being dragged off by bodyguards to an uncertain fate. 'Bloody doongu barskets.'

He saw Wong packing his charts into his bag and strolled over.

'Never used to believe all that feng shui stuff-lah,' he said. 'But I guess it does really work, no?'

'The flow,' said Wong. 'Flow of *ch'i*, flow of cars, very important. That Wu, he keeps saying how important is flow. He boasts about good flow in garage. So when I saw how he made the rooms stick out so bad, interrupt the flow, I knew something funny was there.'

'Maybe better I study this stuff,' said Puk. 'This *ch'i* stuff is what?'

'Scientist call it bio-electrical energy. Philosopher call it life force. Indian call it *prana*. Religious man call it God. I call it *ch'i*.'

'Where does it come from?'

'From centre of Earth. From sun, moon and stars. From sky and from beneath our feet. From outside us. From inside us.'

'Can you see it?'

'I can see what it touches.'

Puk, still filled with amazement at the events of the past few hours, could not stop shaking his head from side to side. 'But how could they possibly think they could get away with it? I mean, someone would eventually have found that secret room that Harris built, even if it was months or years later, wouldn't they?'

The geomancer nodded. 'Yes. I thought about that. I think Harris Wu and Allie Ng plan to steal as many cars as they could – and then they would burn down whole garage, destroy the evidence. I study architecture. Mr Wu use many flammable materials. Unusual for garage. Very suspicious.'

Wong and McQuinnie left Ridley Park in Nevis Au Yeung's Lincoln Towncar, the two of them feeling lost in the sound-proofed, room-sized cabin. They sat with their backs to the driver. Sitting opposite was Foo-Foo, who had offered to drop them off at their office on her way out for a little shopping on Orchard Road. The socialite stared at Joyce, who had become quiet and morose.

'Something wrong?' Foo-Foo asked.

'Naah. Nothing really.'

The young woman played with the ring on her finger. 'It's just – well, life seems so unfair. I mean, I know it's wrong to steal and all that. But still, your husband has got loads of money and cars. He wouldn't have missed a car or two. And – oh, never mind.'

'And younger Curdy very cute.' Foo-Foo looked away as she said this, to spare Joyce's blushes.

'Yeah.' There was a moment's silence and then Joyce real-ised what she had said. 'I mean, was he? I don't know. I didn't notice. I never notice that sort of thing.'

The three of them drove on without speaking for the rest of the journey, and by the time the limousine reached Telok

Ayer Street, the young woman had begun to regain her composure. She had a question for Wong as they struggled up the steep, rather odorous staircase of YY Mansions, as they walked up to their office on the fourth floor.

'One thing I don't understand, CF. If the Curdys' car was green, and the Alfa Romeo was blue, how did they manage to switch them?'

'They put green paint on Alfa, drive it out no problem.'

'But how come Puk and the others didn't notice that the car in the sealed room upstairs was not blue?'

'Curdys very clever. They put yellow tinted windows in. Makes blue colour look like green. Anybody look inside, they see green car. But really is blue car.'

They arrived at the cracked frosted-glass door of CF Wong & Associates. Joyce grabbed his arm. 'Before you go in, I need to tell you something.'

'What?'

'While we were out of the office yesterday, I gave the keys to a friend of mine so he could come and use stain remover on the stain on the wall.'

Wong nodded. 'I know. Winnie sent me fax.'

'Unfortunately, the stain remover made it worse.'

'Also Winnie told me that.'

'So he came back this morning and repainted the wall. He said that was the only way to cover up the stain.'

'Good,' he said. Wong smiled. This was a happy ending to the stain-on-the-wall incident: a freshly whitewashed wall at someone else's cost.

He moved to enter the office. But Joyce continued to tug at the fabric of his jacket.

'Er, CF. I hope you'll like it. He said he thought it looked really nice.'

'I hope he use good quality white paint.'

Joyce swallowed. Her top teeth involuntarily bit her lower lip. She blew her breath out of her mouth. 'Er. CF. He tried painting the stain white, but the red showed through. So instead, he went back to the shop to get more paint. He painted – ' But she didn't get a chance to finish the sentence.

Wong had stepped into the room and gasped to find that the entire west wall of the office had been painted a vivid shade of crimson. Like a wall opposite a Chinese cemetery.

He stared at it for a few seconds. The sight filled him with horror. Blood. Gallons and gallons of blood. A wall of blood.

'I think it's lovely,' said Joyce. 'What do you think?'

Wong sat down in his chair. 'Why do the gods hate me so?' he moaned.

A little computer trouble

In the time of the Tang Dynasty (618–907), there were many secrets in the kingdom.

People made plots against each other. People whispered about each other. People were very careful what they said. People were very careful what they did.

All except one man. Official Guo Zyi took hammer and nails. He nailed his door open. No one in his family could shut it. Everyone passing could see inside.

When people walked past they peeked inside his house.

Now Guo Zyi particularly loved his daughter. She was very bossy. He acted like a servant to her. People saw him combing her hair. People saw him cooking her meals. People saw her shouting at him. Everybody laughed at them.

His two sons said: 'Father, please close the door. Because everybody can see us.'

But Guo Zyi replied: 'I will not close the door. Because everybody can see us.'

A time came when there was a great deal of slander and lies against officials of the city. Many officials lost their jobs. Many people accused each other.

But throughout the period of civil disruption, no one accused Guo Zyi of anything.

If you nail the door of your heart open, Blade of Grass, you can be beyond the power of evil ones who slander and lie. This is great power you can acquire for yourself, with no help from magic or from Heaven.

*An ancient Chinese proverb says: 'He who moves towards
the light does not need the glow of joss sticks.'*
From *Some Gleanings of Oriental Wisdom*
by CF Wong, part 126

Dilip Kenneth Sinha wound down the taxi window, opened
his mouth and drew in a large lungful of air.

It was stinky, pestilent and toxic.

The precise ingredients were hard to pick out, but he could
detect several distinctive odours. Jira, dhania and petrol were
the top notes, with subtle after-tones of garam masala, urine,
dalchini, methi and perspiration. Sumptuous!

He closed his eyes and a warmth rose from the depths of his
soul. The pleasure he felt was rich and wholesome and genuine. Yes, the air in this place may taste vile, it may be packed
with particulate matter, it may be dangerous to health, but
no matter: it was home air. It was *his* air. It was what he had
grown up on and what had formed his body. He took another
deep swig of it and opened his eyes to survey the marketplace
he was passing.

People kept remarking about how Hyderabad had changed.
They had talked for some years about changing its name to
Cyberabad, because of the business community's talent for
technology. But as he gazed at the buzzing, packed streets of
tiny houses, interspersed with large, traffic-locked thorough-
fares, what struck Sinha most of all was how little it had altered
over the decades.

It had always been a city with a bit of bustle about it, and
that physical energy was still there. Groups moved in bright,
vibrant clusters. Most of the women he could see were wearing
lahenga choli outfits.

The only difference was that the number of men scurrying
along the pavements in lungis and shirts of coloured cotton

or printed polyester had fallen. There were now more men in dark trousers, Western ties and white shirts – short-sleeved shirts, naturally. One even saw a not inconsiderable number of male adults in full Western suits. And if you peeled their jackets off, you would find three further layers of clothing. The silk-lined worsted jacket hid a matching waistcoat, shirt and singlet, all four garments bravely being borne in a land where a single light cotton shirt was the only sensible upper body garment.

Sinha himself favoured the single-layer safari suit, as popularised in American B-movies set in Asia.

As the taxi slowly progressed through the maze of market streets to the beginnings of the financial district, he noticed with regret that modern clothing styles had made the business area of the town less colourful than the rest of the city. The office district imposed dark blues, charcoal greys and pinstripe blacks onto the city's naturally colourful soul. It was as if the more sombre the tone of your dress, the more money you would make.

Yet for a thousand reasons, it was still the same old Hyderabad to him. Even here, several shops were still emblazoned with words like 'Shirtings' in antique, ornate fonts, instead of the slick 'G2000' logos you would see in clothing stores in Singapore. Cappuccino might be available in the five-star hotels downtown, but in his favourite canteen – which he had visited for breakfast – tea was still served warm and deep brownish pink, in tumblers instead of cups, with three spoonfuls of sugar already stirred in. And all items of traffic gaily announced their honking presence as they passed, giving the streets the air of a parade, compared to the low, discreet rumbles and roars of traffic in his present haunts of Singapore and Hong Kong.

134

Wong must be enjoying the architectural mix in the capital of Andhra Pradesh, Sinha mused. There were many reminders of the period of the British Raj, with stately colonial buildings at many major junctions. Certain corners reminded him of quarters of colonial Singapore. Yet the eye was regularly caught by other structures, equally grand, but with Islamic and Hindu backgrounds. As the taxi moved along the road leading out of the city, Sinha saw Saracenic, Mughal and mediaeval Indian themes along the houses spanning the wide boulevard.

On this visit, Sinha had spotted one thing he hadn't seen before. Signs on the walls offered NO DEMOLITION VAASTU. In other words, practitioners of the Indian equivalent of feng shui would come and examine your premises with a cast-iron guarantee that the spirits would not decree that your house needed to be pulled down and a new one built in its place. Feng shui with an opt-out clause designed to keep costs low. Even Mr Wong hadn't thought of that one.

Never mind the technological revolution: India remained India.

The room was black. It was so uniformly stained that it was difficult to believe that it had ever been any other colour. Only the presence of thin stripes of yellow wallpaper visible behind burned cabinets revealed that it had once been more brightly coloured.

'Waah,' Wong said.

'Phew,' Joyce agreed.

Sinha merely nodded in response. 'The bomb itself was quite small. But the conflagration it started, as you can see, was sizeable. It caused the complete destruction of almost

135

everything in the room. It turned this space into an instant furnace.'

'Yuck,' said the young woman, her face a mask of horror as she stepped gingerly onto a soft, mushy floor. Underfoot, a layer of moist ash was speckled with indistinguishable chunks of charred material. Eeee. Was any of it human remains? 'And were there many . . . like *people* in here at the time?'

Sinha shook his head. 'Fortunately not. From what I've heard, just the sole victim, Jacob. And he would have been killed more or less instantly. In that sense he was a lucky man. There's a fact worth remembering: if you are going to die from being blown up, make sure you are as close as possible to the bomb. Better a quick end than being maimed and dying in slow agony. As the countdown on your nearest timebomb heads for zero, run, don't walk, directly in the direction of the bomb itself. Then you can be cleanly vaporised.'

Joyce crinkled up her nose. 'Thank you for that pleasant thought.'

She remained a single step in front of the doorway, but the feng shui master walked boldly past her into the middle of the room, raising clouds of ash as he walked. He pulled out his *lo pan* and scanned the room from its centre, taking careful mental note of the positions of the windows and doors.

A pot-bellied man in a green uniform slipped in behind Joyce and walked with careful high-toed steps to stand nervously beside Wong. 'What are you thinking, Mr Wong? Can you find it? Is the ghost here?'

The newcomer's name was Inspector Muktul Gupta, although he was called Mukta-Gupta by his friends. He was in charge of the police investigation. He carried a black stick and there was a large, walrus moustache underneath his pockmarked, bulbous nose. His bottom jutted out backwards almost as much as his stomach protruded forwards, giving him the look of a badly assembled mannequin.

The feng shui master shook his head. 'Need to do some work first. Tell you later.' His small, dark eyes continued to crawl across the remaining surfaces. There was a burnt-out desk, a blackened cupboard and the remnants of the chair that Jacob had been sitting on when the bomb went off.

'It *is* kinda spooky,' admitted Joyce.

The police officer nodded. 'Especially when we are taking into consideration the alleged presence of the alleged ghost and all that.'

Suddenly, Wong's eyes widened. 'Oh,' he said, his body straightening, as he stared into the middle distance, towards the remains of a filing cabinet.

'What is it?' Joyce asked.

'Must leave. Excuse me.' There was real fear in his voice. The geomancer's face had acquired an expression of intense alarm. His eyes were glazed and staring. His spine had stiffened and he seemed about to spring.

'Must go,' he added in a low voice, and raced out of the room.

Joyce moved out of his way as he hurtled past. His clattering footsteps could be heard racing down the stairs.

Wong's retreat had seriously alarmed the police officer. 'I am thinking I'd better see how my men are doing,' Gupta said. His hands clasped behind his large behind, he strode swiftly out of the room, not looking back. Seconds later, the echoing stairwell reverberated to a fat man galloping as fast as he could on his hind legs.

Sinha remained in the blackened office. 'How very curious,' he said. 'I wonder what Wong noticed that I can't see?'

He stepped over to stand in the precise spot where the *feng shui* master had stood – it was easy enough, since Wong's small footprints were easily visible in the carpet of ash. 'Is there a ghost here? I am usually quite sensitive to that sort of thing.' He closed his eyes and tried to feel a presence.

Then he opened them again. The tall Indian astrologer scanned the scene carefully from Wong's point of view. 'Can't get anything. No vibes at all,' he said. He turned to Joyce, whom he noticed was smiling. 'So what do you think upset your master so badly?'

'Nothing,' she said, with an embarrassed giggle. 'Except what affects a lot of people who travel. He's been to the toilet three times already today. I think he's got the trots.'

An hour later, they regrouped at a snack bar called X=Coffee. It was oddly dark for a daytime eatery and was playing Indian pop music at an unsociably loud volume (candy-sweet female voices warbling up and down minor keys with thundering disco-sitar backing). But Inspector Gupta had selected the venue, so the others deferred to their host. Sinha managed to persuade the manager to lower the sound level slightly, as they sat to discuss the case at a stained formica table over strong, sweet, pink tea.

The officer put on his best 'official police statement' voice for the purpose of recapping the story.

'On the morning of November 9 at 11.15 a.m, an emergency call was received informing the constabulary concerning the desirability of them attending an explosion and accompanying conflagration at the Bodwali Building on the third floor of a small office building here in the town of Pallakiri, Hyderabad

West District,' he said in a single breath. 'Since we had officers patrolling that side of Ranga Reddi, it did not take them long. They arrived to find it burning most merrily. But fortunately, the fire had not spread to neighbouring houses but was contained in unit C only.'

'How come?' Wong asked. 'If such a big fire?'

'Both doors to office C were sealed with special airtight doors. Because of the large number of computer-things in the room. They had a lot of air-conditioning to keep the computer-things cool.'

'Computer-*things*?' Wong looked at a police document that included a sketch of what the room looked like before the bomb went off. 'On this picture, only two computer.'

The officer nodded. 'I don't really understand this stuff. There were just two computer *screens,* there, as you say. But there were lots of er, computer things, computer *boxes* you know, around the room. Different sizes. Just boxes with no screens.'

Sinha turned to Joyce. 'You are good at all this technology stuff. What do you call those things?'

'Oh yeah,' the teenager said. 'They were probably like mainframes, or servers, or something like that. How big were they?'

Wong looked at the sketch and indicated a height of about a metre above the ground.

'Servers,' said Joyce. 'Definitely servers. Probably.'

To her consternation, the police officer wrote her words down in his notebook: *Definitely probably servers.*

Inspector Gupta continued: 'Anyway, the late deceased gentleman – what was remaining of him – was found in the office once the fire had been extinguished by the trusty fire services of this locality. He was positively identified by his dental records as being one Mahadevan Jacob, forty-three, merchant of 11/c 15 Jabalpur Court, Nagarjuna Sagar Road. He had rented the office eighteen months ago, and ran his own business there, under the name Data Storage Solutions Hyderabad Ltd. He led a lonely life at work, since he was managing director and all the staff. There was no one else. He had used a temp for a secretary and was sharing the cleaning lady with the rest of the offices in that building.'

'What did the company do?' Sinha asked.

'I don't really know,' the officer said. 'Data storage, I suppose. He hadn't hired any temporary secretaries for a year – this town, as you can see, is being rather on the smallish side, and there were only two ladies who regularly offered their services for typing in the English vernacular. He had no wife or family that we could trace. A bit of a loner. Apparently a lot of computer experts are being like that.'

'What about friends? Or business associates?'

'Since his records were all destroyed by the fire, we were not finding any lists of those either. We assumed that some would come out of the woodwork, but none did. After the report in the newspaper, we found a few people who had been at college with him, or had met him at a computer club a few years back, but we couldn't get much detail on him or on what Data Storage did. It did not seem to be a particularly successful company. For a start, there were no complaints from people whose data had been stored, which was presumably what the firm did.'

Joyce interrupted. 'Geeks get like that. Having no friends. I know a few. They just do email.'

Gupta agreed. 'Anyway, we immediately started an – ' He stopped abruptly as a woman in a sari opened the door of X=Coffee and looked in. 'This way, Mrs Sachdev,' he shouted over the Hindipop.

140

The others politely scrambled to their feet as a confident-looking woman in her mid-thirties strode across the cafe and took a seat at their table.

'These are, er, Mr . . .' The policeman gestured with his arms as if he were about to make introductions but it was evident that he had forgotten all their names.

Joyce took over. 'This is Dilip Kenneth Sinha, that's CF Wong, and I'm Joyce McQuinnie. Very pleased to meet you, I'm sure.'

'Yes, never been good at names,' said the officer, with a grateful nod to Joyce. 'Thank you. And this is Mrs – '

'Sachdev. Call me Lakshmi.'

'Thanks, Mrs Sachdev. Mrs Sachdev occupies the office next to Data Storage Solutions Hyderabad Limited. I asked her to join us today because you may be most interested in her evidence.'

'If I can help in any vay, I vould be delighted to.' She spoke with a clear, crisp voice, given musicality by a south Indian accent which turned 'w's into 'v's and vice versa.

'I've told them about the explosion ten days ago. Could you tell them your side of the story? About the so-called ghost?'

'Of course.' She looked at her listeners. 'About maybe three or four days after the explosion ve got an email from Mr Jacob.'

'The dead man?' asked Wong.

'Correct.'

The feng shui master was constantly amazed by the miracles of technology. 'Email can be used to talk to *dead* people?'

'Apparently yes.'

'It said what?'

'Nothing. At least, nothing interesting. It was really just an ad, urging my company to use the services of Data Storage. You know the sort of thing.'

Joyce piped up. 'Oh yeah, junk email, I get tons.'

Lakshmi continued: 'Anyway, I happened to mention this to a friend, and he said that he had also got a similar email. I checked with more friends – every single person I checked with had got this email. Isn't that strange? Four days after his death?'

Joyce shook her head. 'But it doesn't mean anything. It doesn't mean there was a ghost or anything. It just means that his junk mail is on a server somewhere that is still churning it out. Might go on for months.'

Sinha leaned back in his seat and put his arms behind his head. 'Thank God you're here. This is all rather technical for me.'

Inspector Gupta leaned into the conversation. 'Correct, Ms McQuinnie. We thought the same thing as you. We too are *most* Internet-savvy. So we got an Internet expert to trace where the emails were coming from, and he sent us the address of the ip.'

'The what?' Wong was struggling to keep up. 'This is person or technical term?'

'I understand it is indeed a technical term,' said Gupta.

Joyce's brow wrinkled. 'How do you spell that?'

'I.P.'

She smiled. 'Ah. The Internet Protocol. I see. It's not really pronounced ip.'

'It is in India,' said the inspector, wounded.

'Oh yeah, maybe. But it's like – it's the address that the original signal came from. The address of the actual computer.'

The policeman nodded. 'Yes. This is what it identifies. Anyway, the ip indicated that it came from the late Mr Jacob's computer. Which was a bit odd, because the computer in question was a charred metal box by that time. It was not even plugged in. So people started talking about a ghost.'

Silence descended as this bit of information was digested.

Inspector Gupta continued. 'People got lots of messages over the next few days from the late deceased personage's computer.'

'I don't think there's anything weird or ghostly about this,' said Joyce. 'The email was just bouncing around a bit. Through a network of proxy computers or something. It probably came from Mr Jacob before he died and bounced around a bit before getting to you. Or perhaps it went viral? That's why it got to Lakshmi and all her mates.'

Wong's brow furrowed. 'Went viral?'

'Yeah. Turned into a virus sort of thing. Like a germ. A bug.'

Her answer left him no wiser.

'I think I have gone viral,' he said, wearily getting to his feet and heading for the toilet.

Wong, McQuinnie and Sinha had been summoned to investigate the explosion because the Bodwali Building was one of a portfolio of south and central Indian offices owned by a property developer named Nawal Ajit Kishore, a Singaporean Indian. Kishore served on the board of East Trade Industries in Singapore, and had decided to exploit the connection to augment the work of the local police.

Wong had agreed to the challenging assignment on the basis that Mr Pun pay a larger-than-usual daily stipend and cover the cost of their being accompanied by Dilip Sinha, who had spent a significant portion of his childhood in Hyderabad.

And he had always enjoyed curries. But not on this trip.

Sinha went to talk to some Hindi-speaking witnesses while Wong and McQuinnie trekked across town to see the munitions specialist used as an expert witness by the police department of Hyderabad for all incidents involving explosions. They found him in a back office of a glass-walled building near the Osmania University. Despite the modern exterior, his office was in a musty suite of rooms with lines of old wooden desks.

Finding the right room after some difficulty, they discovered that the expert was a surprisingly youthful man named Subhash Reddy. He was a slightly chubby geek of about twenty-six, with thick hair, a solid moustache and a twinkle in his eye. His lashes were so thick Joyce wondered whether he was wearing make-up.

Reddy had been educated for five years in the United States, and he and Joyce immediately hit it off together. The young woman declared that she loved New York and Subhash explained that he hated it – and somehow the conversation brought them together.

'I just hated Central Park,' said Subhash. 'And those uptown buildings where the rich live.'

'Yeah. It's such a majorly cool place. We saw John Lennon's house.'

'And those silly tourist types who think it's cool to go round in a horse-drawn carriage.'

'Yeah. My sister and me went twice. It was so neat.'

'New Yorkers are just all really weird.'

'Totally. We had the greatest time.'

Wong impatiently dragged them back to the question at hand. 'Please tell us about explosion in Pallakiri town.'

Reddy reluctantly took his gaze off Joyce and twirled his seat around to open a cabinet and find a file on the case. He flicked through the sheets and pulled out a typewritten report. 'It was plastic explosive, tightly packed in a small metal container. He opened the container and the thing exploded. Simple as that.'

'Biscuit tin?'

'Smaller, maybe just three or four inches high. More like a tin of tomatoes or something. But not tomatoes – there would have been traces.'

'No tomatoes?'

'No. There were traces of some meat we haven't been able to identify yet. Possibly pork, possibly beef.'

'Religious motive?'

'Maybe. Maybe not. We also found some silver foil that could've come from a chocolate bar wrapper, and some peanuts. The impression I got was that he had been having breakfast or lunch at his desk when he opened the tin containing the bomb.'

'His food kills him. Very not nice,' said the feng shui master. He had Cantonese blood, and the idea of an exploding meal deeply upset him.

'Not nice. Bombs are never nice,' said Reddy. 'Presumably you have some questions for me?'

Joyce looked at the man's dark eyes. 'Yeah – are you wearing mascara or are your eyelashes natural?'

'I am quite convinced that Delhi belly is all in the mind, Wong.'

An hour had passed, and they were taking a lunch break in a small restaurant. Lazy ceiling fans sent down waves of air that mussed their hair rather than cooled their heads. Sinha had ordered a large repast, much to the annoyance of his digestion-challenged colleague. Within ten minutes of ordering,

145

an aromatic array of six curries was spread in bowls across the table.

Sinha waved his large hands around as he spoke. 'Foreigners expect to get upset stomachs here, so they do. Now look at Joyce. She's young. She has not yet acquired the prejudices of adulthood. So her stomach is fine. Yet what has she eaten? She has surely eaten exactly the same things as you have. The same airline food, the same hotel dishes, the same breakfast. If there were germs in it, you would have the same germs. As for me, I have never felt better in my life.' He took a deep breath, waving his hand theatrically, as if to wave more air towards his large nose.

'Amazing colours,' said Joyce, staring at the neon-vivid curries on the table. 'Like, totally psychedelic.'

She put a tiny portion of each one on her plate and tried to guess what they were. She particularly relished some soft lumps presented in a creamy, lemon-yellow sauce.

'That is a humble potato.' Sinha was filled with pride. 'What a bland and uninteresting vegetable the potato is. No taste, no texture and no visual appeal. Yet curry a potato in the correct sauces and it becomes a succulent, delicious, melt-in-the-mouth treat which is perfect, pressed gently into basmati.'

'Mm-*mm*. How'd you make it?'

'Easy. You simply curry the potato with red onion, dhania powder, mango powder, garam masala, sugar, ginger, jira, dhania, tomatoes, chilli, curry leaves, fennel, all that sort of thing, and gently simmer it for a long time. It turns into what we call a white curry.'

'But it's yellow.'

He was momentarily taken aback. 'We mean white in a metaphorical sense. It has an extremely *subtle* taste. A white taste.'

146

His eyes went out of focus again. 'In all parts of India, the potato is revered. In Hindi – and also in Oriya and Punjabi, we call it *aloo* – that's the name you'll see on the menu at Indian restaurants around the world. In Malayalam and Tamil, they talk of *urula kizangu*. In Bengal, they celebrate the *gal alu*, while the people who speak Telungu talk of the *alu gadd-alu*. The names have one root, but many rich associations. So many titles for one vegetable.'

'And French fries. And chips. Those are names for potatoes.'

'They are? I often wondered what they made those disgusting things out of. Poisonous, I believe.' He pressed a lump of potato with his fingertips into the rice and expertly turned it into a little ball that he lifted to his lips. 'Can you guess what the other dishes are?'

'This one's like lentil soup?' Joyce offered.

He nodded. 'Sambar. We call it sambar.'

'And this is okra?'

'More commonly known here as bhindi or lady's fingers.'

Joyce correctly identified the chicken dish and a fish dish, but was baffled by a lumpy, dark brown meat which was rather too chewy for her taste.

'Beef?'

'Certainly not. This is India. Hindus cannot eat beef. Although many historians believe that the real reasons for the non-consumption of our bovine brothers and sisters were actually more practical than religious. In the fifth century, the number of cows in India was diminishing fast, and it was decreed that the value of a live cow, as an active year-after-year producer of ghee and so on, was far more than the value of a dead cow, as a short-term meal of beef.'

'Is it lamb?'

Sinha shook his head.

'I don't know, then. Is it something rare?'

'Rare in Singaporean restaurants, yes.'

'Crocodile? Tiger? Elephant?'

He shook his head again.

'I give up. It's an unidentifiable meatal substance. Hippo? Rhino? Ostrich?'

Sinha smiled. 'You would call it goat. We call it mutton.'

'I thought mutton came from sheep?'

'In the West, I believe mutton does refer mainly to sheep. But in most of Asia, sheep and goats are considered brethren. In Chinese, I believe they say *yeung* for both. Correct?'

They looked at Wong, but he sat glazed, out of the conversation. He had not made a move to touch any of the food Sinha had piled onto his plate. Indeed, he seemed reluctant to even look at it, as he sat half-turned, staring out of the window.

The Indian astrologer gestured at the mutton. 'Oh come on, try a little *yeung*, Wong. Or "unidentifiable meatal substance", as Joyce calls it.'

Sinha dipped his fingers into the lemon-water bowl, wiped them carefully with a serviette, and placed them under his chin. Joyce correctly surmised that he had paused to make another speech.

'The question is often asked by visitors to India – often, I say, but in truth it is probably not asked as often as it should be, visitors being too likely to accept what they are told without even a modicum of intelligent curiosity these days – anyway, a question which *should* often be asked is this: why is it that a largely vegetarian country can produce such fine meat dishes?'

She sat tight, knowing he would provide his own answer.

'The answer is this. In the period known as the Vedic times, which ran from three-and-a-half to about two-and-

148

a-half thousand years ago, long before your Western spiritual man Jesus Christ was even born, our communities had a thriving and active religious life. The priestly castes energetically sacrificed animals to the gods, and then ate what was left over, so as not to waste it. So there were meat-eaters here for a long time. But then we saw the rise of Buddhism and Jainism – movements which were against any sort of violence to any sort of sentient being (movements which presaged your Western animal liberation groups by millennia). So then, in the fifth century BC, India became the largest vegetarian nation in the world – as it remains today. Because we ate only vegetables, we developed a wonderful range of sauces and creams to enliven them.'

He pointed to a creamy, pale-brown dish. 'But to me, it was the Muslim influence that turned an interesting vegetarian cuisine into the most varied and flavoursome in the world. Arabs visiting India cooked the barbecued meats from the Middle East in the rich sauces and gravies that were common in Indian food. The result was Mughlai cuisine. The final touch: to the cream and ghee of Indian food were added spices, cashews, raisins and almonds. We ended up with meat in rich gravies adorned with aromatic spices and nuts. It was enchantment on a plate. The British fell in love with Indian food and took their addiction back home and it spread round the world. Today, anywhere around the world, just the aroma of an Indian meal instantly fires up the most jaded appetite. It never fails.'

A glance at the feng shui master suggested that this last point was not entirely accurate. Wong remained statue-still in front of his untouched plate, his eyes closed and his brow wrinkled with pain.

The others moved on to dessert.

Sinha remained in lecturing mode, although he ate at good speed as he spoke. 'The entire concept of dessert, as you know, came from the Arabic world.'

'It did?' Joyce asked absently, her mouth full of kulfi.

'Of course. Where do you think it came from?'

'Dunno. Häagen-Dazs?'

'The Arabs came to India and to China, and demonstrated their techniques of crushing almonds and rice, and then sweetening the resultant paste with sugar. Lastly, they added a touch of rose water for scent. The result was the first dessert.'

Suddenly Joyce dropped her spoon onto her plate.

'I've got it.'

Wong, his attention caught by the clang of the teenager's cutlery hitting the plate, looked up. 'You got Delhi belly too?'

'No. I know what killed that Jacob guy.'

Sinha said: 'We know what killed him. A bomb killed him.'

'Yeah,' said Joyce. 'But I know what the bomb was in. And I bet I know what job he did too.'

Wong opened his eyes. 'Tell.'

'He was a spammer. Sitting there with all those computers. And servers. Getting killed by a tin of unidentifiable meat. Remember Subhash said that there were traces of meat?'

The others looked blankly at her.

'The munitions guy. They found traces of unidentifiable meat and a small tin. He was a spammer so someone killed him with a tin of Spam. With a bomb in it. Get it?'

Sinha and Wong looked at each other for aid in comprehension, but found no help.

Joyce raced off to the phone to call Inspector Muktul Gupta.

'She appears to be suggesting some sort of cannibal act?' asked Sinha.

'Cannibal?'

'He was a Spammer and was killed by a tin of Spammer meat, she said. Where do Spammers come from?'

'Spam?' mused Wong, his forehead wrinkled in thought. 'Is a country in Europe. I think.'

'Ah,' said Sinha. 'Now I understand. We call them "Spaniards" here.'

The curious thing about Mahadevan Jacob's office was that it had good, powerful, natural feng shui, every trace of which had been emasculated by bad design. Had an expert in feng shui or a practitioner of Indian *vaastu* inspected the original location, he would have given it a thumbs-up. It was a light, bright, pleasant office, east-facing, comfortably proportioned, and had a good view of the Pallakiri main road and a small canal running to the east of the town.

But the view had been removed and the light turned into a grey glow by cheap, plastic film coating all the windows. The office furniture, clearly obtained second-hand, was all mismatched in style, size and design. The wiring of the various computers had taken priority, as literally dozens of charred cables could be seen lying under the remnants of the desks, chairs and computer equipment.

Wong and McQuinnie spent most of their second day in Andhra Pradesh painstakingly tracing each cable to its destination. Many of them went to a switching box in a locked cabinet to the left of the front door of Unit C. But there were a number of thick wires that appeared to be out of place.

Particularly confusing was a bundle that simply disappeared into a tiny hole in the wall between Data Storage Systems Ltd and Lakshmi Sachdev's office next door.

'Maybe this is ghost,' Wong said.

Meanwhile, Inspector Muktul Gupta had immediately followed up Joyce's suggestion that the victim was a specialist in junk email killed by a booby-trapped tin of Spam – and it led him to a host of answers that neatly filled several gaps in his knowledge. Given a lead by police, local reporters had managed to ferret out more of the facts. By the third morning of their visit, the results were evident in the write-ups in the local papers.

MURDER VICTIM MAHADEVAN JACOB WAS THE SPAM KING OF HYDERABAD, the *Deccan Chronicle* reported that day. He had sent out millions of items of junk email over the past year. He had clogged up the email accounts of unimaginable numbers of people with unwelcome exhortations to buy software, purchase lawnmowers, improve their sex lives, embark on new diets, put their savings into investment plans and so on.

And he had done a lot of it using other people's equipment. The I.P. addresses he had been using were eventually traced to their real origins. Yes, many came from the third floor of the Bodwali Building in the town of Pallakiri, as the police had confirmed from the I.P. trace. But only one of them came from the offices of Data Storage Solutions. The others came from the servers of the other tenants of that floor: Sachdev Imported Fineries Ltd and Bharat Golden Investments Co. Ltd.

Mahadevan Jacob had quietly hacked into the computers of everyone he knew who had an Internet connection of reasonable bandwidth (and a penetrable firewall) and employed them, without their knowledge, to help him send out literally millions of junk email items.

By lunchtime that day, technicians from the Internet service providers had visited the building, and the ghost had been exorcised – or so Sinha said.

'Not exorcised,' Joyce corrected him. 'Deleted.'

The Hyderabad job had been quick and easy. A report was filed with the police and the task was complete. A final meeting was held in the management office of the Bodwali Building. The representative of owner Nawal Kishore was an elderly man named Sharrifudin Azam. 'T'ank you,' the old man said, bowing.

Inspector Muktul Gupta was also grateful. 'Yes, many, many thanks,' he said. 'You have been *most* helpful.'

There was a knock at the door.

It opened from the outside before anyone could reach it and a small, wizened man with sun-roasted skin wandered in. He had a wide grin revealing several gaps in his teeth, and he wore a baseball cap with the slogan *I have a big brian.*

'Hello,' he said, cheerfully, tilting his head to one side. 'Are you crack investigation team being mentioned in *Chronicle*, investigating death of late Mr Mahadevan Jacob, deceased former Spam King of Hyderabad?'

'He is boss,' said Wong, pointing to the police officer.

'What can I do for you?' Inspector Gupta said, thrusting out his chest.

'I am Himanshu Mukherjee. I was merely wanting to express my very-very great delight at how all this turned out.'

The officer gave a short bow. 'Our investigation is proceeding at good speed. Thank you.'

A thought occurred to him. 'Are you a journalist?' He

pronounced it *jarnalist*. 'Are you looking for official statement? Because if so, I cannot be giving you one. Contact with press is all centralised these days. But I can give you the number of our press off – '

'No, I'm not press,' Mr Mukherjee said. 'I am not a jarnal-ist. I am murderer. I killed Mahadevan Jacob. I sent him tin of meat with bomb in it. Spam. Mentioned in paper.'

Joyce gasped. A confession – live, at the scene of the crime. And they were right there, witnessing it.

'Cool,' she said. 'Does that like *so* neatly wrap it up or what?' She theatrically clapped the dust off her hands.

A junior police officer poked his head around the door. 'Inspector, can I have a word?'

'Just a minute, Nitish,' Gupta said. 'Important business is happening here.'

'Quick interruption only,' the young officer said. 'Also important.'

Gupta looked sternly at the youthful sergeant. 'The man in front of me, Mr – '

'Himanshu Mukherjee,' said the confessor.

'Thank you. Mr Mukherjee has just confessed to the mur-der of Mahadevan Jacob. I will be needing to take a statement, as you can imagine.'

The officer at the door nodded. 'Yes, sir. There's a woman at the front desk, sir. She has also confessed to murder of Ma-hadevan Jacob. There may be bit of a row about who actually did it.'

Wong and McQuinnie were talking in a taxi on the way back to the hotel to collect their bags. The air-conditioner in the vehicle was not working, the car was stuck in a rush-hour grid-lock, and they felt trapped in an inferno.

Wong had wanted to get away as quickly as possible, worried that unpaid extra work might be coming their way. 'So they have two confessions. Not our problem. *Their* problem. They are police. They can deal with it. We cannot. This is not feng shui work. This is police work. We go now.'

'Yeah, yeah.' Joyce did not want to argue with Wong. Yet she was dying to find out who had actually done it. Especially since the person at the desk was a young woman – only in her twenties. Was there another story there? Perhaps the murder had been some sort of love triangle? Perhaps the woman and the man had done it together? Still, their plane left that evening. No doubt Gupta could be persuaded to keep them informed about what happened. After all, a senior police officer from Hyderabad must have basic email skills.

Then she remembered that Sinha had once told her that legal cases in India often dragged on for years or decades, so perhaps they wouldn't find out the conclusion of the case for a long time, if ever. It was all rather unsatisfying, but what could they do? There was nothing for it, but to head home.

The car eventually arrived at the driveway of the hotel. 'Yeah, I'm ready,' Joyce said. 'Let's go. Maybe I'll just make a phone call or two while you're packing.' She had Subhash's phone number in a notebook in her bag and remembered how his big, soulful dark-rimmed eyes had stared into hers.

Three-quarters of an hour later, McQuinnie was standing in a queue in the lobby of the Roomy Inn. Subhash Reddy was standing next to her, keeping her company in her final

155

hours in India. They were laughing together at nothing in particular.

Dilip Kenneth Sinha marched into the hotel.

'Hi, DK,' said Joyce. 'You packed?'

'I am not,' the elegant astrologer said. 'The investigation has taken a somewhat unexpected turn. I need to speak to Wong.'

She called to her employer. 'CF! You'd better come here.'

Wong, who lay on a couch rubbing his stomach, not having eaten anything but a single bowl of plain rice in two days, looked up unhappily.

The young woman turned to Sinha. 'He doesn't look too good. Maybe we'd better go to him.'

The three of them abandoned their place in the checkout queue and sat down on the lobby sofas opposite the feng shui master.

'So who was it?' Joyce asked Sinha. 'The weird toothy guy? Or the girl?'

'Who knows?' the Indian said. 'It may have been one of them. Or it may have been someone else. While I was standing there with Gupta, six more people confessed to the murder.'

'What?'

'You heard correctly. Six more people have confessed to the murder. And as I was leaving the station, there were more people heading up the stairs. I suspect the number will have grown by now.'

Wong opened his eyes. He said: 'So now are eight people who say they put bomb in tin of Spaniard meat?'

'At least.'

'Weird,' Joyce said. 'What does it mean?'

'It means that we are not getting on the plane,' Sinha said.

Inspector Muktul Gupta was thrilled to see them back. 'Thank God,' he said. 'This has never, *never* happened to me before. I am really most needful of your help in a very-very bad way.'

Joyce was about to make some quip about too many murderers spoiling the broth, but she looked back at the long queue of people lining up to be interviewed and decided that it might not be funny.

'How many so far?' asked Sinha.

'We took statements from the first thirteen who confessed to the murder. Then, to speed things up a bit, we photocopied a murder confession and got people to sign it. About twenty-eight have signed that version. Judging by the queue out there, we've got another thirty to thirty-five to go.'

'How many will that make altogether?'

Gupta scratched his chin. 'That's about seventy, seventy-five – but there appear to be more joining the queue all the time, so it will be difficult to tell.'

'How can we help?' Wong asked.

'Oh, that's easy,' the police officer said. 'That's *very* easy. See this lot?' He airily waved his hands over the crowd. 'Find out who really did it. That's all you have to do.'

'Piece of cake,' Joyce said, turning around to study the crowd.

'Always hungry,' Wong explained to Gupta. 'Always asks for cake.'

'Young people always want sugary things,' the officer replied, with a distant look in his eye. 'Mind you, so do I.'

157

The three visitors from Singapore arranged to meet Subhash Reddy the following morning at X=Coffee, but had no idea how to proceed. Sinha ate crab curry for breakfast, while Joyce ate a small, pale-yolked egg. Wong nibbled at some dry toast. Little conversation flowed. The problem they were facing seemed insurmountable.

Where to begin? There was no obvious application of feng shui, vaastu or astrological lore. There were no clues. And there was a host of impracticalities in starting any sort of investigation. They were here only for a few days. No way could they interview all the people who confessed to the murder. The list had been closed at one hundred and fifty at 10 p.m. the previous night. And that was only because Inspector Gupta had passed an instant and arbitrary law saying that with regard to murder confessions, no more than one hundred and fifty were allowed, and would-be confessors from any murder from now onwards would be served on a first-come, first-served basis. Any murderer who confessed to any killing after the police-set deadline would not have his confession accepted.

The silence gradually became oppressive as the four of them peered into their tumblers of tea.

'I've got the full list of one hundred and fifty confessors here,' Sinha said. 'Muktul had it sent around to my room this morning.'

They passed it around, surveying it gloomily. How could one identify a murderer when all one had to go with was a list of names and dates of birth?

'Why don't we hang it up and throw a dart at it?' Joyce said. 'How on earth can we find out who did it? I can't even pronounce most of these names. And I don't fancy trying to produce one hundred and fifty birth charts.'

'Same-same,' Wong agreed.

The young woman ran her index finger down the list and stopped. 'Hey. There are some, like, white people.'

Wong looked over her shoulder. '*Gwailo?*' he asked. 'Here?'

Subhash Reddy shook his head. 'No. This is south India. There are lots of names here that come from the West. It's a historical relic. In Kerala, for example, many people are carrying the name George. In Cochin, there is a district called Jewtown. A typical south Indian name might be Minnie Matthew. India is a very mixed place, with all sorts of cultural roots.'

Joyce ran her finger down the list. 'So a guy with a name like, here's one – David George – isn't a foreigner? He's a real Indian?' she asked.

Subhash nodded. 'He's a real Indian.'

Wong took the paper and stared at it. 'Any Chinese names?'

Subhash looked at it. 'Not on this list. But there are Chinese in India. There are lots in Calcutta. Lots in the tanning business, since Indians don't like to handle cowhide.'

The feng shui master looked to Dilip Sinha. 'Can we do anything with this list?'

The Indian astrologer put his fingertips together under his chin and thought. 'I don't know. Like Joyce, I believe intellectual thought is not going to give us an answer in this instance. We need a different method. But something based on chance, like Joyce suggests, is not a good answer. It would be in better keeping with our traditions to look for a mystical route.'

The feng shui master pondered. 'Why so many people want to confess to being murderer? So crazy. Why so many people not like Spaniards?'

159

'It *is* crazy. But I guess the only conclusion is that he was hated. I think it is not Spaniards. I think it is Spanners, right, Joyce?'

'Spam*mers*. With two Ms.'

'Spammers. With two Ms. I see. I must practise. Why are Spammers so hated?'

'I don't know. Well, I do. They fill up your inbox with junk.'

Wong nodded. 'They fill up your inbox with junk. I see. What sort of junk? Old bed? *Lupsup?* Old shoes?'

'Not that sort of junk. I mean computer junk.'

'Oh,' said Wong. 'Old computers. Broken screen, like that?'

'No, not broken screens. I don't mean like physical junk. An inbox is like a computer mailbox.'

'Mailbox? Like on ground floor of YY Mansions?'

'*No.* It's a folder you get on your screen. And they put junk in there. I mean, they put email letters telling you to buy stuff. Advertisements mostly.'

'But why people get so angry?'

Joyce shrugged her shoulders, not knowing how to explain. 'It's – it's really irritating. I mean, I've wanted to murder Spammers before now. You see, you click on the little envelope thing on the corner of your screen, and you think, yay, I've got mail! One of my mates has written to me! You feel all happy. A little number pops up in a box on the bottom left of your screen and says you've got, say, ninety-nine new emails. And you think, cool, because you think they are all letters from like guys or your buddies or your mum or chatroom people you've been talking to or whatever. But then it turns out that ninety-five of them are junk mails telling you to buy stuff. Only four of them are from people you know. It's really annoying. I can't explain how annoying it is. And they are *such* liars – that's the worst thing.'

As she spoke, she became increasingly strident. Wong watched with undisguised fascination.

'The spanners – I mean, the Spammers – really are utter bastards. They have this little thing at the bottom and it says if you click it you won't get any more email, and poor little old ladies who don't know any better click it, and instead of taking them off the list, they send them more and more and more junk mail. Hundreds of pieces a day. They are truly *evil*.'

Wong was still not absolutely clear what the problem was. 'But if you see advertisement in newspaper, you don't get up-set. So why you get upset if you see advertisement in your box?'

'Inbox.'

'Yes, in box.'

Joyce thought for a moment. 'Well, unless you have a fast connection – and that costs big bucks – it takes a lot of time to download emails. Doesn't it, Subhash?'

The young man agreed. 'Joyce is right. It really drives you mad if your precious time and money are being wasted down-loading a lot of junk. Some people who are really poor . . .'

The young woman interrupted. 'Yeah. When I lived in Hong Kong, we had to pay this surcharge called PNETS for every minute we were on.'

'Peanuts?'

'Not peanuts, PNETS. Spelt P-N-E-T-S.'

Wong was looking confused.

Subhash raised his hands to show that he could explain it simply.

'Getting on the Internet is not usually free. It costs money.

Usually there is a charge to the telephone company, and also there are tariffs set by the TRAI – Telecom Regulatory Authority of India.'

Wong was intrigued. 'Ah, this is interesting.' He faced Subhash. 'Can I ask you question? Is it possible that someone only has few minutes every day to download email. And he get very upset because his few minutes taken up by junk emails from the Spaniard, not real emails from lovers.'

'You mean *loved ones*,' Joyce said. 'Not *lovers*.' She suddenly felt herself blushing.

'Sure,' Subhash said to the feng shui master. 'There must be loads of people like that.'

'On this list?'

'Yes. Dozens,' the young man said. 'I think at least half the people on this list don't have their own computers. They use computers at school or college.'

'What if they have no school or college?'

Subhash thought about this. 'Well, then they'd go to Mag-Auntie's.'

'Who's that?' Sinha asked. 'Is it an Internet cafe?'

The young Indian frowned thoughtfully. 'I would say more of an Internet chapatti house, or Internet bhajji house. We call it a short-eats house, you know? It's an *e-choupal* in Hindi slang. It's the place to hang out in Pallakiri.'

Sinha translated: 'Short eats – like a snack bar, or bakery café or something.'

Subhash nodded. 'Yes. The old ladies in this village like to go to Mag-Auntie's. That way, they keep in touch with their children overseas. She lets them use her computers. She charges money. I think at the moment you pay maybe two rupees a minute.'

'So that's not expensive, then.' This was Joyce, returning

162

to the conversation, now that she had got over the embarrassment of having used the word *lovers*.

Subhash sighed. 'I'm sorry to disagree with you, my dearest
sister Joyce, but that *is* expensive.'

Joyce blushed again. She tried to ignore her burning cheeks.
'A couple of rupees a minute? What's a rupee worth? Like a
few cents?'

'For these old ladies, that's very expensive. Some of them
have a budget of a few rupees a *day* to live on.'

'I want to meet Mag-Auntie,' the *feng shui* master said.

Mag-Auntie was nowhere to be seen. She had disappeared.
Her restaurant, an open-air eatery where a dozen people lazily
picked over short-eats and tapped at computers, was being
run by her grandnephew Arti. An enticing smell of charred
chickpeas and fried onions gently wafted from a counter laid
with trays of curries gradually getting cold.

Arti, a blotchy-faced youth of about twenty nursing a bot-
tle that looked like Coke but had THUMS UP written on it,
took a shine to Joyce.

'Hi pretty girl, you 'merican?' He grinned, showing two
missing teeth. 'I show you Internet, good price. Hot pictures.'

Subhash's face darkened. 'Leave her,' he said.

Joyce was thrilled. Could it be that Subhash was jealous?

But then the young man's expression changed. He smiled
and spoke to Arti in the local dialect. As they chatted, Joyce
was aware of the grandnephew sending lascivious glances her
way. She squirmed uncomfortably and moved to stand behind
Wong, who was trying to avert his eyes from the unappetising
food.

Subhash walked over and spoke quietly into her ear: 'I told him that if he tells us where Mag-Auntie is, you'll give him your personal email address.'

'I will do no such thing.'

'I know that and you know that. He doesn't.'

Half an hour later, they were walking through a rural area.

They left the main road and followed a dirt path through a grove of trees towards a clearing. They climbed a small hill, turned through a field of foxtail millet crops, and moved through a row of semul silk-cotton trees into a small clearing at the foot of another hill.

There was something almost magical about the grassy paddock in which they found themselves. It lifted their spirits, and all four of them were suddenly laughing for no reason. The sun glinted through fairweather clouds and a light northeastern breeze flicked forelocks off foreheads.

The glade was astonishingly beautiful. A huge variety of trees lined the clearing, with teak, casuarina, Acacia nilotica, Albizia lebbek and neem jostling together. From behind them, a clump of giant bamboo stalks leaned into the scene, and almost hid a tiny creek that trickled over a natural watercourse.

A small, white, single-storey house stood in the middle of the clearing, with a steep hill to the right and a stone hillock on the left.

On arriving at the spot, both Wong and Sinha were stunned. They gazed at the house, the hill, and the surrounding trees with what could only be described as awe.

The pain that had been a constant presence in the feng

shui master's face for the past two days vanished. He appeared to grow younger.

Wong looked at the house and turned to Sinha. 'The *ming t'ang*,' he breathed.

The taller man echoed him. 'The *ming t'ang*.'

The feng shui master slowly shook his head in wonder. 'Waah. Nearly perfect, no?'

Sinha nodded. 'Yes. Damn near.'

'The house. The hill.'

'The other hill.'

'The *ch'i*.'

'The *prana*.'

Joyce stood open-mouthed and speechless as Wong and Sinha spontaneously started skipping through the tall grass, which was speckled with shoulder-high poppy plants and wild sorghum. They looked like infants, dancing with excitement at the discovery of a new playground.

'*What* are they doing?' she asked.

'I don't know. They're your friends,' said Subhash. 'Do they often do this?'

'I've never seen them do anything like this before. There must have been something in their tea.'

'What does *ming t'ang* mean?'

'It means bright hall. One of the signs of a place with perfect feng shui is that it has a low, open area in front of it where good spirits gather. It's very significant.'

'I get the feeling they like this place.'

Joyce agreed. 'They spend all their lives looking for places with perfect feng shui. They seem to have found one.'

'Come.' Subhash beckoned to her to sit on a large, pebble-shaped rock nearby. 'Tell me about this feng shui stuff. What does it mean?'

Joyce used finger and thumb to wipe the sweat from her upper lip. She sat next to Subhash and looked over at the two grown men gambolling through the glade with their arms in the air.

'It's like this. Deep in your brain is a picture of home.'

'Your own home?'

'No. It's in the bit of your mind they call like the instinctive memory? You heard of that?'

'Yes. We sometimes call it the race memory. Part of our brain that holds things that evolved over centuries and millennia. From when human beings lived in caves and so on.'

'Yeah. That's it. Well, Wong believes that there's a picture there of the perfect home. It's a small place. It's surrounded by greenery – 'cause that was the only colour in those days, they hadn't invented Dulux and stuff. It had running water nearby. It was built into the side of a hill.'

'Why?'

'So the sabre-toothed tigers or mammoths or whatever couldn't get you.'

'Got it.'

'Well, *feng shui* helps us to like recreate that scene. That's why green is a relaxing colour. That's why you feel better with a mountain behind you and water in front. Et cetera, et cetera. Feng shui turns your home into a replica of that dream home deep, deep in your head, sort of thing.'

'Interesting. We have the same idea. We call it *vaastu*.'

'Yeah, same thing.'

Wong and Sinha, having skipped the length of the glade several times, stopped in the middle and stared at the house.

The geography of the scene before them was simple, but breathtaking. The small home appeared to be embraced by two hills. To the east and slightly behind the house was a steep, rocky hill with a small grove of amaltas at its foot. The high branches of the trees were draped in clusters of bright yellow blossoms that looked like gold grapes.

To the west was a smaller hill – really little more than a cluster of igneous boulders. The rocks were phaneritic, their surface peppered with tiny bright crystals. They stretched behind the small home, reaching out to the lower parts of the hill opposite. In front of the rock formation was a single old-growth gul mohur tree carrying a vivid mass of scarlet blossoms.

The two hills, their fingers touching behind the house, formed a perfect Dragon and Tiger embrace, protecting the house and encompassing it with the best fortune imaginable. Further behind the house were tall trees and, beyond, a much larger mountain.

Wong picked out the elements that made the location so magical. 'Green dragon one side, white tiger other side. At back is black turtle. *Ming t'ang* in front. Truly here is heaven.'

'It is really quite remarkable,' Sinha agreed. 'All you need is a red bird at the front, and it would be perfect.'

Wong pointed at the shrubs in front of the house, where several birds could be seen – and one of them was a scarlet minivet, a startlingly bright crimson Indian bird with a jet-black head and cloak.

The two of them started to walk towards the home at the centre of the picture: a small structure with a gently sloping roof. A row of pink cassia trees stood behind it, a profusion of rose-white blooms visible over the house's green tiles. In pride of place at the heart of the area behind the house was a tree that Wong did not recognise. It stood taller than the cassias, with solid branches carrying orange and scarlet clusters of flowers.

In front of the house were several low shrubs, decorating a winding path to the front door. On the right of the stone track were several hari champa bushes, their leaves dark green at ground level, rising to bright lemon green for the newest buds. Even from this distance the apple-fragrance of the bushes could be detected. On the other side of the track was a line of yellow oleander shrubs, known in India as the trumpet flower bush. They were growing wild, with some sprigs standing higher than Dilip Sinha. 'I love the trumpet flowers,' the Indian astrologer said. 'Poisonous to man but very popular with the gods – we use them for decorating temples.'

'That tree is what?' asked Wong, pointing to one beyond the house.

'That's an asoka, a sacred tree for Hindus. It exhales perfume at nights during April and May every year. It is associated with love and chastity. Remember the story of how Sita, the wife of Rama, is abducted by Ravana? Well, she escapes and finds refuge in a grove of asokas.'

'Very beautiful,' said the feng shui master.

'It is. Gautama Buddha was born under one of those.'

As they approached the house, the thick grove of trees behind it appeared to grow taller. 'In feng shui, trees north behind house very favourable. Lots of leaves, lots of prosperity.'

Sinha agreed. 'Works for me too. In vaastu, the north direction is associated with the god Kubera, Lord of Wealth. We associate it with the planet Mercury and Indians place their vaults and money boxes in the north, in the belief that this means they will always have something to put into them.'

Wong took great draughts of air into his chest. 'Feel much better. Feel hungry for first time.'

'I can tell you why,' Sinha said. 'See that?' He pointed to a creeper gently climbing a trellis on the green-dragon side of the house. It had dark leaves, interspersed with thick bunches of flowers of pale violet. 'We call that the garlic creeper,' he said. 'No relation to the garlic you use in cooking, but it has the aroma of cooking. Rather a neat trick by the gods.'

As they reached the house, they noticed how simple it was. The walls of Mag-Auntie's home were off-white plaster and the roof was made of terracotta tiles. There was a shiny satellite dish, draped by a creeper, barely visible behind a chimney stack. The windows were small and square. There was no doorbell.

'Auntie,' Subhash called. 'Auntie.'

No reply.

After politely waiting for a minute, he opened the door and all four of them looked in.

The small room was dark, but a little sunlight came from the windows, and there was some artificial illumination from a computer screen to the east.

'Ah, you have come for me. Finally.'

A small but stocky woman, who appeared to be in her late sixties, turned from the computer game she was playing. 'I apologise – these online games – so addictive, you know.' On the screen behind her, a war scenario was displayed.

She looked at Subhash. 'Do you know *Epsilon Grand Killer Breakout 3*?'

'I play it every day.'

She smiled at him.

He slid into her chair and took over the game.

Before stepping out of the cottage to join the others, she turned to him. 'If I come back and I'm dead, you're dead.'

He nodded without taking his eyes off the screen. Joyce slid into the chair next to him and put her arm across the back of his seat.

The old woman walked out into the glade that had had Wong and Sinha in ecstasy. She was a bulky woman in a shapeless top over a coloured ghaghra. There were a dozen bangles on each wrist. Her black hair was heavily streaked with steel grey.

'I knew you would come for me,' she said.

'Your home is almost perfect,' Wong said. 'Feng shui very good. Very good.'

'It *is*, isn't it? This spot was chosen for me by a great master.'

'He is a great master. His name is?'

'His name is Mistry and he lives north of here. His home is far, far better, even than this. In vaastu terms, it is perfection.'

Wong was amazed. 'I must meet him.'

Mag-Auntie offered to supply him with Mistry's address.

As they reached the edge of the glade, Wong realised that their conversation had entirely the wrong tone. He shouldn't be humbly expressing awe and admiration for Mag-Auntie's home – he should be grilling her to see if she had committed the crime they were investigating.

'You kill the Spaniard?' Wong asked sternly.

'Spanner,' Sinha interpreted.

'If you are referring to the Spam King, Mahadevan Jacob, yes, I killed him.'

Both Wong and Sinha could not help but be surprised at her easy admission of guilt. Taken aback, neither of them knew how to proceed. So they continued strolling, reaching the bamboo grove at the far end of the clearing.

'I killed him – and so did everyone else in Pallakiri, judging by the number of confessions that the police have received,' Mag-Auntie continued. 'I believe it was one hundred and fifty last night – one hundred and fifty-one if you

170

count my admission just now. Unfortunately I am not on the list. I missed the deadline to be registered among the murderers. Mukta-Gupta is at this very moment trying to find a Hyderabadi judge who will legalise his impromptu bit of law making.'

'How do you know this?' Wong asked.

'I lurk in Internet chatrooms. When I'm not playing online games. You find out things surprisingly quickly.'

The three walked slowly along the side of the creek.

'Please explain me. What is a Spaniard? Joyce try to explain, but I find it hard to hear her.'

The old woman nodded. 'Hard for people of our generation. Quite simple. A spammer is the worst sort of human detritus. A spammer is a murderer of hopes and dreams. A spammer is a conman and a thief and a piece of turd from one of the dogs of hell.'

'Ah. So you don't like spammer,' Wong said, without irony.

She thought for a moment before replying. 'Let me tell you a true story, Mr Wong.'

But after that promising introduction, she lapsed into silence. They walked on almost to the edge of a small lagoon at the edge of the glade. She stopped at the edge of the water and began to talk.

'A woman, let's call her Mukta-Leika, earns a few rupees a day. She comes to my shop. She gives a third of her money to me, so she can log on to the Internet to get news of her daughter Amarjit, who is working as a waitress in Telegu. Every day, she and Amarjit swap a few words. It keeps each of them alive in each other's hearts. Oh yes, they could write letters and send photographs, but this daily conversation is a magical thing for them both. It continues like this for many weeks.'

Mag-Auntie's expression darkened. 'But then one day an evil man in the Internet business sells a bunch of email addresses from my ISP to someone else. They sell it to someone else. They sell it to someone else. Each address is worth a tiny sum of money, so small you can hardly measure. Then one day Mukta-Leika comes to log on. She finds that instead of her daily message from her daughter, her email inbox is filled with rubbish. Pictures of sexual acts, abhorrent to us all. Advertisements from people selling items she will never need and could never afford, not if she saved everything she earned for the rest of her life. She tries to stop the flow, but it only increases. Abuse and trickery and lies. So she asks me for help. Of course, I help her. I teach her how to delete the spam emails and find her daughter's letter. But the next day the problem is worse – and it gets worse each succeeding day. Soon, there is so much junk email in her box that her daughter's email cannot even arrive. She spends her full time downloading, but her time is up, and her daughter's letter still isn't there. I give her an extra ten minutes free, but still the junk is coming. There are two hundred pieces of spam, some with HTML, some with pictures, even with video. Even if I gave her a whole hour and bankrupt myself, she cannot cope with searching through the lists of porn and rubbish to find the letter. She gives up. The messages cannot be received. Mukta-Leika is broken-hearted.'

Mag-Auntie turned a hard face to Wong. 'This is true story. It happens every day in my café. There are many, many Mukta-Leikas, with many Amarjits and Rajeshes and Nitishes and other children to contact. It happens in every village in India – and India has a lot of villages. Connections are made between mothers and children, grandparents and offspring, men and women – people with just a few paise to spare. But the spammers arrive and the system can no longer work for them.'

Wong nodded his head. 'Maybe I understand.'

'If this happened to people you know, do you think it would be moral to get rid of the man who caused all the trouble?'

'Maybe yes. Maybe I would murder him myself.'

'In which case I have beaten you to it.'

He bowed his head in acknowledgement. 'Good idea,' he said.

They were at the Hyderabad Airport departure lounge. Mukta-Gupta had come to see them off. Wong explained that they had failed to locate which of the names on the list of one hundred and fifty was the murderer, and had sadly decided to abandon the chase and leave. 'Very sorry.'

But Gupta, bright-eyed, had refused to accept the apology. He replied that he was no longer looking for a murderer.

'You have found one?' Sinha asked.

'I found too many, so I decided that they cancelled each other out.'

'Oh,' said Wong. 'Nice plan. Is it legal?'

'Well, it would have been ridiculous to charge one hundred and fifty people. So I went to a judge and told him the situation. He said that the man was clearly so unpopular that his death was probably a great service to the community.'

'This is true. Judge is wise. Law in India very flexible.'

Gupta grunted his assent. 'In this case, yes. So we dropped all charges. Official reason is lack of evidence. Everybody has been cleared.'

'So the case is over?'

'Yes, only . . .'

'What?'

'People are still coming to confess. Everybody wants to take credit for the murder. I have put a sign up in the police station at Pallakiri: NO MURDER CONFESSIONS. But I am a bit worried about it, to be honest.'

'A bit irregular.'

'Correct.'

'But never mind. The law always has grey areas. Grey areas are very important. Isn't that right, Wong?'

The feng shui master was distracted, having smelt a whiff of curry from the airport café. He replied: 'Grey colour not bad. But you have excess of water influence, Inspector Gupta, so you should use red colour in your office.'

The policeman looked at his potbelly. 'I have excess of something, but I don't think it's water influence. I think it is Navelli's Sponge Cake.'

Twenty metres away, Joyce and Subhash were talking intently to each other.

'Here's my email,' she said, handing him a small card.

'Thanks. I'll write to you very soon. I mean, like, as soon as I get home. Like in half an hour.'

'That'll be nice. I'll reply straight away. I mean, I guess I won't because I'll still be on the plane. But as soon as I get to a computer.'

He looked as if he was thinking about kissing her, but nothing happened. Wong beckoned her, and she awkwardly shook Subhash's hand.

Joyce, a lump in her throat, caught up with Sinha as they strode towards the doors leading to immigration. The question that was ricocheting around her head burst out of her lips. 'DK. Why didn't he kiss me?'

'This is India. People don't do that sort of thing here.'

'So it doesn't mean he doesn't love me?'

Sinha turned to her. 'My dear little girl. In India, if he doesn't kiss you, it means he *does* love you.'

Joyce sniffed and felt a heaviness and a lightness in her soul at the same time. She had the impression that something powerful and wiry, like one of the creepers on Mag-Auntie's house, was growing deep inside her. She turned to wave at Subhash one last time, and then turned away.

Bad marks at school

In ancient times, a thoughtful nun was sad about the transience of all life. She said to her teacher: 'All things decay. Today dawned beautifully, but tonight it will die. Life is only a breath. Man is born to die. What value has existence?'

The teacher said to the nun: 'Go ask the butterfly. Go ask a candle. Go ask a drop of water.'

The nun went to a sacred barna tree, a tree with white flowers which attracted white butterflies. She watched and saw how the butterflies lived only one day each.

The nun went to the temple. She looked at candles burning in front of the Buddha. She saw how the candles went out after only one hour each.

The nun went to a river. She saw how the river was made of a million drops of water. She saw how they passed her town in less than the time it took to sip a cup of tea and never come back.

The nun went back to her school. She said: 'Life is transient like a butterfly visiting a sacred barna tree.'

But the gardener was present. He said: 'No. Butterflies make plants live. Already the barna tree is older than you are. It has been growing for a hundred years.'

She said: 'Life is transient like a candle in a temple.'

But the priest was there. He said: 'No. The fire in the temple has been burning for many centuries. It is one thousand years old.'

She said: 'Life is transient like a drop of water passing a town in a river.'

But the old boatman was there. He said: 'No. The river has been there for ten thousand years. It will be there for ten thousand more.'

And so it is with us, Blade of Grass. Some of us see the butterfly, the candle and the drop of water. Some of us see the tree, the fire and the river.

From *Some Gleanings of Oriental Wisdom*
by CF Wong, part 23

Joyce McQuinnie felt an uncomfortable sourness in her stomach as she stepped through the school gates and walked towards the main entrance. She felt sick. As she walked past the staff car park, she tried to breathe slowly and calm herself. She realised that she was intensely aware of her heart beating: every individual thump seemed to shake her ribcage. Why did schools make her feel so uncomfortable?

She tried to focus on one of the few attractions this assignment held: she was being allowed to do it partly on her own. Since the problem with the fish man's apartment – a problem, which she repeatedly reminded him, was not *in any way* her fault – CF Wong had dropped the idea of letting her handle clients entirely by herself.

In this case, he had made a compromise decision. The head teacher of the international school was a minor non-executive director of Mr Pun's board and was thus entitled to have his premises examined. She was to go for the initial reading, draw floor maps and prepare the basic documents. He would come down a couple of hours later, check all this, make any needed changes, present the findings to the client, and see if he could bully him into pre-booking some follow-up visits, to be paid for separately.

But a *school* – did she really have to spend her day in a place she associated so strongly with misery? She found herself searching for reasons to justify her acceptance of the assignment. It was good to get out of the office, since her attempts to engage the geomancer and Winnie Lim in conversation were always difficult and deflating. And she was always desperately seeking opportunities to prove herself an asset to the company. A job like this, which gave her a degree of personal responsibility, was useful in that regard.

But as she arrived at the scene, her spirits fell again. What a shame that the assignment was in a secondary school so reminiscent of the ones in which she had spent her early teenage years. The unimaginative blocks with their cookie-cutter classrooms, corridors, staircases and playgrounds had only negative associations for her.

As she approached the main entrance, Joyce felt reluctant to join the scrum of children thronging through the doors, so she loitered near the car park. She folded her arms and surveyed the scene. Every school was different, yet somehow they were all the same: the same smell, the same rectangular low-rise blocks, the same tinted concrete yards, the same patchy green and grey playing field.

It was 9.06 a.m. and school had officially started for the day, although there were still straggling knots of children in the corners of the car park, gossiping or waiting for late friends or siblings.

After three or four more minutes, Joyce decided she could delay no longer. Head down, she marched past the row of cheap cars owned by teachers and tried again to force herself to look on the positive side. It was possible that she might meet some interesting people on this assignment. A hunky male gym teacher or two to add to her inadequate, stop-start social life would not go down too badly.

She pushed open the Plexiglas doors. An involuntary shiver ran down her spine as she stepped into the dark belly of the monster.

It was pleasing to discover that the foyer was a cool and quiet space, lined with displays of children's artwork. A notice board stood on one side, covered with pieces of A4 paper, gently flapping in the breeze. A sculpture of Beethoven made out of recycled materials took pride of place on a small pedestal, next to a bronze bust of some unidentifiable local dignitary. There were no hunky gym teachers to be seen. Looking to her right, she found a window at a counter with a secretary on the phone. She waited politely for the woman to finish her conversation.

'Yes?' the receptionist eventually asked.

'Hello! I'm from CF Wong & Associates, the feng shui people? I've come to do some work in, er . . .' She quickly pulled the letter out of her bag. 'Mr LA Waldo's quarters?'

The receptionist blinked. 'You're the feng shui master?' She didn't hide the incredulity in her voice.

'Yes,' said Joyce, wounded and proud at the same time. She straightened her spine and tried to look haughty. 'I *am*. I am going to do the initial readings, and then my colleague, a senior feng shui master, will come along a little later to confirm my findings.'

The receptionist spoke to a spiky-haired boy typing at a computer behind her. 'Eric, go and show this young lady to the head's apartment. You can finish that later.'

The boy slouched out of the office through a side door, perfunctorily introduced himself as Eric Chan, and set off down a corridor at a brisk pace, with Joyce scampering along behind. Her bag, which contained a *lo pan* and a large number of feng shui reference books (she wanted to get everything

179

right and didn't trust her memory), was heavy, but he didn't offer to carry it. Don't they teach them politeness any more? Then it occurred to her that the young man probably thought she was a student like he was, not realising that she was a proper working woman from The Real World, with a real desk and a real office in town.

She suddenly felt it was very important to let him know this. 'You go to this school then?' she asked, trotting to catch up.

'Yeah. We take turns helping in the office. I'm doing nine to ten today. Bit of a pain really.'

'Why?'

'I'd rather be in the lab. Doing computer games. Anything rather than be a slave to Ms Koslowski.'

'Is that the receptionist?'

'Yeah.'

He lapsed into silence without asking her anything about herself. She soldiered on: 'I used to go to a school like this. When I was young. Well, a bit like this. When I was a student, ages and *ages* ago. But not these days. These days, I'm a feng shui expert. I've come to do the reading on your head teacher's room. Does he have bad fortune or anything? If so, it's my job to fix it.'

He half-turned his head to look at her.

'You're a feng shui expert?'

'Yeah.'

'Oh.'

Joyce took this as an insult. 'What do you mean, "Oh"?'

'Nothin'.'

'I'm probably the youngest feng shui expert in town. And our consultancy gets the most exciting cases, too. That's because we specialise in crime scenes. We've done murders,' she said, deliberately using the word without dramatic emphasis, as if it was a term she had to use constantly. *Murders, ho hum.*

This time he stopped walking, freezing so abruptly that she bumped into him.

'Murders? Well, if you're an expert in scenes of crime, you shouldn't be doing the headmaster's quarters. You should be doing room 208A.'

He looked hard at her. She assumed he was sizing her up, trying to decide whether she was telling the truth. Then his head tilted to one side, as if he was thinking about something. He snorted but said nothing.

'What?' she asked.

'Nothing.'

He started walking again, turning suddenly to sprint up a staircase.

Joyce followed with difficulty, her bag getting heavier by the minute. Why did schools always have so many staircases and so few lifts?

When she reached the top, she saw that Eric Chan had slowed down, and was again throwing curious glances her way. 'So does this feng shui stuff really work?'

'Course it does. Otherwise the police wouldn't use it, would they?'

'Police use it?'

'Yeah. I know loads of officers. I work with them. I know their first names, like. Some of them. Inspector Gilbert Tan for example, who I know as Gilbert, and, oh, loads of others . . .'

'Oh.'

'So what happened in room 208A?'

'Nothin'.'

'*Don't* tell me then. I don't care. Schools are such boring places. Nothing interesting ever happens in school. I am *sooo*

181

glad I'm out there in the real world with a real job. Real life is way more interesting. This is like living in a bubble. I pity people like you, stuck here . . .'

Inflamed by the challenge implicit in her words, he sneered at her: 'Huh. There's a lot of real life in here. You'd be surprised.'

'Like . . . ?'

He stopped in his tracks and turned to face her squarely. 'Like this, for starters. One of our students got so pissed off with her teacher that she picked her up and threw her out of the window.'

'Really?'

'Yeah. That *interesting* enough for you?'

'Geez. Violent school, is it?'

The boy considered the question. 'Not really. Just some-times things blow up. You know how it is. That's where it happened.'

He pointed down a corridor to one of a string of doors.

Joyce slowly nodded. So that must be room 208A.

He turned and started walking again. Minutes later, t hey turned a right angle and he pointed to another staircase. 'The headmaster's flat is up there. Students aren't allowed up those stairs. There's a bell. Just press it when you get to the door.'

He turned to go, but she put her hand on his arm to stop him.

'Hang on a minute.'

'What?'

'Why have I been called to feng shui the headmaster's place if someone's been murdered or something in that classroom?'

'The teacher wasn't murdered. Just broke her neck.'

Joyce wasn't sure how to reply to this. 'That's bad enough. But was the headmaster involved?'

'No. I don't know why you're doing his place. Ask him I guess. Gotta go.' He raced off.

Lawrence Angwyn Waldo was a tall, charismatic man. He was old, but handsome in a craggy, wrinkly, Clint Eastwood style. He shook Joyce's hand firmly and invited her in as soon as she had announced who she was. If he was surprised or disappointed that she wasn't the usual elderly male Chinese brand of feng shui practitioner, he didn't show it.

'Come in, come in. What can I do to help you?' His voice was low but crisp, and his accent was refined in a southern-United States kind of way. Something about the precision with which he spoke made her stumble clumsily in her speech.

'Er, nothing thanks! I just need like a little space you know – a table?' Without Wong, she felt out of her depth.

'Will this do?' He pointed to a large, hardwood dining table on one side of a spacious, elegantly decorated apartment. 'Can I get you a drink?'

'No thanks, a bit early for me, ha ha!' She was immediately annoyed with herself. Why had she said that? Made it sound as if she thought he was trying to get her drunk. And that stupid laugh. Why on earth did she do it all the time?

'Cup of tea? Coffee? Juice? Water? Milk?'

'No, thanks, ha ha,' she said, and then regretted it. A drink provided you with something to do with your hands during the first awkward few minutes of meeting someone. Also, had she agreed to a drink, he would have gone off to the kitchen and allowed her to get settled and comfortable with herself.

Having missed that opportunity, she did the usual polite thing of looking around the apartment and making admiring noises. 'Wow. Nice flat!' One of the advantages of being in the feng shui business was that you could be nosey about someone's apartment without coming across as rude. 'Pretty cool!' In fact, the apartment was decorated in a way that she would have described to people her own age as Standard Boring Adult.

'What information can I get you?' Lawrence Waldo asked.

'Er, nothing really! Well, I need to know when you were born and stuff. If you don't mind, that is, ha ha.'

'When was I born? Having just met you, I would say: several decades too late. Ah, but such is life. We move on and others move in and there is never any time for regrets.'

She smiled and laughed, although she hadn't understood what he'd said. He wrote down his birthday and place of birth on a piece of paper and handed it to her. 'There you go. As you can see, I am very, very old indeed.'

'Yeah!' said Joyce. 'Wow, you really are! Thanks. Ha ha.' She took the piece of paper. Her smile remained frozen to her face, although she realised that she had said the wrong thing. She knew she should have said: 'You're not old,' or, 'Goodness me, you weren't really born in 1953?' or, 'Gosh, you're so well-preserved, what's your secret?' She wondered if it was too late to come out with such a comment, and then decided that it was. Why was small talk with some people so difficult? 'It's a great flat!' she said, trying to compensate. 'Now I gotta get my stuff out!' She buried her hands in her handbag, looking for her *lo pan*.

One-and-a-half hours later, Joyce had finished her preliminary readings of the head teacher's flat. It was a medium-sized apartment and there were no unusual influences in it except for a small west-facing extension (good for enhancing income) and a southern balcony with unpleasantly knife-shaped railings (bad for incoming *ch'i* linked to fame and passion).

184

Her mobile phone rang. CF Wong called to say that he had arrived at school and was on his way up to the flat.

Lawrence Waldo, who had disappeared into his office in the main school building for most of the intervening period, returned to the flat. 'Tea break?' he asked. 'Nearly done?'

'Yes, just about! My boss Mr Wong should be here in a min – '

The doorbell rang.

'That'll be him, ha ha.'

'Right on cue. You must be psychic,' the head teacher said, and took two steps with his long legs from the middle of the living room to the front door. He opened it to let the feng shui master into the apartment.

'I am Mr – '

'Mr Wong. Ms McQuinnie's boss. Yes. She told me.'

The geomancer entered the room looking a bit worried. 'Everything is okay? Ms McQuinnie do good job, I hope? Not hurt your fish or anything?'

Waldo, looking slightly baffled at this query, tried to put him at his ease. 'Ms McQuinnie has been very efficient. She has produced vast numbers of sheets of paper covered with notes, which she will no doubt interpret for me when she is ready. Unless that is your role, of course.'

'Ah. Good.'

Joyce was determined to keep control of the assignment for as long as possible. 'This is all very straightforward,' she said. 'It's a neat place.'

'Nothing bad, then?' Waldo asked.

'Well . . .' Joyce looked deeply concerned and slowly sucked her breath in.

The head teacher became concerned. '*Is* there something bad?'

She picked up her charts and pretended to examine them closely. 'I can't see any major *shars* in here, I'm glad to say. But I feel some negative energy coming from outside. From the school block over there. From the direction of . . . It's hard to say.'

She stepped out onto his balcony and Waldo followed.

Wong stayed in the room, wondering what Joyce was up to.

The young woman closed her eyes and advanced one hand in classic mystic style. She reached out in the general direction of the block to their left. 'I feel a lot of negative energy coming from that direction. From the area of the second floor. Maybe kinda over there . . . room . . . two-zero-something or thereabouts sort of thing, you know.'

Wong decided that his assistant had gone mad. 'Er, Joyce maybe I take over and – '

The head teacher interrupted. 'That's interesting. We have had some very specific problems with room 208A just a few days ago. What sort of feeling do you get from there?'

'I'm not sure, but it's very negative. A bad feeling. As if there was some violence there recently?'

The head teacher sat down. 'I'm very impressed. We managed to keep it very quiet, kept it out of the press and so on. Did someone here tell you about it? Be honest.'

'It's amazing what feng shui can tell you,' said Joyce, not wanting to tell a direct lie.

The full story gradually emerged.

Lawrence Waldo began by telling them at great length about what a wonderfully well-managed and happy school he ran. Then he revealed that 'in a rare – *very rare* – instance of school violence', a student attacked a teacher last week. 'It was awful. She was not a big girl, but she was sturdy. She

186

somehow managed to pick up the teacher – who was also not a big person – and pushed her out of the window. Poor Ms Ling.'

'Aiyeeah!' said Wong. 'Teacher killed? What floor?'

'Thankfully not,' said Waldo. 'The classroom was on the second floor. She fell only three or four metres. But she *was* hurt, quite badly. Unfortunately.'

'I felt there was some violence coming from that direction,' said Joyce, who was enjoying her role as a mystic seer. 'Like someone breaking their neck or something like that.'

'She may or may not have broken her neck,' said Waldo. 'Hopefully not. But she landed on her head and was paralysed. Had to be taken away on a stretcher. Very traumatic for all of us. They're not sure if she will ever be able to walk again. Fortunately for her, there were some old PE mats piled up against the wall in that quarter of the playground, and she partly landed on one. If it hadn't been for that, she could easily have died.'

Joyce turned to look at her employer and saw that he was tense and excited. His skinny chest was stuck out and his eyes were bright. She knew that look – it was the expression of a feng shui master who has suddenly discovered a factor that could dramatically increase his earnings for a site visit.

'So you like us to do that room too?' he asked casually. 'Fee for today's work already covered. But that room – that sort of investigation a little bit more expensive, but I can give you good price.'

The head teacher, who was sitting in an old, shiny Chester-field armchair, linked his fingers together and leaned forward, leaning his forearms over his long legs. 'Mmm. I don't know. We've occasionally had feng shui people look at the living ar-eas and the general design of the school, but never in relation to a specific incident like that. Do you think it would do any good? We're not expecting any copycat crimes or anything.'

Wong nodded. 'Of course. If there has been a big problem like attempted murder or something, maybe is something seriously wrong in that room. *Must* be dealt with.'

The head teacher wrung his hands, indecision apparent in his brow. 'Maybe I *should* get you to look in there. What harm could it do?'

'Give you special discount. Thirty per cent.'

'Okay.' Having come to a decision, the head teacher sat up straight, smiled and gave a damn-the-cost wave with his arm. 'Fine. Do it. Send us an invoice. The classroom has not been in use since the, er, incident, so you can do it whenever you want.'

'We start now. Why not? Is it okay?'

'Done.'

Lawrence Waldo rose to his feet, and his two guests followed him up as if there were strings tying their heads to his. 'Thanks.' He held out a huge hand.

Room 208 was a far bigger classroom than anything Joyce remembered from her past. In place of the rows of ink-stained school desks and cheap plastic chairs, there were seats made out of metal tubes, with individual, gently sloped writing surfaces built into them. In place of a blackboard was a white screen. A video projector hung from a pole in the ceiling in the middle of the room, a complex, robotic-looking device that appeared to her to be a prop out of *Star Wars*.

At the back of the room was a plastic concertina wall that opened up to reveal an extra working area, which they discovered was designated 208A. They learned that the classrooms were designed so that there was a 'shared area' between each pair of rooms. Most teachers referred to it as the art space, since it was used for activities that didn't need standard chairs. The shared space contained a row of easels, a potter's wheel, a computer and scanner, and a chest of drawers full of art equipment.

Wong saw that the room faced west and had several obviously negative factors – a painting of a burial mask hung on one wall, a full-length plastic skeleton stood at the back of the room, and a papier-mâché sculpture of a sword hung from the ceiling.

Joyce sat and helped him for a while, but she found herself strangely affected by the sounds of the school. When bells rang, or running feet clumped down a corridor, or there were shouts from the playground, she found herself becoming emotional and unable to concentrate. Again, she could feel her heart thudding in her chest, and wondered if it was doing what she had read were called 'palpitations'.

The worst moment was when a group of children started singing in the room below them. She recognised the song as something she had sung herself, in junior school. What was it called? 'Morning Has Broken'.

After the two of them spent an hour working in 208A, a bell rang and the sound of steps in the corridor became thunderous and continuous. It was lunch break. Young people started hooting and jeering and laughing and shrieking. She heard a girl's voice cackle. She heard strident male voices shouting.

Hormones raging, Joyce felt herself simultaneously re-pulsed by and drawn to the playground beneath them. She eventually decided to slip out of the classroom and wander around the school.

She trotted down the stairs, took a deep breath, and stepped into the throng. She felt as if she stuck out a mile, but nobody

189

noticed her. Again she found herself casting her eyes around to see if the right sort of guys were looking at her. She found no likely candidates. All way too young. *Babies.* She decided that there must be a separate area for older students to take their break. After all, in theory, there must be some students who were the same age as she was, or even older. In Singapore, schools often had young people aged nineteen or twenty, who still wore school uniform.

A little more aimless wandering led her to another playground adjacent to the sports field. There she found several groups of older teenagers, some of whom looked to be her age. Off to one side was a low building with plate-glass windows, through which she could see lanky youths lying around, some doing bits of homework, others reading pop magazines. She strolled over and pushed the door open.

No one looked up as she entered. She suddenly felt desperately alone – the scene powerfully reminded her of her own school days. Her father's constant travelling meant that she had always seemed to be the new girl, the one who didn't belong to any of the cliques, the person wandering around with no one to talk to.

Finding herself embarrassingly tearful, she marched quickly to the edge of the upper playground, where she could stay sheltered by a wall and observe the teenagers move from cluster to cluster.

She noticed one shadow-eyed, dark-haired girl of about fifteen leaning against a wall by herself. She was holding a book and pretending to read, but her eyes were looking into the middle distance over the top of the book at nothing in particular. Joyce immediately recognised a younger version of herself. She wondered whether to go over and talk to her, but what would she say? *Don't worry, it's all right to be a total loser when you're that age. Some of us are just bad at making friends. I was just like that and look at me now. I've got an office and a desk and stuff and I actually get paid . . .*

There was an explosion of laughter from a group on her left near a water fountain. She turned and spotted a familiar face. Eric Chan was leaning against a wire fence, entertaining a mixed group of friends with some stories. She waited till he finished talking.

'Yo, Eric?' she called out, a little too quietly. She repeated it more loudly. 'Eric?'

He looked over and smiled. The young man made brief excuses to the people to whom he was talking, and languidly strolled over to where she stood. 'Hi, feng shui master – or is it mistress? How's old Waldo's flat?'

'Fine,' she said. She felt absurdly grateful to him for being there. And she was also thankful that he had given her information she had used to impress the head teacher – but of course she couldn't say that. 'We're doing room 208A too, now. That's serious business. Criminal charges and all that. Maybe attempted murder.'

'Yeah,' Eric said, taking a piece of chewing gum out of his mouth. 'Everyone in the playground's gossiping about what happened. But they managed to keep it out of the papers. Old Waldo sent a letter home to the parents saying that a "small localised incident of violence by a student against a teacher had occurred" or something like that.' He mocked the head teacher by speaking in an absurdly deep voice, over-enunciating all the consonants.

'Neat. You're good at taking off Mr – Old Waldo.'

'Waldo was *really* pompous at assembly: "The matter is in police hands and it will do no good to the school community for anyone to gossip about it or inform the media."'

'How is she?'

'No one's seen her for days. She's been charged by the police.'

'No. I meant the teacher. I heard she's been paralysed.'

'Yeah. It's pretty serious. Probably will never walk again, they say.'

'What actually happened?'

'You really wanna know?'

'Yeah.'

'Hang on a minute. I'll get an actual witness for you.'

Eric called over to a small group of young people. 'Bug. Bug. *Bug!* Come here. I want you to meet someone.'

A girl with acne on her large forehead and a shiny nose propping up large, round red-rimmed glasses joined them. She eyed Joyce suspiciously.

'Edna was in the class,' Eric explained. 'She saw everything. This is . . . ?'

'Joyce.'

'Joyce is like investigating what happened. In Ms Ling's room, you know?'

'Police?' Edna's voice was low and suspicious.

'Nah,' said Joyce. 'I'm a feng shui expert. We're just checking out the bad vibes, make sure the classroom is okay for when you guys are allowed back into it. That's all.'

'Oh.' Edna still looked uncomfortable.

Eric said, 'Can you tell her what happened?'

'What does she want to know?'

Edna directed all her comments at Eric. Joyce desperately wanted the girl to be on her side. 'I heard the headmaster – Old Waldo's version. It would be really neat to have your version.'

Edna looked down at her feet. 'Okay. Well, it was simple. We're in room 208. At the back of the room is the art area. It's

192

another big space, and we open the sliding doors if we want to make the classroom bigger. But Ms Ling also uses it as a detention area. If anyone is behaving really badly, she makes them go and sit in the art space and shuts the sliding wall thing on them.'

'Like a prison?'

'Yeah, I suppose.'

'So what happened on Monday?'

'Ms Ling said that Sasha was being cheeky. Sasha was being a bit cheeky, but not that bad really. Anyway, Ms Ling is in a bad mood, all nervous and fidgety. Eventually she marches across the room, grabs Sasha by the shoulder and marches her into the art room.'

'Putting her in detention?'

'Don't know really. Just taking her back there to give her a good talking to, I think.'

'Did she shut the door?'

'Yeah. She takes Sasha into the art space and pulls the sliding door shut. Only it doesn't really shut. We're all just sitting there, a bit quiet, you know, stunned by what a bad temper Ms Ling was in.' Edna paused.

'And then . . . ?' Joyce prompted.

'And then Sasha really lost it. She grabbed Ms Ling and threw her out the window.'

'The window of the art space?'

'Yeah.'

'How did you see this, if the sliding doors were shut?'

'They weren't really shut. Not fully. We could see them struggling. Ms Ling suddenly goes: "No, no, put me down!" The two of them fight and they end up near the window. Then she throws her out the window.'

'You saw it?'

'Not from where I was. But I heard it. I heard a scream and a thud.'

'That was the sound of Ms Ling's body hitting the playground?'

'Yeah.'

'Did anyone actually see it?'

Edna picked her nose thoughtfully. 'Yeah. Simone Waldo. She was sitting right by the crack where the sliding wall was open. She saw everything.'

Joyce turned to Eric. 'Is Simone Waldo – ?'

'Yeah. The head's daughter. *Simone*,' he bellowed.

A tall, thin girl with bleached-blonde hair and a bad complexion turned to look at him from the other side of the playground. 'What?'

He beckoned with a short, sharp movement of his head.

She slowly walked over to join them, looking curiously at Joyce.

'She's a kind of investigator,' Eric explained. 'Your dad booked her. She wants to know what you saw. In Ms Ling's room, that day.'

Simone smiled and inflated her flat chest. Clearly she was enjoying her moment of fame. 'Yeah, I saw everything. Absolutely everything. It was like *sooo* traumatic. I gotta go to a psychiatrist. The school's paying. I might be traumatised for life, they say.' She was thrilled at the prospect.

'Tell me in your own words,' said Joyce, recalling a phrase that she had heard television detectives use.

'Well,' said Simone. 'Old Ling takes Sasha Briggs to the art space. They start fighting. Sasha goes crazy. She's a bit mental. That's what they say. She picks up the teacher and pushes her over to the window. Then she heaves her up to the windowsill. Old Ling screams. But Sasha refuses to let go. Sasha pushes her out of the window. She's got this crazy look in her eyes. She's actually mad. That's what they say.'

'Then what?'

'Then Sasha comes out, all distraught. Then she runs through the classroom and runs out, crying.'

'Did she say anything?'

'Sasha?'

'Yes.'

Simone thought about this for a moment. 'I don't think so. I don't remember.'

'Did she say anything while they were fighting?'

'Yeah, she was calling Ms Ling names, "You're bloody crazy" and things like that.'

Edna agreed. 'I heard that too.'

Joyce said, 'Then what happened?'

Simone continued: 'We were all shocked. Somebody went and called another teacher. We all had to wait there. And then the police arrived and interviewed us all individually. It was horrible. We thought Ms Ling was dead. She wasn't moving. Just lying on the playground with her head at a funny angle.'

Joyce thanked Simone and Edna for their help. Time to sit down and make some notes.

She started to walk away and was pleased to see Eric accompanying her. Actually, he wasn't that bad-looking, if you didn't look at the acne on his forehead. It would clear up one day . . .

'Who's that?' she asked, pointing discreetly at the girl standing by the wall.

'Who?'

'That girl by herself.'

'Oh, Becky. That's Rebecca Smiley.'

'Her name doesn't suit her.'

'Yeah.' He shrugged his shoulders. 'Never has done. She's always been a bit of a loner. She used to hang out with Sasha Briggs a bit. Now Sasha's been expelled, she's got no friends.'

They walked along in silence for a while. Joyce decided to keep Rebecca Smiley as the topic of conversation. It was a safe subject, and would show how compassionate she was. 'I feel kinda sorry for her. I was really shy when I was at school.'

'Yeah. I'm shy myself.'

'Rubbish!'

'No, really. I used to be, anyway. When I was like fifteen.'

'That was only like a couple of years ago, probably, am I right?'

'Two and a half, *please*.'

She laughed at his nitpicking, and then abruptly stopped laughing. Mustn't be too friendly. This boy was maybe a year younger than she was. *A whole year.* He was a child. A boy. A baby. She was a working woman with an office – well, a desk, anyway.

'What are you going to do now?' Eric said.

'Find a quiet spot and like write down what those girls said while it's still fresh. And you?'

'Thought I might get something from the canteen.' He paused, apparently working up the courage to ask her something. 'Have you . . . ? I mean, have you, like, had lunch or anything? Would you like to . . . ?'

She was impressed that a seventeen-year-old schoolboy would invite her – a real eighteen-year-old executive working woman with a real job – to lunch. 'I might. Anything good at the canteen?'

'No. It's all crap.'

They both laughed again.

Oops, thought Wong. We did the wrong room. The head teacher's home was straightforward and unremarkable in feng shui terms, but the man's office was a whole different story. How on earth could he work in a room like this? This was the place that was really in need of urgent examination and adjustment.

The geomancer had gone to visit Lawrence Angwyn Waldo to give a preliminary report on their findings about room 208A. Joyce McQuinnie had disappeared without trace.

The head teacher's office was filled with mementoes of visits to other countries. There were spears and shields from Irian Jaya, an antique musket of some sort, probably from the United States, and some sort of curious bamboo thing with ropes and a sharpened end. Wong couldn't work out whether it was a musical instrument or a weapon. He decided, after staring at it for some minutes, that it might be a headhunter's tool from northern Borneo. The entire room was full of spiked or pointed objects, most of which were associated with violence.

The room was terribly cluttered, suggesting that the user was not a clear thinker, and the piles of papers on the filing cabinet indicated that it was not a productive working environment. Some drastic changes were needed. If he were doing this room, first, he would . . .

His thoughts were interrupted as the door swung open and Lawrence Waldo stepped in. He swung nimbly into his large, leather chair. 'Sorry to keep you waiting. Departmental staff meeting. Bane of my life. Never mind. Where's the young lady?'

'Er, not sure. Maybe she is having long lunch break.'

Waldo pressed a button on his intercom. 'Amanda, Mr Wong's assistant has gone AWOL. Can you ask the usual suspects if they've seen her? And then get her sent to my room?'

The secretary's voice came out of the speaker: 'I think she's in the student canteen. I saw her going in with one of the sixth-formers.'

'No problem,' said Waldo. 'I'll get her myself.' He leapt out of his chair and trotted out of the room, moving remarkably quickly for someone so large.

To pass the time, Wong mentally rearranged the room. First, he would throw out all the junk – every last bit of paper and decoration. Then he would move the furniture so that the head teacher was sitting in the northeast of the room, facing east. The *ch'i* energy of the northeast would motivate the man to get his life in order, and the freshness of the eastern energy would inspire him to make a new beginning. The telephone should be moved to the southeast, to enhance communication. The objects of violence would be reordered so they could keep out negative influences.

Less than four minutes later, the head teacher returned, gently pushing Joyce along with a hand in the small of her back.

'The wanderer has been found,' the head teacher said.

Joyce had a big-eyed, surprised look on her face, but was silent.

Again, Waldo threw himself into his seat, and then asked curiously, 'So tell me. What do we have to do? Do we need to install a magic goldfish or something in 208A?'

'Magic goldfish?'

'No, I'm joking. I shouldn't be flip about all this. It's a serious matter. Tell me, do I need to do something to minimise the effects of that ghastly event last week?'

'There are some strange things about this incident,' said

Wong. 'First, the four pillars of destiny for Ms Ling and Ms Briggs are both negative for that day.'

'That's not strange, surely? Both of them suffered very negative outcomes from what happened that day.'

'Yes,' said the geomancer. 'But not so straightforward as that. There's a *shar* by the window of room 208A.'

Joyce, suddenly coming to life, decided to insert a footnote at this point. 'A *shar* is an area of bad fortune. Like I pointed out when I was in your flat?'

Waldo nodded. 'It seems rather obvious that the window did prove to be a point of bad fortune for Ms Ling on that day.'

'But the *shar* is a *shar* of two. And that is the negative number for Ms Briggs, not Ms Ling. The *shar* for Ms Ling is at the other side of the room.'

'I don't understand,' said the head teacher. 'What are you getting at?'

Wong shook his head. 'I don't know. Conclusion is very strange. But I think each of the two women – it is like each one has the birthday of the other one.'

'What? I'm not following this.'

'I think maybe the two birthdays got mixed up in the files,' the feng shui master said.

Waldo smiled. 'That is the conclusion you came to? Very odd. Well, I'll ask Amanda to check. That's my secretary. Sometimes the files do get mixed up, although we keep teachers' records and pupils' records separately, so I don't see how that could have happened.'

'I explain it in detail,' the geomancer said.

Waldo looked less than excited at the thought, although he said nothing.

'Following the flying stars school of feng shui, I made these charts.' Wong pulled out two sheets of paper covered with lines, arrows and tiny Chinese characters. 'Number one, indicating blood, located in west. We also find number six in same square, indicating head. Blood and head. In west of room 208A, where window is. We also have a two, which means someone is not well. Two is *shar* of sickness.'

The head teacher peered down his long nose at the unintelligible scribbles. 'If that's really what that chart says, it seems to have got the fate of Ms Ling down pretty accurately.'

'Yes. But this is not chart for Ms Ling. This is chart for Ms Briggs.'

'Oh.'

Wong warmed to his theme. 'Numbers on birth charts give us a lot of information. Number seven, metal, indicates a young girl. Also associates with eyes. But number nine, fire, links to eyes. Now if we look at this chart – '

Lawrence Waldo looked at his watch. 'That's fascinating, Mr Wong. I hope you get to the heart of it. I'm running late this morning, and I do have a lunch appointment with the chairman of the school trustees board, so I am going to have to run. Anything else I can help you with?'

'No,' said Wong. 'I will do some more work in 208A in the afternoon.'

'Fine. I hope you'll . . .' The head teacher began to say something in a more serious tone, but then his voice trailed off.

'Yes?'

The man stood up and placed his knuckles on the desk. He spoke with gravitas. 'I hope you'll help me get things back to the way they were. I am very fond of both Sasha Briggs and Alma Ling, and value them both as members of this school community. Ideally, I would like to turn the clock back to where it had been at the beginning of last week. But

200

if that cannot be done, I need above all to make sure that this school continues its unblemished record as a school of peerless standards. Do you understand? The school comes first. The greater good of the majority . . . That's what's at stake, here.'

Both visitors nodded.

Waldo shook hands with them and rushed off to his meeting.

Wong turned to Joyce. 'You okay? You very quiet just now.'

'Yeah,' she replied. 'I was just thinking . . .'

He rose to his feet and picked up his case.

'You know, CF . . . When Mr Waldo came to get me just now?'

'Yes?'

'He came to the canteen where I was sitting talking to a guy, and then he escorted me up the stairs and over to here. The odd thing is . . .'

'What?'

'Well, just as we turned the corner to come in here, he patted my bottom.'

'Oh.' Wong wasn't sure how to react to this. He knew that sexual harassment was considered a serious offence these days, but there was no way he would allow a complaint by Joyce to get in the way of a deal with a paying customer. He spoke tentatively. 'You want to complain or something?'

'No,' said Joyce. 'It wasn't a big deal. But it just made me think. I mean, he comes across as such a good man, but that's not what you expect a headmaster to do, is it? Pat a girl's bottom?'

Wong was relieved that she wasn't taking it seriously. 'You're right. Now I go back to 208A.'

'I'm going back to the playground.'

'You're Rebecca Smiley, aren't you? Can I call you Becky?'

'Go away.'

'I only want to – '

'I said, go away.'

Joyce suppressed a sigh. What could she say to make Rebecca understand that she was not the enemy? She had gone back to the playground to find that the former friend of Sasha Briggs had disappeared from her wallflower spot in the upper school playground.

But it hadn't taken Joyce long to find her. Having been a loner herself, it was easy for her to scan the school playgrounds and see the natural places to which someone with a lack of social skills would gravitate. There was a small seated area to the left of the main playground, where some quiet kids were reading books. There were also some benches in front of the school tuck shop. And there was a small alley with a park bench behind the bike sheds. It was in the last of these that she found Becky Smiley, sitting alone with her book.

'You don't have to talk to me. But do you mind if I talk to you? There are things about this thing with Sasha Briggs that have me kinda worried.'

'I'm not listening.'

'I'm not a policewoman. Really, I'm not. Do I look like a policewoman?'

'I don't care.'

Looking away, Joyce mused out loud, 'Hey, you know what this whole awful situation reminds me of?'

Becky didn't move.

Joyce continued: 'Track three of That Guy's Belly's third CD.'

The girl tensed.

Joyce knew she was listening intently. 'The bit in the chorus where they sing, "It's back-to-front and upside-down, the voices in my head they pound-pound-pound . . ."'

She noticed the younger girl turning her head slightly, so continued to sing: '"But I can't explain, I'm in such pain, the world's not fair, whoa, whoa, whoa, yeah." That is *such* a cool song.'

Becky nodded in spite of herself. 'Yeah.'

'The lyrics are like, like, pure poetry.'

'Yeah. They really are.'

Joyce paused and patiently counted to ten in her head. Then: 'I don't suppose poor Sasha ever heard That Guy's Belly.'

'Heard them? You kidding? She had every album they ever made. You should see her bed – ' Becky suddenly stopped. She turned her head away again, evidently upset that she had been tricked into talking.

Silence returned. Joyce decided that she had no choice but to try a long shot. 'You don't have to talk to me. But I've got this theory that everyone has got it all wrong about this Sasha and Ms Ling business. Still, my theory – it's not much use. I'm probably the only person who thinks that. Who's going to listen to me?' Joyce stopped and waited. Again, she counted silently to ten.

Slowly, Becky turned to face her. 'Really?' she said in a tiny voice.

Am I about to tell a lie? Joyce asked herself. Then she looked at the girl's face and decided that what she was about to say was not untrue. There *was* something odd about this case. It was just a feeling she had. She found herself staring at the younger girl's features. As soon as the dark cloud of hostility had disappeared, Becky Smiley's face had an open, honest expression.

'Really,' said Joyce. 'Like totally. I mean it. I really think that there's like a real possibility that people have got it all wrong.'

'Are you really an investigator? You look . . . you don't look like an investigator.'

'I'm a sort of consultant, that's all. Just someone trying to help.'

'Oh.'

Quietness returned. Joyce decided to let it be. Someone started playing tennis at a court nearby. There was a steady *thwack* sound as the volleys lengthened. She could hear some children arguing in the distance. 'Give it back,' somebody yelled.

Becky was hiding something. Could it be an important bit of information about the case? Although Joyce had never been good at holding her tongue, she forced herself to remain silent.

After a minute passed, the young girl spoke again. 'They *have* got it wrong. I'm sure they've all got it all wrong.'

'Yeah. That's what I'm beginning to think, too. But what really happened?'

'I don't know. I wasn't there.'

'Why do you think they've got it all wrong?'

'Because . . . Just because.'

'That's not a very helpful answer.'

'What does Sasha say about it?'

'She's not speaking to anyone.'

'Why not?'

'Because . . .' The schoolgirl sighed. 'I can't tell you. I just *can't.*' She rose to her feet and ran into the girls' changing room.

Joyce, Wong decided, had gone crazy.

On the pretext of checking the confusing birth charts of the main protagonists in the classroom 208A battle, she had searched through the head teacher's files and copied out the home address of Sasha Briggs. The schoolgirl had been grounded in the custody of the aunt with whom she lived. According to Eric, she was on bail until the police decided to lay charges against her. The birth dates in the school files were the same as they had originally been given, so the mystery of their contradictory interpretation remained.

Joyce had suggested they go to visit Sasha Briggs.

Wong had flatly refused to have anything to do with such a dangerous idea. But she pointed out that none of his feng shui readings of what happened in room 208A made sense – and only Sasha Briggs or the injured teacher, Alma Ling, could resolve that problem.

The geomancer amazed himself by agreeing with her. This was after he realised that until he had resolved the bizarre mismatch in the two women's birth charts, he could not complete the report and give Mr Waldo an invoice.

They arrived at the ground-floor garden apartment in Bedok New Town at about 8 p.m. Darkness had fallen. They rang the doorbell repeatedly, but there was no reply.

Wong wanted to leave, but Joyce refused to let him. 'She's in there, I know she is. She just doesn't want to talk to us. But we have to make contact with her. It's really important.'

She led the geomancer around the grass to the back window

of the flat. 'Come on, I'm sure there was a light in this window when we arrived. Don't you remember?'

She tapped at the window, but there was still no response. Then Joyce marched to the French windows and tugged at them. 'It's open,' she whispered.

'You cannot go in,' Wong whispered back. 'Breaking and entering. Very illegal.'

'We're not breaking and entering. We're just trying to make contact with this girl.'

They both heard a click. It sounded like a gun being cocked. They turned to look at each other. Despite the semi-gloom, their eyes passed the same message: *Did you make that sound? I didn't.*

There was a second click – and this time it was clearly recognisable as the sound of a light being switched on. After a second, a fluorescent tube flickered into life. The two of them were bathed in pale blue light and turned to find a young woman in a nightdress facing them from inside the living room. She had a large shotgun pointing at them.

'Put your hands up,' said Sasha Briggs. 'This baby's loaded and I ain't scared to use it.'

'Aiyeeah.'

'Who are you? Why are you trying to break into my home?'

'Don't shoot please. Only we try to help.'

'Chill. We're friends,' added Joyce.

'Yeah? Friends who break into people's houses? I don't think so.' Her finger tightened on the trigger.

Wong closed his eyes in sheer terror. He started murmuring a lengthy prayer in Putonghua.

Sasha lifted the gun slightly higher and took aim at the feng shui master's chest. 'Start running.'

'Becky sent us!' Joyce said.

Sasha paused. She lowered the gun a centimetre. 'Becky?'

'Sort of,' Joyce continued. 'Well, she didn't actually send us, but we're here because of something she said. She told me that everyone's got it all wrong. What happened in the art space. In room 208. She said it wasn't like people said. She said you weren't like that. She said people have got it all wrong about you.'

'Becky told?'

Joyce was about to say yes, but she stopped herself. There was something about the way Sasha used the word *told*. There was some secret between her and Becky – something that it would have been wrong to divulge. 'No. Becky didn't tell us any secrets. She's your friend. You can trust her. The only thing she told us is that it wasn't like people say it was. We believed her. We still believe her. Let's chill.'

Wong decided to leave this conversation to his assistant. In his view, teenagers and women were creatures almost impossible for adult men to talk to. Ducks don't speak chicken, as the Cantonese said. There was little hope that he could follow a conversation between two teenage women.

He carefully backed away and sat himself down in a garden bench to still his heart. He did not like having loaded guns pointed at him. Being shot at was very bad feng shui.

A cicada started its astonishingly loud buzzing, sawing song in the trees somewhere behind them.

'The police don't believe it.' Sasha Briggs, a girl of seventeen with dark brown hair, spoke with bitterness. She had slightly protruding eyes, a large jaw and strong shoulders that looked out of place under the Victorian-style nightgown she was wearing.

'We're not the police. We're consultants. Just helping.'

Wong agreed furiously. 'We are not police. If you want to shoot police, no problem. Go shoot. Not us. I think we go now.' He rose to his feet.

'Shut up and sit down,' Sasha said, lifting the gun again and pointing it at his head.

He sat down, his palms facing her in a posture of abject surrender.

'Can you tell us what really happened?' Joyce asked.

Sasha sat down on the back step suddenly, moving the gun to a level position across her knees. 'You won't believe it. No one would believe it.'

'Try us.' Joyce dropped down and sat on the edge of a plant pot.

The young woman sighed. 'What's the use?'

'Please.'

'Okay. Here goes. Old Ling drags me into the art space and shuts the sliding wall. Then she shouts: "Stop, stop." But I'm not doing anything. "What?" I say. I'm baffled. Really, I'm not doing anything at all. She grabs my arms and digs her nails into my skin. "Ow," I say, but she shouts louder, even though I'm *still* not doing anything to her. It's like she's gone mad.'

Wong was listening intently.

'Then she starts walking backwards towards the window. "Stop it, stop!" she shouts. I'm not doing anything, but she's telling me to stop. It makes no sense. Or at least, it made no sense to me at the time. "What are you doing? You're bloody crazy," I shout at her. I guess I might have said something like that a few times. Then she climbs onto the windowsill, looks down and then just steps off. It's only a few metres down, and there just happened to be a pile of mats down there, so I wasn't that worried. I thought she'd finally flipped.'

'Then what happens?' This was Joyce.

'I don't know what's going on. I decide that Ling has gone crackers. The scratches on my arm are hurting like anything. My eyes are full of tears, I can't see any more. So I swing the door open and march out of the classroom. Nobody stops me. As I'm leaving, one of the kids – I think it was Oliver Choong – is looking out of the window and I hear him saying something behind me. He's like: "I think she's killed her." I run out of school and keep on running till I get here. But the whole time while I'm running, I keep hearing Oliver's words. Then I realise what old Ling has done. She's made everyone believe I tried to murder her.'

The girl burst into sobs. 'It's so bloody unfair.' The gun fell out of her hands and clattered to the floor.

'*Siu sum!* Careful,' barked Wong, wincing.

'It's just a replica,' Sasha said. 'My dad's a collector.'

Joyce gently laid a hand on her shoulder. 'It's okay. Why don't you just tell the police the truth?'

Sasha gave a big watery sniff and then wiped her nose with her hand. 'I told the first policewoman who interviewed me. She didn't believe a word of it, I could tell. She said I might be suffering from delusions. Like my mum. That's what she said. Like my mum.'

'Where is your mum?' Joyce asked gently.

Sasha sniffed again. 'My mum's mental. She's in a home. I don't really blame the policewoman. What I said sounded totally mad. Saying that the bitch grabbed me and dragged me to the window and threw herself out and broke her own bloody neck. I didn't want anyone else to think I was . . . like my mum. Not many people know about my mum. Old Waldo knows. Becky knows. Waldo must have told the police. So after that, I refused to talk to anyone.'

'But you told Becky what really happened.'

'No. I didn't tell Becky anything. I never even got to see Becky. I asked for her, but nobody would let me. Nobody let me see anyone.'

'Then how did Becky know that – that – what happened wasn't like Ms Ling and your classmates say it was?'

'I don't know. Because she's a good friend, I guess.'

Joyce agreed. 'I guess she really is.'

Joyce McQuinnie looked in the mirror. She decided she looked great in the nurse's uniform. It was cut in a not-very-flattering way but she still liked the way it hung on her. She was skinny enough to get away with what she called a 'dumpy-cut' dress. It was a thin white cotton knee-length dress with matching pale blue piping on the lapels, at the end of the short sleeves, and around the hem of the dress.

She put on a light-green surgical facemask and then strode confidently into private room A2. 'Er, hi, Miss. I just need to clean these things with some antiseptic wipes,' she said in a brisk voice.

Alma Ling turned momentarily with irritation in her direction but said nothing. An attractive Chinese woman in her mid-thirties, she sat propped up on her pillows watching a soap opera on television. She was picking her teeth.

Joyce picked up the vast numbers of cosmetics that were arrayed on the side table and slipped them onto the tray she was carrying. 'I'll just put these over here so I can thoroughly disinfect the table.' She took the tray and walked out of the door. She turned to the left and strolled a few metres to the main nursing station, a small office down the corridor from Ms Ling's room.

She came back to the bedside and started wiping down the surfaces again.

'That stuff stinks,' Ms Ling complained.

'The smell won't last long.' Nurse Joyce then busied herself wiping the bed rails and all available surfaces. She worked rather erratically, as if she was trying to kill time.

Ms Ling peered at her suspiciously.

Oddly, the nurse started to blush and bit her bottom lip. Then the beeper attached to her belt started purring and flashed a red light. 'Oh! Gotta go. Back in a minute,' Joyce said, scurrying away.

Alma Ling leaned back on her pillows and went back to watching the television.

Then the phone rang. Annoyed by a further interruption, she snatched up the handset. 'Yes?'

'There's a reporter and a photographer to see you, Ms Ling,' said a female voice that sounded slightly distorted, as if someone was speaking with a pen in her mouth. 'Shall I let them come up?'

'Oh. Right. Yes. Send them up. Wait. I need a few minutes to get ready. Keep them downstairs for five minutes and then send them up.' Ms Ling abruptly slammed down the phone.

The teacher looked to the bare bedside table. 'Shit,' she said. She leapt nimbly out of bed and raced to the nursing station to recover her cosmetics. There was no way she was going to be photographed without her make-up. She was surprised to find that it was dark inside the nurses' office. She switched on the light.

'Surprise!' said a hidden audience of four people: three men and the new nurse. Joyce McQuinnie, CF Wong, Lawrence Waldo and Inspector Gilbert Tan waved in unison.

The head teacher added, 'Glad to see your legs have miraculously recovered, Alma.'

'Shit,' Ms Ling repeated in a most unteacherly fashion. Her legs almost immediately lost their ability to keep her upright, and she dropped in a crumpled heap to the floor.

The glare outside the hospital was so bright that Joyce had to shut her eyes completely. She walked along blinking them open every few seconds and shading her face with her hand until she spotted, through her half-closed eyes, a white Mercedes-Benz with a blue logo. 'Taxi!'

The interior of the car was cool and shaded. A radio was playing 'Unleashed' by Toby Keith. How bizarre that people in steaming, tropical Singapore had such a taste for American country music, she thought.

Wong was happy at last. Now he knew why Sasha Briggs had a birth chart that indicated concepts like 'blood', 'head' and 'sickness' on that date. She had been attacked by a woman who had drawn blood, and had her labelled as dangerously mentally ill. In contrast, Alma Ling's chart said nothing at all about bodily harm, because she had not really been harmed. She had placed the exercise mats under her window, gently lowered herself halfway to the ground and then jumped down the rest of the way, ready to fake a state of partial paralysis.

Sasha Briggs' testimony had made it all perfectly clear.

But there were still several things about the case that puzzled him. Why had the teacher worked so hard to get her student into trouble? Why had the witnesses in the classroom lied? How on earth did Joyce work out what really happened from a set of playground conversations?

'This case very difficult. No motives. People very crazy.'

'Oh, CF, you are so slow on the uptake when it comes to like matters of the heart.'

'Oh. So? What?'

Joyce stared out of the window into the middle distance, trying to work out how to explain it to him. 'Well . . . I don't know for sure what happened, CF. But I think I can guess. It's all about . . . *lurrve*.'

'Lirv?'

'No, lurrve. That's what I reckon, anyway.'

'Who is Lirv?' He vaguely remembered her using the phrase before.

'Lurrve is a bit like love, but it is more dramatic sort of thing. *Heavy* romance.'

'Ah.' They were straying into territory unfamiliar to him.

Joyce turned to her boss. 'You wanna know what I think? I think the headmaster was sort of flirting with Ms Ling and with Sasha. Two-timing them.'

'Two time what?'

'I reckon Ms Ling knew she couldn't compete with Sasha. She's ancient. She's thirty-something. But Sasha's even younger than me. But Ling knew there was one thing Old Waldo loved more than women: his beloved school.'

'So?'

'So she tried to make it seem that Sasha was destroying the name of his school. Pushing teachers out of windows is kinda not the done thing in good schools. She reckoned Waldo would drop Sasha like a hot brick.'

'Oh.' Wong still looked confused. 'So that's why Ms Ling started fight with crazy girl and jump out of window?'

'Yes.'

'But other children see it happen.'

'Not really. They heard it happen. They heard Ms Ling saying, "Stop! Stop!" and they heard Sasha saying, "You're bloody crazy." Only one kid – Simone Waldo, the head teacher's daughter – was sitting by the crack in the sliding wall and actually saw what happened. And she lied about it to make Sasha look bad.'

'Ah.'

'Why? Think about it. She's in Sasha's class. She probably knows that Sasha has hooked up with her dad. She wants Sasha to be in as much trouble as possible. I mean, wouldn't you feel awful if a girl your age was trying to seduce your dad?'

'My father dead.'

'I know, but I was just *saying*.'

Wong was still having trouble trying to make sense of it all. 'But Sasha – after all this happen, why she not tell the truth? Too stupid.'

Joyce shook her head. 'Her mum's a loony. If Sasha goes around telling people that she was alone in a room with a teacher who promptly jumped out of a window, everyone's going to say she's also loony.'

'Her friends tell you this?'

'I think Sasha only told one friend that her mum was a loony. This girl Becky. Becky promised never to tell anyone.'

The feng shui master shook his head. All this had clearly established the truth of one thing he had known for a long time – women are unfathomable, unpredictable and deeply dangerous creatures with whom to become involved. And as Inspector Gilbert Tan unravelled this case in the courts of Singapore, head teacher Lawrence Angwyn Waldo would start to discover the truth of this for himself.

Wong comforted himself with the thought that he was one of the last masters educated in the old, politically-incorrect school of feng shui, which specified that the yang principle meant strong, positive, life and male, while the yin principle meant weak, negative, death and female. The ancients knew what they were talking about.

The adventure of the offstage actors

An ancient text from the Zen masters tells the story of a man who climbed a holy mountain to talk to the hermit who lived on top. The hermit was the number-one sword fighter in the world.

The student reached the peak and lay down at the feet of the hermit. He said: 'I must learn the art of sword fighting. How long it will take?'

The hermit said: 'It may take ten years.'

The student said: 'I have many things to do back home. If I work two or three times harder than other students, how long it will take?'

The hermit said: 'Then it will take twenty years.'

The student said: 'I do not understand. Why will it take longer if I work harder? I am eager to learn. What if I work night and day and holidays too?'

The hermit said: 'Then it will take thirty years.'

The fastest way to do anything, Blade of Grass, is the correct way. If you do something in a hurried way, it will take longer.

From *Some Gleanings of Oriental Wisdom*
by CF Wong, part 24

CF Wong read through his story one last time, tweaked a few words here and there, and closed his book with a thud. He picked up his battered briefcase and slid the tattered volume into it. Then he placed the bag with tender care – since it contained his most valuable possession – between his shins, and went to sleep. Ah! The satisfying, easy slumber of the hardworking man who has done his work, done it well, and been generously tipped for it.

The massive kid-leather marshmallow chair in the lobby of the Bangkok Oriental Plaza gently drew his body into it as the jacuzzi in his suite had done earlier. He felt himself descending fast, tumbling head over heels into a state of happy oblivion. The buzz of hotel business around him faded fast, and he only half-heard, as if at a great distance, the whir of multiple wheels as luggage trolleys trundled across marble floors and thick Persian rugs. The air-conditioning, as is usual in hotel lobbies, was set at flash-freeze. But the frequent blasts of super-heated air coming from the main entrance doors compensated for the chill.

This particular job, Wong dreamily mused, had been particularly successful. By which he meant they had done enough to justify their payment from Mr Pun, and gathered a nice, fat tip as well – and all for a minimal amount of work.

He and his assistant had been assigned to do what Joyce called 'a parachute job' – flying in to a new country to do a quick survey for a member of Mr Pun's board, and then getting out fast. The task had been to check the feng shui characteristics of the star dressing room at a swanky new auditorium in Bangkok. The man due to use it was Khoon Boontawee, a Thai movie star who had appeared in thirty-six movies, in every one of which he played a good guy with a naughty streak, or a naughty guy with a streak of goodness. Tonight was the premiere of his new movie, *Street Fighting Dragon*, in which he played the golden-hearted son of an evil gangster leader. The date, the Friday of a holiday weekend, had been selected by the star's manager to maximise income, although it was an inauspicious day on the star's own calendar. So Khoon Boontawee's mother, who was half-Chinese, had insisted that a genuine Hong Kong feng shui master be imported to alleviate any negative influences.

And the job had turned out to be easy. He and Joyce had been flown in on the Thursday night and been booked into the Plaza. After a huge buffet breakfast on Friday morning, they had been whisked to the theatre. The negative influences had turned out to be obvious to identify.

Khoon Boontawee was born under the sign of the thunder tree with green as his colour and three as his number. By moving to the new auditorium, he was unfortunately travelling in the direction of his own key number, which was like trying to squeeze magnets of the same pole together. The dressing room itself had an over-abundance of southern energy, giving rise to a risk of the user suffering from emotional swings and an excess of passion – not something that actors generally lacked.

The remedies were simple to organise. Wong had arranged for Khoon's costumes and personal effects (and the truck which carried them) to travel in a different direction for an hour and approach the hall from a more suitable direction in the early afternoon.

And he had assigned a team of staff to swiftly make changes to the huge dressing room to soften the energy. Southern *ch'i*, if correctly tempered, was associated with public recognition and fame, which would be ideal for a star. Six potted plants were arranged in the room so that tree energy could support Khoon's fire energy, and the fibreglass chairs were replaced with bamboo and wicker furniture. Drapes, throw rugs and tablecloths of red and green were added to complete the happy marriage between fire and forest influences. Khoon, he was sure, would walk straight in and feel happy and relaxed.

By six o'clock that evening, everything was complete. It had been a busy few hours, but the work had been straightforward, the theatre staff efficient, and the whole exercise satisfying. Especially now that a tip of one thousand US dollars in a red envelope was in Wong's inside breast pocket, courtesy of Thai media tycoon Pansak Jermkhunthod, who was on the board of East Trade Industries in Singapore and chairman of Star City Ventures.

They had nothing to do but lounge in the lobby and wait for their car to take them to the airport. Joyce had gone to the hotel shop to buy souvenirs, leaving her boss to doze in the voluptuously over-soft chair. He was soon snoring.

'Mr Wong. Mr Wong.'

He opened one eye. A silhouette was standing over him, its back to the evening light glowing through the hotel's glass doors.

'Unh? You are taxi driver?'

'No, it's me. Suchada Kamchoroen. Deputy manager from Star City Ventures. We met this morning?'

Wong failed to recognise the woman, but assumed she was one of the executives to whom he had been introduced at the theatre that morning. He tried to struggle to his feet but his old bones failed him. 'Ah, yes, Ms Such – er. Very nice you come to say goodbye. Your theatre very nice. Dressing room all fixed. I think you will have plenty good luck, no problem now on.'

The manager, an angular dark-brown woman in her late thirties, squatted down to his level so that he wouldn't have to stand up. 'Mr Wong, I think we have a problem. I want to ask your advice.'

219

'Yes, of course. You want me to check your office? We have taxi coming to take us to airport, so maybe not too much time. Maybe next time I come to Bangkok I check your office.'

She shook her head. 'A problem has come up at the theatre. I need to talk to you urgently.'

'But we have taxi coming, flight tonight – '

'Don't worry about your flight. Our staff can look after you, take you to the airport. We can put you on a later flight, or a flight tomorrow if need be. It's a – a serious problem. We were told that you have become quite famous in Singapore for solving, er, difficult problems. We've got a real difficulty here, and the police aren't being much help. We will pay you extra, of course. We'll pay you anything you ask.'

That last sentence filled the feng shui master with a bottomless well of sympathy for whatever new problem had arisen at the theatre. He suddenly sat up straight, his eyes wide open. 'Too bad. Sit down. Tell me the problem. We can delay flight. I can fix, I'm sure.' A vision of himself scribbling a figure with many zeroes into his invoice book appeared in his mind.

She delicately lowered her silk-clad body (two-tone red and gold Jim Thompson shot silk cut in Dolce & Gabbana business-suit style) onto the sofa next to him, but before she could speak, Joyce arrived.

'Oh, hi, Kam. Did you come to say bye? Look what I got.' She hoisted three shopping bags into the air, not without difficulty. '*Loadsa* cool stuff. You wouldn't *believe* – '

'Hi, Joyce. I'm glad you've done some good shopping. But I'm here on serious business. We have a really big problem at the theatre and I need your help.'

The young woman quickly wiped the smile off her face. 'Oh, dear. Yeah, right, fine. Anything we can do, just ask.' She draped her shopping bags around her feet and dropped heavily into the chair opposite, trying to compose her features into an expression of intense concern.

Suchada Kamchoroen spoke quietly: 'Khoon has disappeared.'

'Disappeared,' Wong echoed.

'I mean, like *completely* disappeared. We don't know where he is. We think something bad may have happened.'

'Ooh. Maybe he's just late,' Joyce said brightly. 'Some people are like that. I'm late for *everything*. And I'm not even a movie star. It's, it's . . . it's just my way,' she finished, rather lamely. 'Besides, it's only ten past six. When does the premiere begin? Like eight or something, right?'

The auditorium manager nodded. 'It begins at 7.50. But Khoon was due to arrive at the theatre at 4.30 for a half-hour press conference, along with two of the other actors. They never made it. None of them. Khoon was due to do a series of three ten-minute one-to-one interviews, from 5.15 to 5.45. He missed those, too. There's a pre-show cocktail party about to begin, at which he is supposed to be guest of honour.'

'Hmm.' Joyce screwed up her lips in thought. 'Maybe he forgot. People do that, too. A lot. I forgot a really, *really* important exam once – '

Suchada shook her head. 'They didn't *all* forget. They were in a group.'

'You telephone him?' Wong asked.

'That's the most worrying thing of all. All three actors had mobile phones, and so did the driver who was bringing them to the theatre. None of them has answered their phones in the past two hours.'

Joyce put her worried face back on. 'Geez. That seems a bit like totally suspicious.'

'It's as if all four of them have vanished off the face of the earth.'

Wong asked, 'Where were they last time seen?'

'We know they left the house where they were staying at about 3.40. They were staying at the private home of our chairman Pansak Jermkhunthod. Khoon was travelling with his two co-stars, Ing Suraswadee and Warin Krungwong. Nothing has been heard of any of them since.'

There was a sudden musical bleating noise. A mobile phone was ringing. Suchada tugged a small, white Nokia cellphone from her Prada Tessuto handbag. 'Excuse me. Yes, hello, Kamchoroen here.'

After a few seconds, she stiffened with excitement at the words she heard.

Wong and McQuinnie tried to eavesdrop but Suchada spoke in short, sharp bursts of Thai, responding with excitement to what she was hearing. The only words they understood were the last two: 'Yes, bye.'

She rang off. 'They've found the car and the driver. But all three actors have gone. The police have interviewed the driver. He says the car was attacked. He is in a bad state. The actors . . . they've been kidnapped. Oh, Mr Wong – our luck is not good at all today.'

The premiere of *Street Fighting Dragon* went ahead without a hitch. But while four hundred people sat motionless in the theatre – indeed, a number were fully comatose – the nearby offices of Star City Theatre Ventures were a hive of activity.

Senior Bangkok Police Major-General Thienthong Sukata, a liver-spotted man with a pear-shaped head, briefed Ms Suchada and her elderly boss, Plodprasad Sardsud, on the discovery of the car in which the actors had been travelling. Plodprasad had very dark skin and wrung his hands continuously as he listened, his head bowed and eyes fixed to the floor.

Wong and McQuinnie sat quietly behind them.

The vehicle was discovered on the outskirts of the city, having veered off the road and hit a tree, where an officer on patrol found it, the policeman explained. Plodprasad groaned, while Suchada sat in silent misery.

The feng shui master insisted that they speak to the man who had actually found the car.

A few minutes later, Major-General Thienthong introduced them to a brown-uniformed man of about thirty with astonishingly tiny hips, the sight of which filled Joyce with sick envy. His name was Sergeant Chatchai Suttanu and he claimed to be able to speak English, although he had a pronounced Bangkok accent.

'Car was Chevrolet Zafira. Actor's car. Car was travelling along quiet roat just off New Petchburi Roat when another car speet up and came lewel wid them, you know?' he said. 'And then someone from insite nubber two car fire – '

'Wait, please,' interrupted Wong. 'Who told you this?'

'Drywer,' Sergeant Chatchai said. He looked down at his notebook. 'A man name, ah, Khun Boonchoob Chuntanaparb.'

'Thank you.' Wong began to write the name down, but quickly realised it would be impossible. He scribbled out what he had written and replaced it with: 'Driver Mr K.' Then he remembered that *Khun* meant *Mister* and scratched the whole line out.

The officer continued: 'Anyway, bomb was fire from that assailan' car into Chevrolet Zafira of moowee s'tar. It was fire with big power and s'mats true clows wi'dow, bang!'

'Bomb?' asked Wong.

'He means a missile,' said Major-General Thienthong.

'What sort of car was it?' asked Suchada Kamchoroen. 'The car that fired the missile.'

'Drywer Khun Boonchoob do not know what sort of car. He set it was grey car, four doss. It was hard to get detail fom him. He was wery shock, you know?'

'Which window broken?' the geomancer asked.

The officer looked down at his notes again. 'Gas bomb t'ing went true fron' side wi'dow, and lantet in emp'ty patsenjer seat nex' to drywer. Stray away it startet giwing off large amoun' of gas wit lout hissing noise. Gas smell wery bad and make all patsenjers in car to s'tart coughing and have painful ice. In back, moowee s'tar Khun Khoon grap door hander and open door to ex-cape, but dit not go out of car. Car was goin muts too fas'. Somepoty – maybe Khun Khoon or may be other man actor Warin Krungwong – shout to drywer to s'low-s'low car, so they can jum' out. But now other car was behine other car – '

'The assailant's car was behind the actors' Chevrolet,' Major General Thienthong inserted.

'Yets, bat guy car was behine actor Chevrolet and was bumping it from behine. So drywer he coot not s'top car, or even s'low-s'low car.'

'Wow,' Joyce exclaimed. 'Sounds like a movie.'

'In fact, it sounds a bit like the movie that is being premiered tonight,' said theatre director Plodprasad, apologetically. 'There are two car chases in it. It's an action movie,' he added disdainfully, and then appeared to regret his comment. 'Sorry, that's off topic.'

Major-General Thienthong gave him a stern look before nodding to Sergeant Chatchai to continue.

'Assailan' car was behine actor car, smat'ing it from behine, again-again-again. This make it *wery* hard for drywer to s'top. He poost down hart on foot brake and pull up han'brake wery muts. Car s'pin roun'-roun'-roun' go off site of roat. It hit barrier and s'crape site wall of s'chool and s'mall-s'mall sop-house sellin' durian and other fruit. It go a bit more and than s'top about fitty-sisty metre along roat. Fron' site car all broken into tree.'

'I hope no one was hurt,' said Joyce.

'No one on s'treet was hurtet,' Sergeant Chatchai assured her. 'But drywer hit his het, go s'leep. Maybe from crass, maybe from gas, don't know. He wake up ten minute after. All moowee s'tar gone, snatch away.'

Plodprasad was shaking his head in amazement. 'All very amazing. Very movie-like. One of the Bond films had a good car chase in Thailand. Now, which was it? Can never remember the name. I think *Man with the Golden Gun*. The one with Mary Goodnight. I can remember her.'

'Perhaps the driver was lying. Perhaps he was in cahoots with the kidnappers,' Joyce suggested.

'No.' Sergeant Chatchai was adamant. 'Drywer was in s'tate of shock. His arm hat burn mark from when gas bomb explote. He hat big cut on his het, loss of blut. I do this job many year. I can hear people who tell lice. He was telling troot.'

Major-General Thienthong turned up his palms in a gesture of futility. 'So that is our challenge. No description of car. No description of kidnappers. But we have to find them.' He turned to Wong. 'If you can help, I would be grateful.'

225

Straight after breakfast on Saturday morning, Wong travelled with Sergeant Chatchai in a police vehicle to the house where the three actors had stayed. Their plan was to study the scene there and then retrace the route the car had taken from the house towards New Petchburi Road.

It took nearly an hour to reach the mansion on the outskirts of Bangkok. The house was a fortress. A long row of iron railings six metres high, backed by a thick hedge, kept out the rabble. Their car followed a seemingly endless outer perimeter wall for eight minutes, after which they came to a gateway bounded by two large pillars topped with stone eagles more suited to an American military academy.

Guards opened the gate electronically for them, and they drove up a winding driveway to a grand, steep-roofed house hidden in the trees.

The country home of tycoon Pansak Jermkhunthod was huge, beautiful and completely absurd. It was a villa designed on the lines of an over-sized temple, or perhaps a royal palace a Thai king might have built for himself circa 1830. It had multiple layers of roofs, the lowermost ones held up by painted, carved pillars.

Spiky and triangular, the building made Wong shiver. To him, the impression was one of rising fire energy, blasting over-rich yang energy upwards. Pyramid-shaped buildings were always unsuitable for personal dwellings, he believed. Only temples or churches had the right to point to Heaven with such casual effrontery. Yet an attitude of self-worship was all too common among the rich, and it was not surprising that the same conceit could be found in the design of their homes. No wonder many wealthy people were unhappy.

From his viewpoint in the driveway it looked as if the internal walls were lined with heads – how revolting. He squinted and realised that they were probably *khon* masks, repulsive heads of Thai gods with exaggerated lips and eyes, and teeth hanging down over their chins. How could anyone think that decapitated beings could add charm to their home? No lake was as deep and unfathomable as the human mind, he mused.

He fondled the charm around his neck, bowed his head, and stepped into the palace.

Joyce, meanwhile, had been told to relax and go shopping, but had decided against it – largely because she had no money left. There was another consideration: the possibility that she might get to hang out with movie stars. Now that was something not be missed.

Just outside the offices of Star City Ventures, she was interviewed by a young reporter from the *Bangkok Post* called Phaarata Sittiwong. The press, thronging around the doors, were hungry to speak to anyone who had the slightest connection to the case. In an attempt to prove to the reporter who interviewed her that she had not wasted her time, Joyce blurted out that she herself was part of an imported team investigating the incident.

Twenty minutes later, the two of them were on their way together to interview driver Boonchoob Chuntanaparb, who had been sent by police to recover at his home in a village on the outskirts of Samut Prakarn, just outside Bangkok.

Joyce was pleased that she could understand Phaarata's Thai-accented English, which was far clearer than the police officer's, although she pronounced *with* as *wit* and *world-wide* as *wort-white*.

In a coughing, light-blue taxi filled with images and statu-
ettes of the Buddha, Phaarata explained that Samut Prakarn
Province was at the mouth of the Chao Phraya River which
ran through Bangkok.

'Bangkok is really a very old place,' she said. 'It was built in
the 1620s, but first it was on the west side of the river at Phra
Pradaeng. Two hundred years later, King Rama the Second
commanded his men to move the whole city across the waters
in boats.'

'Hmm, hard work.'

Joyce stared out of the stained taxi window. Although only
a short hop by plane from Singapore, Thailand was totally
different. There was an out-of-focus quality about it – the
edges of the roads merged into the sidewalks and the sidewalks
blurred into shops and restaurants. But the streets were a happy
riot of colour, people were cheerful and brightly dressed, and
they moved relatively fast, despite the fierce heat.

'It's nice, this place,' she commented absently. She found
the jostling rows of mismatched buildings oddly attractive.
Many streets featured long strings of ugly, blockish shops
interspersed with absurdly ornate temples. Homes tended to
be small and cottage-like, or large, grand, and half-hidden behind high walls. The streets, whether in the urban areas or on
the long stretches of palm-fringed roads between, were lined
with utility poles bearing a huge number of trailing wires. It
appeared to her as if the whole of Thailand had been swamped
in hundreds of thousands of kilometres of spaghetti cable
dropped from the skies.

It took almost an hour to arrive at the built-up centre of
Samut Prakarn. Joyce was delighted when Phaarata suggested
they transfer into a tiny three-wheeled taxi for the rest of the
ride. The vehicle into which she climbed was a cross between

a motorbike and a rickshaw, and had a blue and white striped awning over a small plastic sofa. 'These bike things are *soo* like cute.'

'Tuk-tuks.' The reporter ordered the driver to go to a temple called Wat Chai Mongkon. 'This you must see. It's very beautiful. Very old. Built in 1350.'

'Wow. That's like – well, really, *really* old. I used to live in Hong Kong where nothing's old. In Hong Kong, if a building is thirty, no one wants it and no one can get a mortgage to buy it and they have to pull it down.'

The buzzing, insect-like vehicle scuttled awkwardly around several corners, its engine straining and stuttering, its gears making an ear-piercing racket. But it weaved in and out of the traffic efficiently and they quickly found themselves in front of a bright, white temple with a multi-layered golden roof.

'It's just gorgeous,' said Joyce. The temple was a clean, well-kept structure with six separate layers of overlapping, sloping roofs, each of which had its own upward-sweeping architectural flourishes. 'Why has it got so many roofs? Do things leak here a lot?'

'That's the way they made them. It makes a place more grand to have roof on top of roof, people believe in Thailand. Protects us from bad influences, lift us nearer to heaven.'

The reporter scribbled an address on the front of her notebook and tore off the page for Joyce. 'If you get time before you have to fly back, go to see the Wat Asokaram in Tambon Taiban. It's not far. It's worth seeing. It has bones of Buddha inside. It was built in 1955 by Phra Suttithamarangsrikhampeeramaethajarn.'

'Who?'

'Phra Suttithamarangsrikhampeeramaethajarn.'

'That's easy enough for you to say.'

'What?'

'It's all right. I was just making a joke.'

They hailed another tuk-tuk and scooted along Phrakhon-chai Road before tipping right into Sukhumwit Road and left into Phraeksa Road. Ten minutes later they were in a more rural area and the reporter led the tuk-tuk to a small house by the roadside on a street with no name and no kerb. Instead of ringing a doorbell, Phaarata stood outside a small terraced home and shouted through the window in the local language. To Joyce's ear, the language sounded as if it was entirely made of *cheh* and *keh* and *meh* sounds and had to be spoken at breakneck speed.

Unable to understand a word of the conversation between Phaarata and Boonchoob Chuntanaparb's mother, she cast her eyes around and looked at the curious world in which she found herself. The building was one of a row of miniature homes in a dusty, baked landscape where tiny slices of lush jungle were cramped by large factories and industrial buildings.

This is how some people live, she thought, suddenly amazed. I could live like this if I wanted to. There are many different ways people can live. This is one of them. This is their choice. It could be my choice. There are many choices. How big the world is. The thought made her simultaneously excited and terrified.

She turned back to face the discussion as the voices became louder and more animated. She still couldn't follow what was being said. But the tone of the conversation made one point abundantly clear: Boonchoob was not there. Eventually the reporter thanked the woman of the house, bowed politely in her direction, and turned to her companion.

'He's gone out?' guessed Joyce.

'No. He never arrived home. He seems to have fled.'

'Aha!' said Joyce. 'Weird – and suspicious, right?'

'Weird? Why do you think that?'

'Well, think about it. If he's run off, it means he's probably guilty of something. We just gotta work out what.'

Phaarata shook her head. 'No. He is not guilty of something. Not like how you say. Sometimes when there is a car crash, the drivers flee. It happens.'

'Why?'

'Drivers, they think they are going to be in trouble. Especially big trouble if their passenger is someone important. Or if they destroy someone's expensive car.'

'Oh. So you think he ran away because he thought he would get into trouble?'

'I'm sure. His passengers were stars and the car was wrecked. It is no surprise he ran away.'

'Where will he go?'

'In Thailand, very easy to hide. This is a big country. Many small-small villages. Some in the forests, jungles. He will hide for a few weeks, few months, until all this fuss is over. Then he will quietly come back. It's the Thai way.'

Joyce nodded. 'Oh. I see. Well then, I guess this lead turned out to be a dead end. I just hope my boss is having a more successful time.'

Wong had not had a successful time.

He had left the grotesque, head-filled mansion and been driven back to Bangkok in a police vehicle. There he had met up again with Suchada Kamchoroen, who had taken him out of the theatre for some lunch at Anna's Café in Soi Saladaeng, close to Silom Road's busy office and shopping area.

Phaarata delivered Joyce to the group at the café on her way back to the newspaper office.

Hot and sweaty, the feng shui master's assistant was rapturous about the drink she was handed. 'I used to hate these,' she said noisily slurping a cendol. 'I think it was the idea of beans in a soft drink. And also the yucky feeling of lumps of jelly mixed in. But now I like them. I think I must have become truly half-Asian or something.'

On the way back into town, Phaarata had given Joyce a quick Thai lesson and she was anxious to share what she had learned. The words filled her with giggles. 'There are thirteen words for *me* or *I*. The word for *me* if you are a guy is *pom*. Can you believe it? And if you are speaking to your younger sister, the word for *I* is *pee*. If you are talking to a mate, you say *goo*, and if you are a woman talking to an older person you say *noo*, which means *mouse*. Who made up this language, anyway? Whoever he was, you can tell it was a *guy*. It is like *soo* sexist.'

Wong wasn't listening. He was frustrated. There had been no obvious clues at all at Pansak's luxury home. A lengthy examination of the rooms the three stars had occupied revealed little of relevance. A detailed questioning of the servants had only raised three small points of interest, and two of them concerned the car, not the house.

First, both Khoon Boontawee and Warin Krungwong may well have had a very pleasant stay at the house – their rooms were well-designed and suited their profiles adequately. The actress, Ing Suraswadee, might have been slightly less comfortable – she had an L-shaped room with an indentation in the south, crushing the *ch'i* and making it difficult for her to achieve recognition for her achievements while she was there.

Second, it appeared that the car had stopped somewhere, briefly, between leaving home and being attacked. The evidence for this was that two servants indicated that when the car left, Khoon Boontawee and the actress Ing Suraswadee were sitting in the back seat, and Warin Krungwong was sitting next to the driver. Yet when the attack happened, the driver's statement revealed that Warin had joined the others in the back of the car. Where did they stop and rearrange themselves, and, more to the point, why?

Third, during the drive from the house to the spot where the car had been found, Wong had timed the journey. It took seven-and-a-half minutes. Officials said the traffic might have been slightly heavier the previous day, so it may have taken about nine minutes. Yet the official record of events suggested that close to twenty minutes passed before the crash. What happened in the intervening ten minutes?

Realising that her boss was not in a communicative mood, Joyce put her personal stereo headphones into her ears. Wong, detecting the *shh-chka-shh-chka* sound he so hated, shuffled further away.

The young woman decided to scan the two English newspapers. They had similar front page headlines: KHOON KIDNAPPED and TOP MOVIE CAST SNATCHED. The *Bangkok Post*, the *Nation* and the Thai language papers all had front-page photographs of the three actors too and speculation about what might have happened, with illustrations of black-masked villains snatching drugged stars from a car.

She then picked up Suchada's voluminous files, which contained detailed profiles, photographs and other information about the missing actors. 'Phwoar,' she said, looking at a bare-chested picture of Warin Krungwong. 'Tasty or wot.'

Suchada nibbled her fingernails, tense and confused. 'How on earth did they do it without being seen? That's what baffles me. The kidnappers would have had to lie in wait, catch up with the car, shoot the gas canister thing into it, ram the car off the road, stop their own car, grab the actors, and then race off. They managed all of that without being seen, on a busy road in the biggest, most traffic-congested place in the world.'

'Outside Bangkok not so congested as inside,' Wong said.

'Yes, but the difference is not much these days,' Suchada replied.

'Phwoar!' said Joyce even more loudly, discovering a picture of Warin in a loincloth. The others looked at her. 'Sorry.'

She flicked through the rest of the photographs at speed, rapidly falling in love. While Khoon Boontawee may have been the big name among the three, Warin Krungwong was much more enticing. 'He's kind of a hunk,' she said to the theatre manageress, slipping her headphones off. 'And look at his expression. His eyes always look teary. And his hair flops over his forehead. That's the sign of a truly brilliant actor.'

The Thai woman laughed.

'You find the others,' Joyce told Wong. 'I'll rescue Warin. Is that a deal?'

The feng shui master continued to ignore his assistant.

'How was your trip to see the car driver, what was his name, Boonchoob?' Suchada asked.

'Oh. No good,' said Joyce. 'He scarpered. Apparently drivers in Thailand do that a lot. When they've crashed.'

'Sometimes,' Suchada said, shrugging.

Wong, desperate for a lead, looked over at his assistant. 'You find anything interesting at house of driver? You go where?'

'We went to a place called Samut something. Actually, it's a funny word, Samut. My mum's from England, and in the north of England "summat" means "something".'

'What?'

'In England, summat means "something".'

234

'But what?'

'Something. It means *something*.'

'But wha – never mind.'

Joyce continued: 'And they call the temples "wats". That's funny too, if you think about it. You know, *what* and *wat*.'

'What?'

'Yeah.'

At this point, Wong tuned out of the conversation, which was beginning to hurt his head. 'There is video shop on next street, to east side. Why not you go see if you can find Khoon Boontawee movies? Do some background study.'

'Good idea. Or maybe movies with Warin, even better.'

She picked up her bag and sauntered out of the café. The *shh-chka-shh-chka* noise faded.

The feng shui master breathed a sigh of relief and got back to staring at his *lo shu* charts for the three actors and the driver.

Major questions remained unanswered. He looked at the route map between Pansak's house and the link roads to the New Petchburi Road. Somewhere on this route, the car stopped, the passengers swapped seats, and assailants appeared. But at which point? And most important of all, where did they take their victims? The questions gave him a headache.

And he felt terrible for another reason – an issue that no one had yet raised. It would only be a matter of time before it occurred to one of his paymasters, he thought grimly. Why had he, one of Singapore's allegedly top-rated feng shui masters, been so wildly wrong in determining Khoon Boontawee's fortune? The birth chart, which Wong had checked and double-checked, said that the film star's Friday would turn out fine – but it had been a disaster.

He was checking flying star natal charts for all three actors for a third time when Joyce returned from the shops carrying three disks in thin plastic film. 'VCDs are really cheap here, aren't they? I hope the quality's okay.'

'Hmm: No guarantees,' Suchada told her.

Wong looked up, irritated that the teenager was back so soon. 'You buy disk of *Street Fighting Dragon*?'

'Naah, that's not available yet. Give 'em a chance. It was only premiered last night. I got some movies with Warin Krungwong in them.' She held up some disks of action movies. 'Actually it was really hard to find them. Had to go to loadsa shops. Warin doesn't actually star in any movies. He's always the co-star. But there's a picture of him on the back of this one. I wonder if he would sign it for me?'

'If we get him back,' said Suchada.

'Oh, yeah.'

Joyce sat down and asked the theatre manager to translate the text on the back of the VCD packs.

'This one sounds the best,' said Suchada. 'Khoon stars in it, but Warin gets a mention in the review. "Warin's emotional performance as a power-crazy cop is electrifying. He well-deserved his best support actor nomination."' She flipped another disk over. 'This one's good – I've seen it. Warin plays the pilot of an aircraft with a hijacker on it. The plane crashes and he – '

'Aiyeeah,' Wong complained. 'Can you go read video box someplace else?'

'Okay, okay,' said Joyce. 'Keep yer hair on.' She stood up, ready to move away.

But the feng shui master's eyebrows suddenly rose. 'Aiyeeah!' he said again. '*Gung-hai-la!*'

Joyce was pleased for a chance to show off that she actually understood a Chinese phrase. 'What do you mean, "Of course"?' she asked. 'Of course what?'

236

The feng shui master urgently needed to go back to the theatre as quickly as he could. Traffic was gridlocked, so Suchada led them to a jetty where they could get a river ferry.

On the geomancer's instructions, Joyce had phoned Sergeant Chatchai, summoning him for an important meeting. The slim officer appeared ten minutes later on his motorcycle at the jetty.

'*Sa-wat dee*,' he said with a little bow.

'Good thing you were close,' said Joyce. 'Traffic's awful.'

'I not close,' Chatchai replied. 'But on this wery fas'.' He gestured at the bike. 'But mus' be quick-quick. Wery busy today.'

With a spray of water, the ferry arrived beside them.

'Come,' said Wong. 'We talk on boat.'

They clambered unsteadily onto the rocking vessel. After the feng shui master had found his feet and wobbled to a seat, the four of them sat in a row at the back.

Wong pulled out Joyce's video cover showing Warin Krungwong. From his other pocket, he produced a thick marker pen. 'Here is one movie star. Now watch please.'

He started scribbling on the photo with the marker.

'Hey, that's mine,' Joyce objected. 'You're spoiling it.'

Wong continued to draw until he had added a peaked cap to Warin's head. Then he drew glasses on him and blackened his cheeks. He added a moustache. After surveying his handiwork for a moment, he added epaulettes to the shirt and drew a collar and tie. He turned to the police officer. 'Is this the driver you interview?'

Sergeant Chatchai studied the photograph for a long time before replying. 'May be drywer,' he said, slowly. 'Yes, may be drywer.'

The feng shui man looked the officer in the eye. 'Please think carefully. You said you thought driver was telling truth. But maybe actor was playing role of driver. Maybe quite good actor was playing role of driver.'

Wong pulled out a fuzzy mugshot of a thin-faced individual with buck teeth. It looked like an employee's ID photo blown up with a computer. 'Or was this the man you interview?'

'No,' said Sergeant Chatchai. 'No see this guy before.'

Suchada put her fingernails to her teeth in nervous excitement. 'So you think maybe the driver he interviewed was *Warin*? Warin with a load of make-up? How did you know?'

'I did not know,' said Wong. 'But I suspect something is not right. Sergeant Chatchai here said driver does not know what kind of car bashes him. This very strange. For drivers, cars are whole life. Usually they know *every* type of car. That makes me think driver's story not true. Also, driver said Warin was in back seat. But servants say he was in front. Then I know that the man police talk to is liar.'

Silence descended as the four of them dealt with the implications of this revelation. If the main premise on which the entire case was based was false, all assumptions changed. The boat chugged briskly down the Chao Phraya River, its engine throbbing a powerful rhythm.

'That's why the police couldn't find any witnesses to the kidnap,' Suchada said. 'Because it didn't happen.'

'There was no assailan',' Chatchai said.

'There was no kidnappers' car,' Suchada added. 'That's why police couldn't even find skidmarks on the road.' She yanked her phone out of her bag. 'I need to tell Mr Plodprasad this right away.'

A little over ten minutes later, the four of them were on the stage of the second auditorium at Star City Ventures. There were more than a dozen people walking around with costumes and parts of theatrical sets. A woman wearing a huge papier-mâché mask, supported by a man on either side, was carefully walking along a white line chalked in the middle of the stage. Preparations were in hand for a production of *West Side Story* in *khon* masked-dance style.

Suchada had given a rundown of Wong's thinking to her superior.

'So you think the driver police interviewed was Warin? But what happened to the real driver? Who did what to whom?' Plodprasad asked. 'I'm confused.' The old man wearily sat down in a front-row seat.

Wong, whose legs were also hurting from his over-active day, sat down next to him. He explained: 'Warin sat in front passenger seat and switch on some gas thing. Silent, quiet, dangerous. I think maybe he roll it under his seat and point it backward so gas go on back-seat passengers first.'

'Khoon Boontawee and Ing Suswadee.'

'Yes. Mr Khoon and Ms Ing get dizzy, go sleep quickly. Warin very clever. He close off chauffeur dividing panel, privacy panel, to keep gas in back-seat area.'

Suchada agreed. 'That makes sense. So Khoon and Suswadee are out cold before they know what's going on.'

Wong nodded. 'As soon as victims asleep, Warin get rid of gas canister. He get driver to take him to hideout near Samut Prakarn.'

'So the driver is in cahoots with Warin? Is that what you're saying?' Plodprasad's fuzzy white eyebrows rose against his dark brow.

'Don't know exactly,' the feng shui master replied. 'Maybe actor is paying driver lots of money. Anyway, they hide unconscious bodies. Driver he disappears, runs away. Warin he dress up, pretend he is driver, he goes and gently crashes car into tree and then give statement to first officer who comes along.'

'Who just happens to be Police Sergeant Chatchai Suttanu,' said Plodprasad.

Sergeant Chatchai proudly pointed to himself. '*Pom.*'

'Then he goes back to kidnap house and waits.'

Suchada asked: 'Waits for what?'

'For us,' says Wong. 'Waits for investigators and media to start working. All going to plan perfectly. Suddenly, small, not very good, action movie is front-page news on every newspaper. Story of mystery disappearance is on TV, even probably on international news in oversea countries. Everybody talking about three stars. Everybody know their names.'

'Is that what he wanted? Just publicity? It's a great stunt, but you can hire PR companies to get publicity for you.'

'No, he wants more than that,' says Wong. 'Look at VCDs of Joyce. Warin always number two, number three. Always support actor. Khoon Boontawee always number one, always star. But in this real-life movie drama, Warin want to be number one.'

'So how is he going to do that?'

'Because he is playing special role. Role which will make him very famous. He is going to be hero who escapes from kidnappers and rescues colleagues. Rescues Khoon and Ing. Who are in support roles only. Warin going to be number one star in this story.'

240

Plodprasad looked from Wong to Suchada and back again. 'It all sounds rather fanciful to me. But who knows? Whatever you say, I guess there is nothing to do but sit and wait.'

Sergeant Chatchai left to recover his motorbike and get back on patrol, but his seat in the front row of the theatre was almost immediately taken up by another officer. Major-General Thienthong's third (and favourite) daughter had a minor role in the dance-drama being rehearsed and he was delighted to spend the day at Star City using the kidnapping incident as an excuse.

The lights dimmed. The overcrowded stage was suddenly empty. A run-through of a *khon* scene started to unfold on stage.

The noble God-King, Phra Ram, danced across the stage. His face was an intricate mask of finely-painted red-lined features on a white background, topped with a glittering gold crown.

Suchada whispered to Joyce: 'The masks are made with up to twenty layers of paper. We use a special paper made from tree bark called *khoi*. It takes years to learn how to do it.'

'They're gorgeous.'

'All the teeth on Hanuman – that's the monkey-general over there – are made from real ivory, and the jewels in his crown are made from glass and semi-precious stones.'

They watched scenes from the *Ramakian* for almost two hours.

Then they heard the doors at the back of the auditorium creak open. Someone had entered the theatre. Wong turned his head to see a young woman wave urgently from the back. It turned out to be Plodprasad's secretary. She skipped nimbly down the stairs, her face flushed with excitement.

'Call for you, sir, very urgent.'

'Who is it?' Plodprasad asked.

'One of the kidnapped actors, sir.'

The group sitting in the front row rose to its feet as one man. Everyone stared at the secretary.

'It's Warin Krungwong, sir,' she said. 'Shall I transfer the call down here?'

'Let me speak to him,' said Major-General Thienthong.

Wong raised his hand. 'No. Let Mr Plodprasad speak to him. But, Mr Plodprasad, tell him that media is here. Media wants to take picture of him. He will like that, I think.'

The secretary returned to her desk at a sprint to transfer the call to the telephone in the star dressing room that Wong and McQuinnie had feng shui-ed the previous day.

Minutes later, a light flashed on the green handset on the dressing table, and Plodprasad picked it up, at the same time pressing a button to activate a built-in speaker.

'Krungwong, is that you? Can you speak English – the international media are here.'

'Sardsud. Thank God! Call the police, we've been kidnapped.'

'I know. The police are here too. We've been looking for you for the past twenty-four hours. Where are you, man? Are you safe? Are the others with you?'

'We're in some sort of old barn in Samut Prakarn. I saw a sign on a factory out of the window. But we're safe.'

'What happened?'

'I don't remember very well. We were being driven along when some car comes up and fires a gas thing into our car. We all black out. Next thing I know, I wake up to find I'm all tied up in a locked room with no windows. I woke up about two hours ago. Ing and Khoon are with me, but they're still unconscious.'

'How did you get away?'

'I managed to wriggle out of the ropes that were holding me. Then I kicked down the door. Then I dragged poor old Khoon and Ing out of the building. Ing is coming round a bit, although she is still very dizzy and delirious. She can walk a bit. Khoon is still out cold. I had to carry him to safety. So much for the Street Fighter Dragon. Ha! He must have a pretty weak metabolism.'

The police officer took the handset from the theatre director. 'Mr Warin. This is Major-General Thienthong Sukata speaking. I'm going to send some men over to get you. Are you in any immediate danger?'

'Depends on when and if the kidnappers come back,' said Warin. 'And if they decide to search the area for us.'

'Stay low and hidden. We have cars in the area that can reach you within minutes. Can you give us more precise directions as to where to find you?'

'Yes, I think so,' said Warin. 'I know this area a bit. Go to the main roundabout on the way in to Samut Prakarn from Bangkok and take the third left by the old farm. I think if you go straight for a couple of kilometres, you'll see an old brick barn on the left-hand side. That's where we're hiding.'

'We're on our way.'

'Be quick.' Warin rang off.

Plodprasad held up one finger for the police officer's attention. 'Get your men to take them to hospital first, give them a good check-up. If Mr Wong's theory is right, and it is looking good so far, my guess is that Khoon and Suswadee will be full of gas fumes, and Warin Krungwong will be mysteriously clear of them.'

Major-General Thienthong Sukata marched out of the green and red dressing room, leaving a stunned and inert group behind him. The frozen tableau was broken when the theatre general manager came back to life with a chuckle.

'Ha ha *ha!*' Plodprasad shook his head, suddenly laughing. 'Woo hoo! You know what the strangest thing about this whole incident is?'

'What?' Joyce asked.

Plodprasad wiped tears out of his eyes. 'After all these years, poor Warin has finally turned in a performance worthy of winning the best actor award. But unfortunately, nobody filmed it.' He started clapping.

Suchada Kamchoroen joined in the applause.

Joyce raised her hands and clapped. 'Yaaay, Warin. What a star!' She turned to Suchada Kamchoroen. 'It's a bit of a shame, really. He really was a *major* hunk. Can I keep the photograph?'

Wong was the only one who failed to react in any way. He sat in the wicker chair, tapping his finger against the dressing table, still unsettled.

The Thai woman draped an arm warmly around his shoulder. 'Not celebrating, Mr Wong?'

'Cannot work out why my *lo shu* charts for actors all wrong,' he said.

Suchada smiled, and patted the feng shui master's bald pate. 'If that's all that's worrying you, it's a question I can answer in two seconds flat.'

'You can?' He looked up at her.

'Sure. You obviously haven't spent much time with actors. Actors are one group of people you will never be able to do successful birth charts for, Mr Wong.'

'Why?'

'Because they lie about their age. Every single one of them. Every single time you ask. I guarantee it.'

Wong blinked. Of course! Boontawee wasn't a 1971 thunder tree earth dragon. He was much older. Something quite different. Same with the other two. They were actors. They needed to stay young for ever. How could he have failed to realise this!

The feng shui master picked up his *lo shu* charts, rolled them into a bundle, dropped them in the dressing room bin, and allowed himself a smile.

The case of the late news columnist

In ancient China lived a very bad king named King Zhou. He always drank too much wine. When he drank too much he became suspicious. He became dangerous.

One time he spent the whole night drinking wine with his friends. He became very drunk. They became very drunk also.

The next morning he woke up. He did not know what time it was. He did not know what day it was. He did not know what his duties were for the day. His friends also did not know.

King Zhou said: 'Don't worry. I have one wise and capable official in my government. His name is Ji Zi. He knows everything about running my kingdom.'

The king told his servant to go and ask Ji Zi what day it was.

But after the servant went, King Zhou became suspicious. He said: 'Ji Zi very smart. Maybe too *smart.'*

The servant reached the house of Ji Zi. The servant said: 'The king drank two bottles of wine and has forgotten what day it is today. Can you tell him?'

Ji Zi replied: 'Tell King Zhou I drank three bottles of rice wine last night. I cannot remember anything. I cannot remember my own name even.'

The servant told King Zhou what Ji Zi said. The king stopped being suspicious of his official.

Blade of Grass, always be smarter than people think you are.
The best way to do this is to act more stupid than you are.

This is even truer in times of danger. If a forest has a
beauty contest, the judge will choose the tree who stands up
tall. But when the woodcutter is walking around, the tall
trees wish they could bow their heads.

From *Some Gleanings of Oriental Wisdom*
by CF Wong, part 31

A guttural banshee howl erupted from Madam Xu's room.

It was a heart-stopping wail reminiscent of nothing but a pterosaur losing a game show final. The dying cry rose sharply and petered out slowly into a cracked whimper.

Alarmed, Joyce raced out into the corridor and hammered on the door. She was wearing a fake DKNY (it said DNKY) oversized T-shirt and had a ring of toothpaste around her mouth.

'You okay in dere?' she asked indistinctly, the toothbrush rattling against her teeth.

There was no reply.

She knocked again, and then took the obstruction out of her mouth to speak with more volume. 'Madam Xu? Something wrong? I'm coming in.'

She noticed with horror that she had spat Colgate Sparkling White With Tartar Control against the door and was instantly aghast, feeling a powerful urge to return to her own room to fetch something with which to wipe the door down.

Dismissing that thought as impractical in the circumstances, she reached for the brass-plated handle, repeating: 'I'm coming in.' But it was locked, so she was left rattling it uselessly.

Joyce used her fist to bang on the pale satinwood door as heavily as she could, splattering more toothpaste on it, this time from the toothbrush in her hand. Bugger! She gritted her teeth. Did Colgate Sparkling With Tartar Control damage wood varnish? Would they be charged for this?

'Chong-Li? Chong-Li? You okay?'

Still no reply. She wondered what to do. Should she call the hotel reception, get a spare swipe-card? Or perhaps call an ambulance – the animal-like squawk she'd heard had chilled her to the bone, and suggested that some *thing* in there was attacking Madam Xu. Or should she call security? Someone with a gun might come and shoot whatever it was!

But what if the people she summoned to open the door were men and Madam Xu was not properly dressed? Or had her teeth out? Or had no make-up on? She would never be forgiven.

Wracking her brain for alternatives, Joyce recalled that the guest rooms had connecting balconies. It might be possible to clamber from one to the next.

She raced back through her room and out onto a tiny terrace. Taking great care not to look down, she gingerly lifted her right leg as far as she could and heaved it across a tiny space on the left side of her balcony so that it hovered over the floor of the terrace of the neighbouring room. She could see nothing but concrete in front of her eyes, and was surprised that it had pores in it, like skin. She tilted her toes and stretched her leg until it touched the floor on the other side, and then carefully shifted her weight so that it was on the side to which she was moving.

She jumped down, painfully scraping her thigh against rough cement as she did so. Relieved to see Madam's Xu's French windows partly open, she placed her fingers on the cold left doorjamb and yanked. It swung open.

Stepping inside the chilled, low-lit room, she found Madam Xu, fully dressed, lying flat on her back on the bed, eyes open and staring blankly at the ceiling. The room was filled with a thick cloud of floral perfume.

Had Madam Xu been Guerlained to death?

'Madam Xu! You okay?'

The figure on the bed did not move. Joyce froze in horror. Was she dead?

The young woman started feverishly biting her fingernails, unable to take another step forward. She felt an overpowering urge to back out to the balcony, to disappear and let someone else take responsibility for this problem.

No! she told herself. *Every second counts.* Gathering her courage in both hands, she forced herself to move closer to the supine body. She passed her hand over the woman's mouth and was relieved to find her still breathing. Then she waved her fingers over Madam Xu's open eyes. Gradually, the dilated pupils drifted down and focused on her.

'Phew! You're not dead?'

Out of the corner of her eye, she noticed the telephone was off the hook, its handset dangling on the floor. Maybe the Chinese fortune-teller had had a call that had given her a terrible shock.

'What is it? Have you had some bad news or something?'

Getting no response, Joyce gingerly picked up the handset to see if anyone was still on the line. 'Hello? Anyone there?'

'*Hello mees. Who arr you?*' said a male voice with a Filipino accent.

'My name's Joyce. I'm travelling with Madam Xu. I'm afraid she's not very well at the moment. Can we call you back?'

'I guess you can.'

'So, like – who are you?'

'Metro Police Chief Deputy Director Danilo de los Reyes.'

249

'Oh. Okay. Metro Police – ah. Maybe I'll get a pen. Hang on a mo – ' She glanced around for paper and something to write with and was pleased to find both on the bedside table. 'Okay, I gotta pen, can you say it again?'

'Metro Police Chief Deputy Director Danilo de los Reyes.'

She started to repeat his name back to him as she wedged the handset between her shoulder and ear. 'Metro. Police. Chief.'

'Deputy Director Danilo de los Reyes.'

'Deputy. Di – this pen doesn't work at all. Sorry.' She angrily scribbled blank circles on the page. *Bloody useless.* 'Maybe I'll just remember it. Deputy Daniel, Director de Los Angeles – er?'

'Metro Police Ch – never mind. My men are in a car heading to the hotel. They'll bring you to me. What's wrong with Madam Xu?'

'Don't know. I think she's fainted. What d'you say to her? Did you give her really bad news or something?'

'I suppose I did. I told her that Gloria Del Rosario was found dead last night.'

Joyce gasped and sat down on the edge of the bed. She felt that all the breath had been sucked out of her.

'Miss?'

'Geez. That's – that's – terrible.'

'Yes,' said the police officer. 'It is, as you say, terrible. Especially since, I understand, your companion Madam Xu and a man named Wong were among the last people to see her. We have her appointments book and they visited her apartment yesterday morning, correct?'

'Yes, they did. Me too. I'm kind of an assistant. We spent most of the day there.'

'Fine. Well, I guess I need to tell you not to leave town. We'll need statements.'

'We're supposed to be on a flight at lunchtime.'

'Cancel it. My men are on their way. They'll be at your hotel in a few minutes. We'll want to take you all down to the station for some questions. I'm afraid I can't tell you how long it will take. But I want you to stay in Manila for a few days. Very important.'

'How did she . . . ?'

'Jumped off the roof of the newspaper building early yesterday evening. Goodbye.'

Joyce, too shocked to reply, slowly lowered the phone.

Wong, like Madam Xu, reacted badly to the news, and appeared to be in physical pain. His eyes were screwed up into wrinkled ovals and his whole face had acquired a shar-pei look about it. The fortune-teller was moving in a zombie-like way, breathing slowly and heavily as if she was in a trance.

Joyce was also kind of shell-shocked too – but her reaction was not nearly as dramatic as that of her companions. She was more surprised than upset. She wondered if there was something wrong with her. It was very worrying. *I am incapable of feeling emotions. I have been permanently damaged by my upbringing. I need serious therapy. I should have got some chocolate out of the mini-bar.*

'You guys are really shook up, aren't you?' she said as the three of them sat in the back of a police car on the way to the station.

Wong bowed his head once in agreement.

'I know how you feel. It's kinda weird to spend some time with someone and then to have them like *die*. It's just so, like,

251

utterly, totally, utterly . . .' She was lost for words. Mind you, the truth was that they hadn't spent much time with Gloria Del Rosario – barely ten minutes. They had met her at the apartment at 11 a.m. the previous day. She had shown them in, given them coffee, and then gone off to work. They had spent the day at the apartment, and left two written reports for her.

'The end. It's the end.'

Joyce looked at Madam Xu, who had spoken in a watery croak of misery.

'End of what?'

The older woman turned sad eyes to her. 'End of my career.'

'Oh. Why?'

'Think about it, young lady. I did a fortune-telling session for a client yesterday. I told her all sorts of things about her future. That very evening she dies. No one will trust me ever again. This is very bad. I have been exposed as a charlatan. I am ruined.'

Wong agreed. 'Yes. Very bad. For me too, same reason. Very, very bad. *Too* bad.'

Joyce nodded. 'I see. A kind of credibility thing. People won't hire us. If this gets out.'

Wong shook his head in amazement. 'How come I did not see this? *Ho gwaai*. Too strange. This is marketing disaster. Maybe we have to change price strategy. Very bad news for me.'

Joyce began to realise that her companions were not remotely concerned about their client, but were worried only about how much damage the death would do to their earning power.

As the police car jerked through the Manila traffic, surprise gave way to a kind of anger: How dare people hold them in any way responsible for what happened! How could they have

252

foretold Ms Del Rosario's death from a visit to her flat yesterday? All they had done was analyse the influences from various directions and make some adjustments to the placing of furniture in the room. The woman had never actually *asked* whether she was going to die that night. She had hardly even been there. Had she asked, Wong or Madam Xu could – perhaps – have told her.

Madam Xu opened her eyes. 'I think I will change my name,' she said.

'Gypsy Rose?' suggested Joyce, although she had no idea where the idea came from.

The interview with the Manila police was painful but mercifully short. The three visitors from Singapore were separated and individually grilled for three-quarters of an hour about all their contacts with their client Gloria Del Rosario – from initial phone calls and faxes, to the time spent in her office, to what they could remember about the conversations they had with her.

Afterwards, Wong and McQuinnie were reunited, given cups of extremely bad coffee and made to fill in several forms. They were informed by one of the officers that Madame Xu had fainted during questioning, and had been taken back to the hotel, where a relative of hers who lived in Ermita had been summoned to tend to her.

They were then summarily dismissed.

But they had hardly set off along the shabby third-floor corridor when a young policewoman raced after them, her shoes clattering loudly on the linoleum floor. She summoned them back with beckoning fingers, like someone trying to persuade a cat to come down off a roof. 'Sorry,' she said. 'The boss wants to see you. Something's turned up.'

Her shoes still clacking, she led them to a dingy office occupied by the senior officer Joyce had spoken to on the phone.

Metro Police Chief Deputy Director Danilo de los Reyes was a man in a white shirt and dark tie who seemed much too short for his lengthy name. As they entered, he quickly switched off some music, silencing Rey Valera in the middle of a passion-filled yelp. The officer spun back in his black leather executive chair to greet them.

'Hello, Mister Wong, Miss McQuinnie, sit down. I just want to ask you a few questions.'

Over the next ten minutes, de los Reyes went over the same material as had the earlier questioners, focusing mainly on Ms Del Rosario's mood and state of mind the previous day. But certain of his inquiries indicated that he suspected foul play. He asked repeatedly whether she had talked of having enemies, or expressed fears about the future.

He seemed frustrated by the lack of information he received. As he spoke, he squirmed in his chair, which made a series of squeaks. 'She *did* have enemies, we know. All journalists who take the kind of risks she took have enemies. She didn't pull her punches in her columns.'

No reply to this comment came from the visitors. Wong, who answered monosyllabically or not at all, still looked drained and taciturn.

Joyce, who had seen a *lot* of movies, felt obliged to ask the obvious question. 'I know what you're thinking! You're like, did she jump or was she pushed?'

De los Reyes twirled his thin moustache like a Victorian villain.

254

'Could be.' He spoke carelessly, as if this was just one of a myriad theories running through his mind.

'Like bizarre, totally.'

'Look at this.' The police officer flicked a sheet of paper over to his two guests, who were sitting directly opposite his desk in a pair of low wooden chairs, like a pair of naughty schoolchildren sent to see the headmaster.

'Here we have the final letter that Gloria sent. Short and sweet, as you can see. "Goodbye Ferdinand. My final, final deadline approaches. It's been good. See you on the other side." Ferdinand refers to Ferdinand Cabigon, the editor of the newspaper.'

'Geez,' said Joyce. 'A real live suicide note. Maybe.'

De los Reyes corrected her: 'A suicide email. Sent on the office intranet minutes before she went up to the top of the building and then, er, descended.'

'So she did top herself.'

'That may be what that email suggests. That's what we were given last night, when we were called to the building after she, er, was found on the ground near the rear entrance. Suicide was our initial thought but we sealed off her office last night, in preparation for a more rigorous examination this morning. We had a team of people going through her things, and we found this other letter a little while ago.'

He held up another piece of paper – this time in a plastic bag.

It occurred to Joyce that Danilo de los Reyes was the only person she had ever met who pronounced the 'r' in the word *letter*.

She leaned forwards to look at a small, handwritten note on lined paper torn from a notebook. She read the words out loud for the benefit of Wong: "You should have just printed a correction, bitch. But you refused. I'm sorry, Glowgirl, but that means you get your comeuppance. You've written your last column."'

She fell back into her seat. 'Glowgirl?'

'Ms Del Rosario's nickname. The envelope was postmarked Thursday, so was likely to have arrived on her desk yesterday. It looks like a threat. Later that night, she was found dead. It may be that the two things are connected.'

Silence returned to the room.

The geomancer coughed, coming to life. He scratched the straggly hairs on his chin. 'A correction,' he said, interested. 'So she wrote some bad stuff about someone. In the newspaper. Someone want a correction. She say no. So someone push her off roof?'

De los Reyes nodded. 'That *may* become one of the hypotheses.' Evidently, he was a cautious man.

'But why she write suicide note then?'

'Maybe it wasn't a suicide note. Maybe she just knew that someone was going to kill her, and it was a goodbye. Or maybe it refers to something else – maybe she was planning to change career or something. Who knows?'

Joyce thought hard. Gloria was a columnist facing threats. She had been involved in some sort of dispute that involved her writings.

'I got it!' she said. 'You just go through all the stuff in her articles for the last few days and see who she really pissed off. Bang – you got him! Easy!' How well-suited she was for detective work, she thought proudly.

De los Reyes grinned. 'Ah, to have the sweet confidence of youth,' he said. 'For you, life is so *seemple*.'

Joyce was initially pleased at this comment, but then noticed that his smile was the one adults give to cute, small children. A blush began to form on her cheeks.

'In real life, it's a bit harder than that,' de los Reyes continued, his hand idly straying towards the pause button on his stereo which would enable Rey Valera to finish his yelp. Remembering himself, he withdrew his hand.

'Ms Del Rosario wrote a sort of daily snippets column, so would regularly insult three or four or five people a day. Given that the column ran six days a week, we are talking about hundreds, if not a thousand aggrieved members of the community a year. And it's quite possible that someone was taking revenge for something she said about them last year, or the year before.'

Joyce thought about this. 'Naah,' she said, shaking her head. 'I don't think so.'

The officer stiffened and lifted his eyebrows, as if to say: *You're telling me my job?*

'I know lots of grudgy sort of people,' continued Joyce, anxious to establish herself as equal to any law-enforcement professional in the room. 'My dad's one. He holds grudges against people for years. And sometimes he does get back at them ages later. But if he's going to take like *physical* action against them, he does it straight away. He once hit me so hard I flew across the room and hit the wall and broke a tooth.'

Danilo de los Reyes gave her a tentative nod. 'Not everyone is like your daddy, Miss. But having said that, you're probably right. People who commit crimes of violence very often are reacting by impulse. They are fired by anger. It is possible, of course, to plan a murder a year or two in advance, but such murders are a small minority of the total universe of murders.'

'Universe of murders?' Wong did not like the sound of that phrase.

'I was using the phrase in the mathematical sense, referring to the group of all murders, which we could then divide

257

into smaller sub-sets, such as planned murders and impulse murders.'

De los Reyes' eyes strayed back to the stereo. Clearly he felt a desperate need to resume his fix of romantic music. 'We'd like you two and Madam, er, Zoo, to stay in town, if you can. We may need to call on you again.'

'Cannot,' Wong said. 'Must go home to Singapore. No work here. Plenty work there.'

If we don't lose it all, Joyce thought to herself.

'I'm sorry,' said de los Reyes. 'You *must* stay. You can co-operate by choice or we can require you to stay.'

Six minutes later, the two of them stepped out of the police station into a hot, grey Manila day. The sky was overcast. A tooting, multi-coloured jeepney shot past, over-filled with tired families carrying shopping bags.

The pair stood on the front step of the police station, stunned and indecisive. What to do? Their assignment was over, and Wong and Xu's careers were at stake – but it was not clear whether there was anything at all they could do about it.

Out of the corner of her eye, Joyce noticed a luxurious red car parked down the road start to move. The vehicle, a Ford Fairlane Ghia Sedan, glided along the kerb and stopped almost silently in front of them.

'Give you a lift?' said a black-garbed man in sunglasses. His cheeks were pockmarked and there was a scar through his left eyebrow.

Wong glared nervously at him and took a step back.

'No, thank you,' Joyce said, instantly haughty at the driver's cheek.

'Get in, Mr Wong,' the driver said. 'And you, miss. There's money in it. My boss needs to consult you about something.

We'll make it worth your while.' He flicked off his sunglasses, which were the rimless, wraparound type from *The Matrix* movies. 'I'm a friend of Gloria's. Santos is my name.' He was in his mid-forties, and the hair just above each of his ears was grey.

'Certainly not,' Joyce said.

'How much?' Wong said.

'Hundred thousand,' said Santos.

'Dollars?'

'Get real. Pesos.'

Wong's eyes flickered as he did the maths in his head. 'Pesos *two* hundred thousand. For one day consultation.'

Santos appeared to be considering this. 'Okay, two hundred thousand. But for three days consultation.'

'Two hundred thousand for two days,' said the geomancer. 'Plus expenses. Final offer, best price.'

'Done.'

To Joyce's intense disgust, Wong climbed into the stranger's car and she – strongly against her instincts – found herself with no choice but to follow suit.

The office of the chief executive editor of the *Philippine Daily Sun* would have been dull and seedy, but was redeemed by the framed newspapers – all with dramatic, banner headlines – that lined the walls.

Wong and McQuinnie were ushered into the room by a tearful middle-aged woman named Baby Encarnacion-Salocan, who introduced herself as the editor's secretary. Despite her first name, she was at least in her late forties, if not fifties.

'Please sit down. Mr Cabigon will be here in a minute,' she said, sniffing. Turning to go, she brushed against the editor's desk and a pile of papers slumped to the floor. Joyce dropped to her feet to pick them up. 'I'll do it.'

'Thank you, dear,' she said. 'My eyes are so red I can't see.'

'No worries, Ms En – er . . .'

'You can call me Baby.'

'Oh! Right! Thanks, er, Baby.'

She went back to her desk outside the office and sat there, quietly weeping.

Joyce watched her curiously, and felt more than ever that she was a freak, somehow born without the ability to feel emotions.

The feng shui master stared at the newspapers on the walls and noticed that none of the headlines made any sense at all.

2 PARAS BRODS, SIS IN ABUSE RAP

SOLONS CODDLING DRUG LORDS, SAYS COJUANGCO

35,500 QC FAMILIES TO GET LOTS

'What does it mean?' he whispered to Joyce.

'What does what mean?'

'The newspaper title. Any one. Don't understand.'

Joyce peered at the framed newspaper nearest to her. GMA CONDOLES BANGUS SOLON. 'Don't know. Maybe they're in the Filipino language.'

Wong peered at the text. 'But the small writing is in English.'

'Yeah, but the headlines ain't.'

The door swung open. They both looked around as Ferdinand Cabigon entered the room, closely followed by Santos.

The editor was a chubby man of about fifty, with sloping shoulders and a pale brown suit the exact colour of his skin. 'Hello, Mr Wong, Ms McQuinnie, I'm so glad you could make it. We need your help and, as I'm sure Boy has explained to you, we will be willing to pay for it.'

Wong's eyebrows rose. *Boy?*

Santos, tucking a stray strand of hair over his ear, explained. 'My name is Undungan Santos Junior, but most people call me Boy.'

The editor hitched up a trouser leg slightly and nimbly placed one buttock on the edge of his desk. He gestured with his hands as he spoke. 'As you may have guessed, the death of Ms Del Rosario last night has affected us very strongly.'

'Yes, very sad, very sorry,' said Wong.

'But this is the *Philippine Daily Sun*,' Cabigon said grandly, as if the statement carried obvious associations with it.

'It is,' cheer-led Boy Santos Jr.

The editor waved his fist at no one in particular. 'We're not going to take this lying down. We are going to do a re-creation of Gloria's last days and last hours. And we are going to get our top investigative reporting staff – that's Boy, here – to do a daily series of articles on the investigation, the suspects, the way the probe is going, all that sort of thing. And we're going to find out what happened and who was behind this.'

'And us?'

'And you, Mr Wong . . . well, judging by the reaction of journalists phoning us for comment, people are intrigued by the angle that she had an apartment full of mystics in her apartment a few hours before she died. Some say that you and Madam Xu must be useless at your job, because you did not predict her death. Others say you actually caused her death. We haven't decided which angle to go for.'

Wong was outraged. 'Not true! We were in restaurant with Madam Xu's cousin last night. At time she died. Can give you name of restaurant. In Makati City.'

Cabigon shook his head. 'No, I don't mean that they think you pushed Gloria off the roof. They think that you used your black magic to make her kill herself.'

261

'I got no black magic. I am feng shui master, not magic man.'

'Whatever. To the reader, all this stuff is all the same. Magic, occult, witchery. They love it and hate it at the same time. They are deeply suspicious of it but they're endlessly fascinated by it. The main thing, from our point of view, is that they can't read enough of it. We need more.'

Santos folded his arms and sneaked a glance at his watch, apparently impatient with his long-winded boss. 'I want to get moving as fast as I can on this one, boss.'

Cabigon nodded to his colleague but continued to address the feng shui master. 'Mr Wong, you and Madam Xu have become part of the story, whether you like it or not. So we want to keep a tight hold on you. We'll pay you two hundred thousand pesos to stay on our side. That means that you supply material to our reporters, and our reporters only.'

'What material?'

'Oh, nothing really. They'll produce the material. You just have to okay it.'

Joyce butted in. 'You mean they'll make up stuff?'

'Not exactly *make up stuff*,' said Boy Santos Jr. 'We might speculate a bit, but the basic facts will be absolutely true. Unless we get stuck.' He gave her an apologetic, slightly sheepish look.

Cabigon picked up a sheet of paper from his desk. It was some sort of contract in small print. 'The main thing you have to do to earn the money is this: sign this pledge not to talk to any other media. This murder will be the most talked about thing in Manila this month, with a bit of luck. We own the victim. We own the scene of the crime. That means we are also going to own the story. And to do that properly, we need to own you, too. We printed extra copies early this morning because we were all over the broadcast news. Circulation is going to climb from today onwards.'

He thrust the contract at them.

Joyce spoke to Wong in a stage whisper. 'Should we be signing this? I think we should be asking them some tough questions first.'

'Yes,' said the feng shui master, and looked up at the editor. 'When do we get paid?'

'Half now, half in three days,' Cabigon said.

Joyce folded her arms and said, 'What if we don't sign?'

The editor smiled. 'We would stop being so friendly to you. We'd say goodbye. You'd be free to go. If we can't find a decent suspect, we might even try to pin the murder on you. Suspicious foreigners. Wouldn't be hard. I'd avoid that outcome if I were you. Manila jails – they're not very comfortable. Ask Boy.'

Santos looked very uncomfortable.

'That's not fair,' Joyce objected. She turned to stare at the investigative reporter, suddenly realising that the editor had identified him as a former jailbird. What had he been locked up for? Was he dangerous?

'Maybe not,' said Cabigon. 'But it would sell a lot of newspapers. "Sun Nabs Sus Mystics". Anyway, don't worry about it. Mr Wong *is* going to sign.'

'He is,' Santos said in a more conciliatory tone. 'Look, it would do you no good not to. If you guys did refuse to co-operate, I'll tell you exactly what would happen. Our rivals would try to sign you guys up. You'll probably get an approach from Rogelio Marasigan of the *Times* or Eduardo Aras of the *Herald* or one of the others. Their operations are not nearly as classy as ours.'

Wong scratched his chin. 'But what about their budget?'

Cabigon glanced at Santos. 'I'd say much smaller than ours on this one. What do you think, Boy?'

'Yes, much. We're going to slaughter them on this story. Gloria was killed on our premises. It's not worth them investing much money in this. I doubt they'd offer very much. Not two hundred thousand, anyway.'

'Okay, we sign,' said the feng shui master.

As he scrawled tiny Chinese characters at the bottom of the sheet, Santos took a seat and started flicking through a pile of papers he had brought with him.

Cabigon went around the back of his desk and sat down. 'Let's talk news angles,' he said, handing the *feng shui* master a copy of that day's newspaper.

The murder of Del Rosario, of course, had been front-page news, with the *Philippine Daily Sun* giving up its whole front page to the story.

Wong was pleased to note the headline was in a form of English he could understand, although the sentiment it expressed baffled him. Why talk about the weather?

SUN WILL

NOT STOP

SHINING

Santos turned to Wong and McQuinnie. 'You guys are going to be stuck here in this office for the next few days, so you might as well make yourselves useful,' he said. 'Job one will be to identify the suspects.'

Joyce was still feeling uncomfortable about the way the newspaper people had strong-armed them into being on their team, but decided that she might as well use her formidable powers of deduction to help solve the case.

'I've already worked out how to do it. The police think she may have insulted someone in her column,' she said to Santos.

'So we need to get like all the back issues of her column for the past few weeks or months or whatever. Then we find out who it was. I worked it out while the police were consulting us about what they should do.'

'Got 'em,' said Santos, pointing to the top sheet of the stack of paper in front of him. 'This is the total list of everyone she has written about in the past three months.'

'Oh. Good. Then we need to make a list of all the people she was like really mean to.'

'Got it,' Santos replied, holding up a sheet of paper tightly packed with names.

'Oh. Great,' said Joyce, feeling out of her depth. 'I guess you've done this sort of thing before.'

'Yeah, Miss,' he said. 'A few times.'

'So then what? I guess we should work through the list of suspects. Divide them into more likely and less likely.'

'I been working on that, too,' Santos said. 'I've graded them all. I've been using a point system.' He held up a large sheet of graph paper and showed his audience of three that it contained long lists of names, with tiny scribbled numbers next to each. He had something of the attitude of a magician demonstrating an illusion. Editor Cabigon placed a pair of reading glasses on his nose and squinted.

'It's a two-part system,' Santos said, addressing his remarks mainly at his boss. 'They get marks out of ten for each part. In the first column, I've written a number to indicate how insulting she was to them. Like, if Gloria just printed something stupid or embarrassing they said, they might get a two or a three. If she called them crooks or liars or wrote something that caused actual problems for them, they'll get six or seven points. If what she wrote caused their share price to collapse or some agency to investigate them or some deal to be aborted or some divorce to take place, that person gets nine or ten points. That's *that* column.' He pointed with his pen to the list of small red numbers alongside the lists of names.

Then he pointed to a list of blue numbers. 'These other numbers indicate the person's ability to retaliate. If she is rude to some priest or something, he'll probably forgive her so I put a zero here. If she insults someone who can't really fight back – I don't know, like a teacher or a social worker or something, that person might get a two or a three. If she insults a business person, the mark goes up to five or six or seven, and if it is some sort of tycoon with known connections to the under-world, I gave that person an eight or nine or ten.'

He looked around the table to make sure everyone under-stood the system.

'That's brilliant,' Joyce said, clapping. 'So all we have to do is see who gets the highest marks and we got 'im!'

'Done that, too,' said Santos.

The young woman was speechless with admiration.

'That's this list here.' He held up a third sheet of paper, which contained about thirty names. 'She insulted all these people in a pretty nasty way – she attacked them with what my grading system rates as an eight-to-ten point attack. And all of them have an eight-to-ten probability of being well-connected and rich enough to fight back.'

The editor reached for the sheet of paper and scanned the list of names. 'Great work, Boy,' he enthused. 'Some nasty gentlemen here.'

Then he raised his eyes and focused on the middle dis-tance, apparently seeing headlines floating before his eyes. TOP TEAM IN SUN JOURNO DEATH PROBE – SUSPECTS SHORTLISTED – NAMES TO BE NAMED. Have we got a running news feature logo?'

'Yeah,' said Santos. 'Graphics are doing one. Gloria's face and a sort of blood dripping thing. It's not bad.'

'Looks like we're on the boil,' Cabigon said. 'You can have Reynaldo and Billy and Imelda. I'll leave the rest to you.'

'Got it,' Santos said.

The editor dismissed them by pulling a handful of letters from his in-tray and starting to read them.

In the corridor outside, the investigative reporter walked along with his head hunched downwards. 'And what exactly am I going to do with you guys?' he asked. He seemed to be directing the question to himself.

'I don't know,' said Joyce, whose attitude to Boy Santos Jr had been transformed by the discovery that he had followed the same logic as she had in identifying a way to solve the mystery. 'Whatever you want. I'm good at interviewing people. I've been on a few murder cases. And Wong has solved loads of cases. He's a bit famous in Singapore for it. Really, truly.'

'Okay. We'll get you to do some checking. And what about the old guy? Does he speak enough English to be any use?'

'I stay here in newspaper office,' Wong said. 'I want to study old newspapers. Where is newspaper library?'

'I'll get one of the cadets to take you down.'

'Thank you.'

Joyce was assigned five names out of a list of thirty to investigate. She spent an hour in the newspaper library, collecting basic data. The five were all businessmen aged twenty-nine to fifty-eight living in Manila.

She spent several frustrating hours on the phone, attempting to schedule interviews over the next day or two. All the businessmen had secretaries or personal assistants who tried to dismiss her.

'Mr Lin doesn't take visits or calls from reporters, and especially not from your newspaper. If you want to learn about our company, we can send you an annual report.'

One was a little more helpful. 'If you send in a written request with all the questions written down, one of our staff may be able to answer them.'

But none of them agreed to meet her.

Then she went back to the newspaper library, to see if she could learn more about the five individuals from what Boy called 'the cuts'.

Meanwhile, Wong had stayed in the library throughout the day, reading newspaper after newspaper, working his way through several months worth of the *Philippine Daily Sun*, and then moving on to other newspapers, including the *Philippine Daily Inquirer* and the *Philippine Star*. He scribbled pages of notes.

Five-thirty – the designated hour for Wong, Boy Santos Jr and herself to regroup with the editor – came around all too fast, and Joyce felt that nothing had been achieved. As she walked towards Ferdinand Cabigon's room, she was embarrassed to reveal what little she had to show for the hours she had spent making calls and poring over cuttings. What on earth would they put in tomorrow's newspaper?

Santos was not in the least bit down-hearted. 'It's going great,' he told editor Cabigon. 'Head: REPORTER HAD ENEMIES, COPS SAY. Story: The fearless reporting of murdered *Philippine Daily Sun* columnist Gloria Del Rosario led to her having a host of enemies, a top police chief confirmed yesterday.'

'Yeah, yeah,' said Cabigon. 'But how about going on the investigation angle?'

'I'm saving that for the sidebar, until we get stronger results,' said Santos. 'Head: TOP NAMES IN MURDER PROBE. Story: Some of Manila's biggest names in business and politics are being investigated by a *Philippine Daily Sun* team and a crack team of police detectives in a bid to solve the murder which has rocked the country.'

Joyce listened to the discussion with fascination. She thought they had spent a dull day and obtained no significant results, but the way Santos phrased it, the investigation was powering ahead and results appeared to be just hours away.

The following morning, Wong decided to take a break from his reading, and headed to Gloria's apartment in Mandaluyong on the west side of Manila to see what had gone so tragically wrong on the feng shui front.

Although access to the apartment was officially off-limits, the police had finished their investigations and moved on. The newspaper had supplied a security guard to loiter in the area to stop anyone – meaning rival reporters – from entering. When Wong showed the guard his temporary staff badge from the *Philippine Daily Sun*, he was allowed through.

On the Friday morning, Gloria had said that she wanted them to tell her if the apartment was suitable for a home office. She was apparently thinking of leaving the newspaper business and working from home, although she hadn't explained why.

The apartment was mostly blue-grey and was in the southeast sector of the building. Although due east was associated with busy, active work, the *ch'i* of the southeast had a similar energy, albeit noticeably gentler – and thus perhaps more suitable for a mature writer who had passed the youthful workaholic ace-reporter stage.

Wong had produced a plan to gently redesign the apartment to make it more comfortable, and also to provide space for two functions: a living area and a home office.

For the second of these, he had drawn up plans for a curved surface set into a corner, at a forty-five-degree angle to the walls. This gave the desk a southern position, which would have allowed Ms Del Rosario to tap into the south's fiery *ch'i* energy. As a woman whose career was concerned with being in the public eye, she needed to produce work that caused her to shine.

He had also added to the report a list of adjustments she needed to make – such as purchasing a purple mat to go under her chair to maintain the fire energy. He had mapped out a plan for how she should arrange her furniture, right down to the items on the desk (journalistic awards and pictures of loved ones on her right, computer in the centre, plant on the left and something representing finance in the northeast quadrant).

The whole process seemed straightforward enough, as did the *lo shu* charts he drew up for her birthday. But clearly he must have overlooked something important.

As he was on his knees, looking to see if there was something under one of the items of furniture he had missed, Madam Xu entered the apartment with the security guard at her side.

'On the floor, Wong? You'll simply ruin your trousers, not that they are really worth saving.'

'Ah! Madam Xu. You better? Recover fully I hope?'

Upholstered in a red outfit with gold brocade, she looked larger than life. She placed her large handbag on the dining table.

'Never better, Wong. Just had to get over the shock,' she said, pulling out a handkerchief with which to pat her neck.

'Damage to the self-confidence muscle is always painful, but fortunately my personality is massive enough to absorb even the most devastating of attacks. I am a rock, I am an island, as Confucius said.'

She sat down and started pulling objects out of her bag: various packets of cards, charts, rocks, a crystal ball and some metal trinkets. Her job had been difficult on Friday. Because Gloria had to go to work, she had left a handprint and some personal effects for Madam Xu to analyse. It was always harder doing readings from inanimate objects in place of a live client.

'The glass showed me silver clouds on Friday – but I am wondering whether they were really grey clouds. It is such a small difference to the eye, but of course a huge difference in the interpretation of the subject's fortune. There were also streaks of colour on the underside of the clouds, as one sees during the sunset. I took them for orange streaks, implying emotional times – but now I wonder whether they were red for danger.'

Madam Xu picked up the print of Del Rosario's hand. It was an Air Hand: a square palm with deeply etched lines and long, artistic fingers. The overall shape of the hand implied quick-wittedness and deviousness: both good qualities for a newspaper columnist, one would have thought. The Mount of Mercury, the area of the palm just below the little finger, was rather small and flat, implying poor ability at interpersonal relationships, while the Mount of Jupiter, under the index finger, appeared firm and high, indicating a powerful drive for success.

Ms Del Rosario's head line and heart line were so close that they actually combined into a single line for more than half their length. Such circumstances were notoriously difficult to read. If the lines were truly united, they could indicate a single-minded individual whose heart and mind were in perfect accordance. But more often they indicated something much more negative: an imbalance in which one line swamped the other. But which was dominant?

Madam Xu started at the handprint and sighed. This was a hard decision to make, even when the person's hand was right there in front of you. To try and examine the question from a palm print – well, it was almost impossible.

What remained undeniable – and it was devastating, however brave a face she put on it – was that she had used all her predictive arts to look at someone's future, and got it completely wrong.

Wong rose to his feet, having found nothing unusual under the furniture. 'Very strange,' he said, picking up Gloria Del Rosario's natal charts for the seventeenth time. 'We mess up real bad.'

Joyce marched purposefully into the car park. The words of Boy Santos Jr were ringing her ears. *A good reporter never takes no for an answer.*

Velma Palumar, the secretary of businessman Jaime Mangila Jr, chief executive of Bagolbagol Industries, had flatly refused to allow any access to her boss. Velma would not take a message, accept a fax, allow written questions, or even agree to send her any written information of any kind.

This had made Joyce depressed, then hostile and finally suspicious. What had these people got to hide? If they were straightforward business people, they should accept straightforward queries from honest members of the media (she was, after all, presenting herself as a reporter working on a feature on behalf of the *Philippine Daily Sun*). It was all decidedly fishy.

Before leaving the office, she had asked Santos, 'What sort of word is Bagolbagol anyway? Sounds weird. Sounds like a monster from a children's book.'

'I'm not sure,' the reporter had replied. 'But remember, this country has lots of languages. As well as English and Tagalog, we speak Ilocano, Pangasinan, Kapanpangan, Bicol and loads of other languages.'

Santos had telephoned a friend, who told him that Bagol-bagol was a Cebuano word for 'Skull'.

'Phew! *Definitely* a baddie then,' Joyce said. 'Who but a *major* villain would call their company Skull? He might as well just walk around with a placard saying, *I am a baddie* or something.'

There had been very little information in the files about Jaime Mangila Jr, although the piece that Gloria had written about him had painted him as very mean indeed – it said that he had been dating a beauty queen while his wife had been in hospital dying of cancer.

Most of the other references to him in the newspaper library had been to deals his company had done, which revealed very little that made much sense to her. In one article, it reported that he had bought twenty-one per cent of a company of which his family had majority ownership. In another, it said that he had used nominee companies controlled by people 'working in concert' to shore up his share price and had been censured by a commission overseeing dealings on the Manila stock exchange.

The only article that contained anything about him that stayed in Joyce's mind was another one of Gloria's: a piece she had written a year earlier. It was a news feature about car number plates of the rich and famous in the Philippines. Jaime Mangila Jr drove a white sedan with the number JMJ 4444, it said. Joyce knew that the number four was associated with death in several Chinese cultures. This had confirmed the businessman's Probable Bad Guy status in Joyce's eyes.

So she had travelled to Mangila's office to see if she could find his car and catch him going in or out. Santos had explained that such an action was called 'doorstepping' in journalistic slang. She had no intention of cornering a possible murderer by herself. She merely wanted access to him. If she could ask him a few questions while he was getting into his car, she might find out something useful – but more importantly, she would surely impress the hell out of the others on the investigative reporting team.

Applying the old adage that a person with a clipboard can penetrate any space, she bought a cheap one from a stationary shop and marched straight into the garage at Consol Towers, where Bagolbagol Inc. was based on the thirty-fifth floor. The guards at the entrance did not give her a second look.

It took surprisingly little time to find Mangila's car. At the back of Lower Ground Level Two she found a roped-off cluster of long, expensive-looking cars – mostly BMWs and Mercedes-Benzes. But there was one car in the most convenient parking space (right next to a private elevator) which was a white sedan: a Lexus. As she approached, she noted the number plate: JMJ 4444.

Glancing behind her to make sure the coast was clear, she raced over to the car and hid herself behind it, realising that she might have to wait several hours. She placed a newspaper on the ground to sit on, put in her earphones, and started reading some magazines she had bought at the hotel kiosk.

It took Boy Santos Jr four hours to get Joyce out of the holding cell at the Makati police station.

She was livid with the Manila police force and spat fire continuously as the paperwork for her release was completed. Santos tried unsuccessfully to hide his amusement at the girl's fury.

Joyce knew that to some extent it was her own fault, since she had wanted to namedrop her senior police contact, but could not remember his name and title. And her failure made her even more angry.

The past few hours had been difficult. The driver of Jaime Mangila Jr had discovered her fast asleep behind the car and called security guards and the police. She had explained that she was investigating the tycoon on suspicion of murder. This had resulted in the local patrol officer deciding that she was most probably a backpacking substance abuser high on something. She kept hearing the word 'shabu', which confused her, since to her it meant 'Japanese hotpot'.

'You shabu?' the officer had asked her in broken English.

'Yes – and tempura,' Joyce had hollered. 'But what the hell does that have to do with anything? Could we talk about Japanese food later?'

Her explanations that she was on a law enforcement mission were ignored. 'Daniel something!' she'd said to the officer who dragged her away. 'He'll vouch for me. I'm on an investigation! He asked me to stay a few days. Just look in your staff list. There's bound to be a Daniel something. He's short and he likes really sappy music. If you won't call him, call the *Philippine Daily Sun*. Ask for the editor.'

Joyce was even more furious when Santos revealed why it took so long to get her out of jail.

First, Ferdinand Cabigon had refused to okay the expense needed.

'Rotter,' the young woman said as she and Boy walked down the steps outside the police station.

'Cabby said the monies that needed to be paid for you to be released had to come out of the two hundred thousand pesos promised to Wong.'

'Meany. So we had to pay out of our own money?'

'Well . . .' Boy appeared reluctant to answer.

Joyce turned to face him. 'So what happened?'

'Well, I'm afraid your boss refused to agree to this.'

'*What?*'

At first, anyway. It was only after that old lady – what's her name?'

'Madam Xu.'

'After she told him that leaving you to languish indefinitely behind bars would mean he would get into trouble with *his* boss.'

'Mr Pun.'

'Yeah. Only when she took that line, did he finally agree to it.'

'Bastard. *Bastard.*'

Joyce was further amazed to discover that the cash Santos had to pay was not a bail payment to the police, but a payment to the security company – a subsidiary of one of Jaime Mangila Jr's firms – which had captured her.

'It's not exactly a bribe. It's a goodwill payment to make them drop the charges,' he said. 'Sort of like an out-of-court settlement. Companies here have to make a lot of these informal payments.'

By the time they got back to the offices of the *Philippine Daily Sun*, Joyce had descended into a state of sullen silence.

Santos led her into a large conference room. She slumped in a corner chair. She decided she would never speak to Wong again for the rest of her life.

The journalist informed her that the investigative reporting team had narrowed the list of likely candidates down to four possibles, in addition to Joyce's nomination of Jaime Mangila Jr. Their names were Sudang Bueno Sr, Manuel Hernandez, Hamlet Humaynon and Jesus Maria Ramirez, and all were Manila business people.

Santos and McQuinnie were joined in the conference room by Wong and Madam Xu. Joyce looked daggers at her boss and beamed smiles at the fortune-teller. The main editorial conference of the day was about to take place.

At 6.30 p.m. exactly, twelve senior journalists marched into the room, including the news, features, business and sports editors and various layout and production staff. Baby Encarnacion-Salocan sat slightly away from the table to take notes.

Santos explained in a whisper to Wong that this was the daily meeting at which preliminary decisions were made as to which stories would appear on which pages.

Fashionably late, the brown-suited chief editor appeared, took his seat at the head of the table, and the discussion began.

Santos spoke first, explained that the investigation was proceeding slowly. He said he could come up with some angle that would justify one of the front-page slots for the next day's paper, but he had no real breakthrough to report. 'We'll put in some sort of holding story. We've got a nice interview with one of Gloria's old boyfriends, but that's about it. She Knew Too Many Secrets: Glowgirl's Lover. We're going to need much more time for something meatier,' he said.

The journalist explained that it would take another two or three days research to produce features on the short-listed suspects which would be interesting enough to print – yet not actually defamatory. And even then, there was no guarantee that they would uncover evidence to identify any particular one of them as Gloria's likely murderer.

That was when Madame Xu spoke up.

'We do not need two or three days,' she said. 'Why, we barely need two or three minutes.'

'What do you mean?' Santos asked.

'You have done the lion's share of the work. Now I will do the final part – the thing that only I can do. I will use my psychic powers to find out which of your five candidates did the murder. It will save you a great deal of time. Give me the list.'

Santos looked askance at Cabigon. 'Is this a good idea?'

The chief editor shrugged his shoulders. 'Psychic powers,' he said. 'Never tried it. Could be a good angle.'

'Sidebar maybe,' said Santos. 'Or a filler we could use at the weekend.'

Cabigon played with his moustache. 'I don't know if we can use psychic identification as providing enough proof to even hint at someone being a suspect in print. It's a bit, you know, unorthodox. Unless we do it as a funny.'

'What do you mean?' said Madame Xu, who was irritated that her generous offer to solve the mystery had not been greeted by the ecstatic cries of gratitude she felt it deserved. 'Surely psychic proof is the one type of proof that cannot be argued against? If I have identified him as the villain, then there are no other options. He must be sent to jail forthwith.'

Editor and staff swapped glances that said: *She really is crazy.*

'He has to go to trial, first,' Santos explained gently.

'No, *I* would have to go to trial for libel first,' the chief editor interrupted. 'If I printed that some businessman was a murderer because a psychic said so. No. With all due respect, Madame Xu, we need the sort of evidence that can stand up in court. The fact that you think someone did it – with all due respect – is simply not proof.'

The fortune-teller thought about this. 'If you say so.'

There was silence for half a minute. It was broken by Santos. 'So we'll go with Gloria's boyfriend for tomorrow's lead and start more detailed investigations into these five, I guess?'

'Wait a minute, wait a minute,' said the Chinese fortune-teller. 'Don't you want to know who did it?'

Santos looked to Cabigon and then back at Madam Xu. 'The editor has just said your prediction wouldn't be enough proo – '

'Yes, he said that, but wouldn't you like to know anyway? Just for fun. It would make your investigations much easier and much quicker too, if you already know who did it. Then you could just investigate *him* only. Save loads of time all round.'

Santos looked at Cabigon. Their eyes continued their earlier discussion: *We could humour the old girl.*

'Okay,' said the chief editor.

The reporter said, 'We need to be quick. I have a phone interview to do.'

Cabigon looked at his watch. 'And I have a meeting to go to.'

'Yes, yes,' said Madam Xu. 'No need to be impatient. It's worth taking a little time over this to get it right.'

She sat down and placed her crystal ball down on the table. Then she put on a pair of reading glasses through which to stare at it. She picked up her little canister of *chim* and started shaking it. 'I'm combining methods to go as fast as I can,' she told the onlookers, as one sliver of engraved bamboo popped out.

She ran her hand over the list of five names. 'Hmm, interesting,' she mumbled.

She went back to her crystal ball and gazed deep into it again. 'This is called scrying,' she explained. Then she closed her eyes, put her hands on her tilted-back head, and took a series of deep breaths. Once again she opened her eyes and ran her hands over the list of five names.

'Got it,' she said. 'Got it.'

Santos's gathering boredom lifted. 'So which do you reckon it is?'

'It isn't *any* of these,' Madam Xu said. 'This is a list of innocent people. Well, probably innocent is not the right word for a group of business tycoons, but they are certainly innocent of the crime of which we are accusing them.'

'That's not very helpful,' said Ferdinand Cabigon, suddenly annoyed. He looked at his reporters. 'Well I still think it was somebody on that list, whatever your spirits say.'

'Oh, it wasn't just the spirits that told me that the murderer was not someone on that list. They merely confirmed what I learned from another source. My source was flesh and blood. It was, in fact, Mr Wong here.'

All eyes turned to the feng shui master.

The old geomancer looked surprised to be receiving such attention. 'True that it is not one of the people on the list who did it.'

'So who did it?' Cabigon asked impatiently.

'And more importantly, have you got some evidence, some proof?' Santos said, exasperation in his voice. 'We have a newspaper to fill.'

Wong leaned back in his chair. 'The murderer of Ms Gloria Del Rosario was very clever,' he said. 'Clever in two-three ways. First, he knows that people will think that someone she insulted killed her. She is a reporter. So killer reinforces this idea by leaving a message that she should have printed correction. So everyone think she wrote something wrong about a man and refuse to print correction.'

Wong intertwined his fingers in front of him. 'So first thing we realise is that murderer probably is someone she did *not* write about. He is someone whose name is absent from her column. Murderer wants to send us in wrong direction.'

Joyce forgot that she had pledged never to speak to her boss again: 'So the note about the correction was a red herring?'

'Red earring?'

'Herring.'

'Don't understand.'

'It's a type of fish. Comes from Norway or something.'

The geomancer nodded. 'Thanks. But I think no fish involved.'

He pointed to the piles of newspapers on the conference room sideboard. 'I check through all the gossip columns in all the newspapers. Nearly all have same names at same parties. Same politicians, same business people, same celebrities. I make list of all names which appear in three main newspapers over past six months.'

He pulled out a sheet of paper and pointed to some tiny, tight blotches. 'This is my list.'

'It's very short,' said the sports editor, a short fat man sitting next to Wong.

'Yes. It shows seven people who were mentioned at least six times in other gossip columns but *not even one time* in Gloria Del Rosario's column.'

Santos started to look interested.

'I ask intern to do research on these six,' the feng shui master continued. 'Find out which companies they involve in, who is shareholders? We find that five out of six are connected some way with man called Billy Valesco Ong. They are on boards together. They are listed in consortiums together. In photographs file, they are at cocktails together.'

There was silence in the room. Nobody dared to move a muscle. Wong had spoken the name of the publisher of the newspaper, a scary individual who once sacked a senior staff member for misspelling the name of the Ong family dog.

'So now we decide what is the real story,' the feng shui master continued. 'Fact is, Mr Ong does not like his friends to be embarrass in the newspaper. He has certain loyalty to them. But he has no direct contact with editorial staff. So he ask someone else to make sure these peoples' names do not appear in gossip column in negative way. He ask person who stands between board of directors and reporters. This man is chief editor.'

Every eye turned towards Ferdinand Cabigon.

'This is ridiculous,' said the editor. 'There's no censorship in this newspaper. No more than in any other newspaper, anyway. I have complete freedom from the proprietor and make my own decisions. He has never interfered, not once.'

Wong continued. 'So editor had series of little interviews with chief gossip columnist of the paper. He tells her if she wants to keep her comfortable little job and big pay packet, she better be very careful to not mention name of any of proprietor's friends. Gloria she say, okay. But she feel very bad. Other reporter in other newspaper write about them. But not her.'

'This is probably true,' the sports editor said. 'Her column did seem to get very tame in recent months.'

'Shh,' Santos scolded him, his eyes fixed on Wong.

'After some time, Gloria worry this will be noticed. She decide she will not censor herself any more. She tell editor she will no longer keep proprietor's friends out of column.'

'This is crazy,' Cabigon objected, becoming red in the face. 'All make-believe from beginning to end. I think you better leave now, Mr Wong.'

The feng shui master held up his hands. 'Not finish. Ms Del Rosario and editor have big fight on Friday. Editor sacks her. She tells him she is more happy to leave job than to stay in job and censor herself. She say she will write her last column that night.'

The editor had begun to sweat profusely.

'Before her column go to sub-editor and layout desk, editor reads it,' Wong continued. 'He sees it is confession. Confession that she censored herself. Because editor ask her to. Her column destroys her reputation. But also it destroys *his* reputation. On Friday evening – '

Ferdinand Cabigon rose to his feet and shouted at the visitors. 'That's enough. This is slander. You and your crazy friends will get out right now.' He tried to speak with authority, but his voice shook. He turned to his staff. 'Throw him out.'

Boy Santos Jr rose to his feet. 'I'll throw them out. But first I want to hear the rest of what Mr Wong is saying. About what happened on Friday evening.'

Journalist and editor stared at each other.

Cabigon opened his mouth. 'I – '

Santos interrupted. 'Free speech. Isn't that what newspapers are all about? Sit down,' he ordered. 'Boss.'

The reporter looked to his colleagues for support. Several of them nodded.

Cabigon reluctantly took his seat.

Wong continued: 'So editor call her to executive office on top floor – he says he wants to give her goodbye gift. She go upstair with him. He asks her to wait. Then he run downstair. He type suicide message on her keyboard to him. He clicks "send" button. He rush upstair to executive floor. He take her up to the roof to show her something – then he push her off. He goes to executive toilet to wash his hands, make sure no fibre from her clothes on him. He goes downstair back to his desk.'

There was a scraping sound. Ferdinand Cabigon had pushed his chair back again. All eyes turned to him. His face was wet and his eyes staring.

'Stay,' Santos said.

'Soon, body is found, splat, dead on ground,' Wong continued. 'Many photographer, reporter, they run downstair, out of building, have a look. They see Gloria is dead. Mr Santos he run upstair and run into editor's room to tell him Gloria dead. At that moment, editor press send-and-receive button and receive her final email. He reads it, pretends to be very shocked.'

Cabigon shrieked at Wong. 'There is no proof of this. There is no proof of this at all. It's just a wild story. She never wrote any final column. What you've said is pie in the sky.'

'No, it isn't.' The quiet voice came from his secretary, Baby Encarnacion-Salocan.

Everyone in the room turned to stare at her.

'Gloria thought you might just delete her final column, so she sent an extra copy to me. I kept it. She treated me decently. So did Mr Wong and his assistant. So I printed it out and passed it on to him.'

Madam Xu clapped her hands. 'So that's how you worked it all out. Damn clever of you Wong. I thought for a moment that you must be psychic, to know so much detail about what happened. But you had the full story from the victim. That's cheating, Wong.'

Santos rose to his feet, and with the help of the business editor and the sports editor – the two bulkiest men in the room – escorted Ferdinand Cabigon back to his office, where he was incarcerated until the police could be summoned.

Back in the conference room, Wong was defending himself from Madam Xu.

'Column of Gloria did not tell me everything. Just bit about how editor ask her to censor herself. How she decided to leave job instead.'

Joyce leaned into the conversation. 'But how d'you know about how he pushed her? She couldn't have written all that down. And how come you suddenly know how to send emails?'

'How to do email I don't know. Baby told me all that stuff. I just repeat it.'

Ms Encarnacion-Salocan bowed her head. 'I was sitting outside the editor's office the whole time. I saw him rushing in and out. I checked the send and receive times on Gloria's intra-office emails. Remember, I'm the editor's secretary. I have top level clearance. It was easy for me to work out what had happened. Gloria was my best friend. She confided in – ' The woman burst into tears.

Madam Xu was still annoyed with Wong. 'You had too much help. This doesn't count.'

Boy Santos Jr re-entered the room and turned to the visitors. 'Thank you for your help.'

'Thank you is very nice,' said Wong. 'But we still get paid, I hope?'

'Don't know. Cabigon signed the contract. If what you say is true, and he gets arrested, the owner might nullify things he signed. Especially as you make him look bad. Hard to say.'

The feng shui master looked depressed.

Joyce's mind was whirling with the excitement of the past days: a murder, an investigation and a spell in jail – she felt bonded with Santos. 'What an amazing three days. I never realised being a reporter was such a complicated and exciting job.'

Santos smiled at her. 'It can be. But sometimes it all seems to go out of control.'

'But even then – I mean, it's amazing how you always find the right thing to put in the paper.'

The investigative reporter sat down next to Joyce. 'Thanks, Joyce. But you know what? For the first time since I started this job, I have absolutely no idea what we should be putting on the front page tomorrow.'

At Ninoy Aquino International Airport, Wong peered at the piece of bread that Madam Xu had purchased for him as a snack. Joyce was in the airport CD shop.

'This is what?'

'Authentic French cuisine, according to the *table d'hôtel*,' she said.

'Looks funny.'

'Adobo Croissant, it's called. Try it.'

He took one bite – and then set it aside, wiping all traces off his lips with his napkin.

'Not hungry,' he said.

'Me also,' said Madam Xu.

The case had been interesting, but the two Chinese mystics were still depressed about how wrong they had been when examining Gloria Del Rosario's apartment. How could two so-called experts in the predictive arts have missed something as large as the imminent death of their subject?

'I'll buy you a much better snack, Mr Wong,' said a voice.

They looked around to see Baby Encarnacion-Salocan. The editor's secretary sat down, explaining that she needed to tell them something before they left the Philippines.

She told them that she had been miserable for the past six years, working for a wily and increasingly untrustworthy boss. She had desperately been seeking changes in her life, and wanted to quit the newspaper and start working independently.

'I vacated my flat and moved in with Gloria three months ago. When she said that she was entitled to a free session from a top feng shui expert from Singapore, I asked her to accept,' she said.

'So birthday was your birthday, not birthday of Gloria?' Wong was wide-eyed.

She nodded. 'Gloria accepted Mr Pun's offer of a free feng shui and astrological consultation, but she gave you guys my birth date instead of her own. That home office area was mine, not hers.'

Madam Xu, shocked, put her fingertips to her lips, barely daring to believe her ears. 'And that handprint . . . ?'

'That was my hand,' said Baby.

'Thank God.'

'So when you both predicted that the apartment's inhabitant would enjoy a full and rich life, you were talking about me, not poor Gloria,' Baby continued. 'I'm sorry to have deceived you. I couldn't have afforded to employ you myself. It was because of the lies Gloria and I told that you got mixed up in all this.'

Madam Xu was stunned. 'So I have not lost my abilities after all,' she gasped. 'And Mr Wong the same. We got it right!

Thank you for the best news we have had in days. That news earns you a big kiss and a hug.'

The two women clutched each other tightly.

Wong looked alarmed and slipped away.

Epilogue: Letters from friends

Feng Menglong was a sage who lived in recent times, four hundred years ago. He wrote a book called Zhinang.

In his book he said men always strived to have easy lives. If any obstacles came their way, they would get off the path of righteousness.

Feng Menglong wondered why Heaven made it so difficult for men to attain enlightenment. While he was thinking about this, he encountered an example of the problem.

One farmer of his acquaintance wanted to study and reach enlightenment. But his land was too dry that season and he had to spend every day carrying water to it.

The farmer said: 'I would study and acquire wisdom and become enlightened if I did not have so many troubles in my life.'

The difficult times continued. The farmer carried water every day and forgot his pursuit of the truth.

But other people in the village continued to study and seek enlightenment. Their fields became dry and dusty and the soil was blown away by the wind. The farm became a mound of lushness surrounded by baked hollows.

Then one day, after a long drought, the rains came.

The water sprinkled the mountaintops and ran down the sides. The water filled the deep hollows of the land.

Feng Menglong saw that the lowlands had much more water than the plateaus.

He realised that a life with highs and lows is richer than a life with only highs.

Blade of Grass, learn from the words of Shanneng, a Zen master during the Southern Song Dynasty. He said: 'When hardship is over, we look back and discover a certain joy in it. But if you can discover the joy while the hardship is happening, your winter will be as filled with as much wonder as your summer.'

From *Some Gleanings of Oriental Wisdom*
by CF Wong, part 33

CF Wong sat at his desk and flicked through his invoice book. It had been a busy month, and he had not had time to sit down and go through his accounts for several weeks. Things were looking bad. He phoned his patron, Pun Chi-kin.

'Wah, Pun-saang, so much properties this month, in so many different country. I think three trip in one month too much, cannot do good job, always too much hurry-hurry, no time for my other work, aiyeeah, big problem.'

'I have every confidence that you can cope, Wong.' The property developer's voice was smooth and velvety on the surface, but was there just a hint of iron underneath?

'Also, some job very difficult. Not easy. Take many days.' The feng shui master tried to avoid a note of pleading, but it was difficult. 'Maybe we look again at my retainer, Mr Pun, see what is suitable fee, can-or-not?'

Mr Pun gave a low growl in response. After a few seconds, he continued, 'I realised you had a lot of work this month, visiting the board members, Mr Wong, but I thought you would be grateful. I know you never miss a chance to hit clients with extra fees for extra services. No doubt you lined your pockets, as you normally do.' There *was* metal in his tone – not iron, but something harder and more dangerous: tempered steel.

'Oh, no, sir, no-no-no. Your board members get free service, everything included. Only sometime they force me to take extra money, I say no-no-no, don't want. But they force me. Bad face for them if I say no.'

'Ye-es.' Pun was sceptical. 'Whatever. Anyway, I have certain concerns about the way you carried out some of the assignments this month.'

Wong froze. 'Oh. I do something wrong, boss?'

'Mr Wong, one of my board members is dead and another is out on bail on charges of fish-theft. This makes things awkward. I accept that you had no direct involvement in the death of Ms Del Rosario, but I cannot say the same for your role in the arrest of Mr Tik.'

'Ah, Mr Tik.'

'Yes, Mr Tik.' Pun gave a long sigh. 'If, in future, you discover business people related to my company are engaged in wrongful acts, it would be wise to quietly forget what you see, do you understand? Or at least, tell me about them before you tell the police. I'm a conservative man, and I like things to go on exactly as they have for many, many years. Arrests of board members are awkward and unpleasant for me. Understand?'

'Yes, Mr Pun.'

'I am deducting a certain sum of money from your monthly retainer this month to help you learn that important lesson.'

The words were like a knife in Wong's stomach. He sat down heavily.

'Still there?'

'Yes, Mr Pun.'

'Now, you say you want a review of the overall level of your retainer?'

'Yes, Mr Pun.'

There was silence on the other end of the phone. It seemed to go on for a long time. When Wong had begun to wonder if the line had gone dead, the businessman came back. 'I'm glad you asked. I've been thinking about reviewing the costs of your operation. After all, this is a period of heavy deflation, as you know. Deflation should be applied uniformly, I've always believed.'

The feng shui master was suddenly alert. Deflation? What means deflation? Was this good news or bad? Must check, quick. Wong, with his free hand, quickly plucked his English dictionary from the bookshelf and started flicking through it. 'Sorry, Pun-saang. Please wait. Urgent call on other line.' He pressed the hold button, inflicting a monophonic version of *Greensleeves* on his chief paymaster.

Finding the page, he read it carefully, his lips moving: 'Deflation: lessening of monetary value; economic condition in which money loses spending power resulting in a reduction of costs; the opposite of inflation.'

Wong considered this, the space between his eyebrows screwing itself into a tight grid. Did this mean what he thought it meant? Money going *down*?

Must act fast. He pressed the hold button again. 'Maybe no need for review of cost jus' yet,' he said as pleasantly as he could. 'Can manage okay jus' now. Three-four trip oversea in one month no problem. Sorry about Mr Tik.'

'Well, Wong, glad to hear it,' said Pun, his voice dry and unamused. He rang off.

Aiyeeah. The feng shui master crossed his arms and slumped forwards across his desk. After a minute, he jerked himself upright and reached for the bag of curried fishballs he had purchased as a late-afternoon snack.

But Winnie Lim was wiping her lips with a tissue, having scoffed the lot.

An hour later, the geomancer was sitting at his favourite table at the night market. He had brought two books with him to provide cheerful reading: his invoice book and his receipts book. There was nothing more comforting than flicking through payment stubs.

He smiled as he reached a group of stubs stamped with the word PAID. He had seen three separately billed extra clients on the Australia trip – little old ladies from Perth who had wanted their homes feng shui-ed. There had actually been a fourth offer from that Mrs Lavender, but he had reluctantly turned her down because she kept brushing her pendulous breasts against him and giving him lascivious looks. Not safe to go to her house. It occurred to him that he could have agreed to it, collected the money and then sent Joyce to do the work. Ah well, too late.

The biggest disaster was the Manila trip. First, the client had died, so there was going to be no hope of follow-up visits. Second, Wong had spent the best part of three days working long hours in the offices of the *Philippine Daily Sun* and been paid nothing at all for it. He should have insisted on full payment in advance.

As he compared his earnings with the days spent working, he found that the disappointing Manila trip was partly compensated for by extra profits earned in Thailand. He had received a fat tip after finishing his official assignment of redoing the dressing room, and another one after the unofficial job – solving the mystery of the missing actors.

The India trip had produced no extra fees, but had been worth it for another reason. His visit to the home of Mag-Auntie outside Pallakiri had powerfully brought home to him the similarities between feng shui and vaastu. Until then, he had always been slightly disdainful of Indian geomantic arts, considering them to be more superstition than science.

But that glade! It was so perfect, so paradisiacal, so much the archetype of the original Pure Land of Zen. Truly it proved that the human mind all over the world was programmed to react positively to a home with ideal geomantic conditions. Mag-Auntie had given him the address of her vaastu master, a man called Mistry, and he was already planning another trip to India for the purposes of visiting him.

But how to finance it? India was far away and airline trips there were expensive. And if he did not want to eat street food, he would have to stay in a fancy hotel, preferably one with Chinese food. It would cost money. He needed a client there to finance his visit.

As dusk fell, the night market became busy. The chefs started work.

Dilip Kenneth Sinha and Madam Xu arrived moments later, as if the venue's cooks and diners had shared a bus.

'Go easy on the garlic and spice tonight,' said Madam Xu. 'I am meeting a client after dinner at 7.30.'

Sinha shook his head. 'I'm afraid, dear lady, that we shall have to order for you separately. Wong and myself can no longer taste food that has not been spiced. Years of ill usage have damaged our palates beyond the reach of subtle flavourings.'

The fortune-teller took out a small flannel and wiped down the surface of the table in front of her. 'Well, we don't have to have Indian. We could have Chinese – Szechuan for you and Cantonese for me. You could have your chilli crab.'

'Correct. Or we could go for Malay. We haven't done that for a while.'

Wong nodded. 'Lontong,' he said. 'Need lontong tonight.'

'Good choice,' said Sinha. 'There are few things as comforting after a long day's work as rice cakes and eggs swamped in a spicy cream sauce. I suggest that we have, on the side, a plate of otak-otak. There's something about the pleasing stink of fish paste that sets the world to rights.'

'I fancy a roti john,' said Madam Xu.

'Panggang,' said Wong.

The lengthy discussion of what to order was an important part of the ritual. Despite the delay it caused to the actual meal, the meal tasted far better if its various components had been carefully compared, analysed and matched.

The consensus was to go for Malay cuisine. Its Thai influences of shrimp paste and chilli would satisfy Wong and Sinha's macho cravings for burned tongues, while the more subtle flavours of lemongrass and coconut milk would be suitable for Madam Xu's delicate palate.

Once ordered, the food started to arrive quickly. Barely eight minutes later, Wong was holding a bowl of lontong and shovelling soaked rice-cakes into his mouth. Sauce dribbled down his chin.

The three members of the investigative advisory committee of the Union of Industrial Mystics ate in silence. As one of the great sages said: To he who has been made to wait, dinner is Heaven and Heaven is dinner. For a moment, the three-legged stool made up of Heaven, Earth and Man was at peace. Wong was a happy man.

Then Joyce McQuinnie slipped on to the stool next to him. 'Yo, boss man.'

Shh-chka-shh-chka-shh-chka-shh.

'You looked a bit blue in the office,' she said. She was talking unnaturally loudly, as she often did when she was wearing headphones and having a conversation at the same time.

'Blue?' Wong looked down at the back of his hands peering at his veins, which were sometimes bluish. They were the same brown as usual, although one was stained with lontong sauce.

'I mean like, you know, *down*.'

He glanced down at his feet. His ankles, a sliver of which showed between his sheer Shanghainese socks and his trouser legs, were also the usual shade of brown.

'I meant down in the dumps.'

Wong looked at her. 'Which dumps?'

'No dumps. I meant – never mind. I bought these. Thought they might cheer you up. Winnie forgot to empty the letterbox this morning and I found them sticking out.' She handed him two envelopes. 'One of them is from Nevis Au Yeung. The other's from – '

The feng shui master grabbed the first envelope and tore it open in one swift movement. Au Yeung the billionaire! Number 39 on the *Forbes* rich list for Asia. A billionaire had written to him. What sort of tip might a billionaire give to someone who had performed a good service for him? It could be millions. It could be a spare apartment or house or car. It could be a yacht. How much could he sell the yacht for?

Inside the courier packet was a small, white envelope bearing the name – no, it must be a mistake. He narrowed his eyes and glared closely at the handwriting on the front again. No mistake. The envelope was addressed to 'Joice, c/o Mister Wong'.

'For you,' said Wong crossly, handing it over.

'Oh. Really? Well, this one's definitely for you, anyway.' She tossed him another envelope.

The young woman laughed to find that her letter was from Foo-Foo Au Yeung. It was a note inviting her to lunch. She read it out loud for Wong's benefit. '"Nevis has given me $100,000 to go and find a Chitty. He has always wanted a flying car. Would you like to meet for lunch? We can spend some of the money on lunch, and the rest on shopping. He'll never notice."'

Joyce was thrilled. 'Cool. Shopping with someone else's money. I could put up with that for an afternoon, no sweat.'

Wong tore open the other envelope and squinted at it.

It was a letter on lilac scented paper from Mrs Jackie Lavender of Perth. *Dear CF*, it said, *I never really got a chance to say goodbye. And you did, quite possibly, save my life. I owe you a debt of gratitude and I always pay my debts. I've decided I'm going to visit Singapore to express my gratitude in a personal way. See you soon, my dear little man. Perhaps we could do some light exercise together?*

The feng shui master closed his eyes. He remembered the ancient Chinese proverb: From a hungry tiger and an affectionate woman there is no escape. But that in turn reminded him of his encounter in the Sing Woo supermarket. After fifty-six years of life on earth, he was still being showered with trials and tribulations.

Why did the gods hate him so?

> *More than a thousand years ago, a scholar went to see a great master of a school in a city called Chang'an.*
>
> *The scholar said: 'Master, I come to you to be led to a state of enlightenment. I believe only you can deliver me to such a state. I need transcendence.'*
>
> *The teacher looked at him and said: 'I need to shit.'*
>
> *The scholar was confused. He said: 'Why do you say this to me?'*

The master said: 'I don't want to move. So I wonder if you can go to the toilet and shit for me, please?'

The scholar: 'But I cannot do it for you. You have to do it for yourself.'

The master said: 'Yes.'

And the scholar understood.

Blade of Grass, every student must undertake his own personal journey. There is only room on The Way for one person at a time.

When does the journey end?

The Zen masters tell the story of the famous poet Bai Juyi.

He went to see the Monk Niaowo and asked him how he could become One with Heaven. Monk Niaowo said: 'Do good. Do not do bad.'

The poet Bai Juyi said: 'That is so simple. A child of three knows it.'

Monk Niaowo said: 'A child of three knows it. But a man of one hundred cannot do it. Enjoy the journey, for the journey is the end and the end is the journey.'

From *Some Gleanings of Oriental Wisdom*
by CF Wong, part 34